MILE-HIGH MADMEN

AIR AFFAIR

LESLIE VOLLARD

Cover design by Dar Albert at Wicked Smart Designs

Published by Oliver-Heber Books

0 9 8 7 6 5 4 3 2 1

1

*W*as there anything lonelier than watching your fiancé flirt with another woman at your own engagement party?

After draining her third glass of champagne, Rory decided she'd had enough.

"I'm leaving," she murmured to Evelyn, as she glared at her husband-to-be who had his arm around the curvy, red-headed singer from the band. Only the pianist remained on stage, playing a ragtime ditty as partygoers flung themselves around the dance floor of Belmont Park's Turf and Field Club, drunk on her father's largesse. As usual, Papa looked on like a king from his throne, surrounded by his usual court of aspiring robber barons and power brokers. And also as usual, he was ignoring his future son-in-law's flagrant transgressions.

"Shall I kill him for you?" Evelyn asked.

Rory put down her glass on a high-hat table draped in purple linen with gold trim and turned to her best friend to see a sly smile on Evelyn's heart-shaped face. "Edward or Papa?"

"Either. Just say the word. They'll never know what hit them."

Rory didn't doubt for one moment that her friend could carry out her threat. Evelyn Carnegie could kill with a look, even wrapped in frothy yellow charmeuse and chiffon with her chestnut tresses crowned with a ridiculous diamond tiara. It was almost enough to make Rory smile.

Almost.

"Kill the knight in shining armor who is rescuing me from my scandalous past?" Rory pressed her lips together as she watched Edward's hand slip to the singer's buttocks and squeeze.

"It's ludicrous that men can behave like that," Evelyn said, pointing her chin at Edward, "and women are still expected to remain pure until the day they wed. Any word from Archie?"

Rory winced. "Not a one. The coward is still hiding in London." Papa was never going to let her marry the son of his business nemesis, not even after she and Archie were caught by a photographer in flagrante delicto. And she was almost relieved, given how little spine Archie had shown since it all came out in the open. What an idiot she'd been to fall for him! He was so adamant about wanting to marry her before everything fell apart, but the minute things went wrong, he disappeared without a word to her, claiming to all who would listen that *she* seduced *him*.

"Worthless rat. You're better off without him."

Rory couldn't agree more. She reached out and grasped Evelyn's hand. "You're a good friend."

Evelyn pressed her hand back. "Yes, I am. Now go stare at some airplanes until you feel better."

Her friend knew her all too well. "Will I see you at the suffrage rally tomorrow?"

"You know you will."

Good. Rory was looking forward to marching with a crowd of passionate, angry women. She might not be able to choose her husband, but at least she could vent her frustration through political action. Papa didn't approve, but he hadn't forbidden it either, thanks to Aunt Alva's intervention. It was one of the few outlets she had for her frustration with the rigid constraints of her life.

"If anyone asks where I am, say I'm powdering my nose." Rory glanced around the opulent room, decked out in royal purple and gold at her father's command. After all, this was his demesne. In the low light of electric chandeliers, the crème de la crème of New York society glimmered and sparkled like ghastly courtiers as they ignored her plight completely and lost themselves in the festivities.

Rory slipped into the shadows and slunk out the door of the castle her father built to keep out the riffraff at his famous racetrack. Princess Belmont, the gossip rags called her. At least until the debacle with Archie. Then they called her much worse, but she wasn't going to think about that.

Nor was she going to think about how she was being bought and sold like one of her father's horses. Papa wanted a friend in the Senate, and Edward wanted the Belmont money. It was a business exchange. Her father said it was to protect her tattered reputation, but there was no disguising the nature of this union. It was a joint venture between men, and she was merely property changing hands. A shiver ran down her spine.

Papa didn't treat her brothers like this. They got to choose who they married, within reason. But then the rules had always been different for them. Papa doted on them in a way he never had with her. Unfortunately, none of them would speak to her after the incident with Archie. She'd never been close to them, but it hurt, nonetheless.

Airplanes. Think about airplanes. Even if only for a brief respite before she returned to her gilded cage.

The hangar called out to her from across the racetrack. She couldn't stay away. Ever since the postal service set up airmail operations on the racetrack grounds, she'd taken every opportunity to peek inside at the miraculous machines that let one soar through the clouds like a bird. The siren call of freedom and danger was one she could not resist. She'd studied them, gobbling up every article she could find about airplanes and flying. The Wright Brothers' achievement at Kitty Hawk was nothing short of a miracle, and she was hooked.

There were even lady pilots. She'd seen Katherine Stinson do an air show in Mineola a few months before, and she thought her heart might explode with longing. Never had Rory wanted anything so much in her life as to climb into one of those glorious machines and fly it herself, escaping the cage of her life and soaring free.

And so here she was, padding carefully manicured grass toward the makeshift wooden barn the postal service used as a hangar for its brand-new airmail operation, trying not to make a noise. In the distance, a radio played the latest ragtime hits. Was someone still awake and guarding the place?

She slowed her steps, breathing in the smoky air of Queens. It was little better than an ash pile these days with all the wartime manufacturing. Her father complained that the poor air quality was bad for his racehorses. "Well, Papa, after you've married me off, you can spend all the time you like with your precious horses," she mumbled.

There was a rustle nearby. She stopped and held her breath.

Was someone there?

For what felt like an eternity, she stood completely still, listening for the slightest hint that she might not be alone. If she got caught sneaking out of the party, Father would lock her in her room and throw away the key until the wedding.

A tense moment passed.

Nothing.

She was imagining things. It must have been all the champagne.

Slipping in through the hangar's barn door, which was slightly ajar, she stood still for a moment, letting her eyes adjust. The only light came from an office window with its shutters down at the opposite end of the hangar. Everything else was cloaked in darkness. Gathering her courage, she wound her way past the hulking shadows of six biplanes, until she found one with a ladder to the rear cockpit. In the meager light, she could see that the front cockpit was filled with sacks of mail.

The polished wood propeller of the JN-4 gleamed with a reflection of the light from the office. A "Jenny" they called it, fitting, given its feminine lines. Dual wings, held together with posts and a web of wires, cast complex shadows on the wall of the hangar. Just looking at it sent a thrill right down to her toes. Someday, she would fly one of these beautiful contraptions. She would find a way, no matter what her husband might think.

Walking around the wing, temptation overtook her, and she climbed the small ladder resting against the curving body of the plane and nestled into the rear cockpit straddling the rigid wooden control stick. Fortunately, no one was here to see how improper she looked with her gold satin dress bunched between her silk-stockinged legs.

Grasping the stick with both hands, she imagined what it would be like to wield this machine, soaring above the clouds, trembling, and vibrating with the roar of the powerful Hispano-Suiza engine. She longed to feel its thrust, pressing her back in her seat with inexorable force, the wind caressing her face, chasing away the sultry heat of the summer's night.

Why did men get to have all the fun? This might be called a Jenny, but it was hard to imagine a more masculine invention than this aircraft. Surely the soft, skillful hands of a woman would best know how to tame such a beast. She inhaled deeply, smelling leather, oil, and the feral tang of the steel engine sleeping in the fuselage.

A quiet thrum of giddiness ran through her veins as she ran a finger lovingly down the instrument panel.

Yes, this was just what she needed to shake off the horror of the party. Closing her eyes, she was a bird in the sky, the whole world spread out before her. Weightless. Free.

Her reverie was interrupted by the unmistakable rasp of a match. Her eyes flew open, and her heart skipped a beat as an orange glow appeared in the darkness several yards away. The pungent aroma of a fine, Cuban cigar tickled her nose.

She froze.

"Well, hello, princess," said a rich baritone, as fine and mellow as a caress. It was a voice made for radio. If only it wasn't pronouncing her doom.

"To whom do I have the honor of speaking?" Rory asked, exaggerating her aristocratic mid-Atlantic lilt, pretending she wasn't absolutely terrified. Could she brazen her way through this? It would be a disaster if this got back to her father. And who knew what this strange man's intentions might be?

"Lieutenant Hank Hawley, at your service." He gestured with his cigar as he sprawled on a rickety wood folding chair leaning against the wall of the hangar. How did she miss him in the shadows?

Standing slowly, he sauntered into a shaft of light, and she was free to take a long, appraising look. He was in white shirt-sleeves, the fabric clinging to his muscular chest, leaving little to the imagination. The loose khaki pants of an army pilot's uniform ballooned around his thighs then tucked into knee-high boots.

His sleeves were rolled up to his elbows, revealing powerful forearms. He had a tattoo she couldn't make out on the arm holding the cigar. His shirt was unbuttoned at the neck, and she could see a hint of hair just above the V of his neckline. In short, he looked like he stepped out of one of her dreams.

After all, how many times had she fantasized about being whisked away from her coddled life by a brave and dashing pilot? If she was alone in her bedroom, she might have imagined undoing the rest of his buttons, one by one, until she reached the waist of his pants. And then…

Oh God. She must have drunk too much champagne. Stiffening, she shook her head and sat up straight, attempting to clear her wayward thoughts. If she was going to get out of this, she needed her wits about her.

"I'm not going to hurt you," he said, his chocolaty voice soothing her as he put his hands up. "Frankly, I'm wondering whether this is real. Maybe I'm dreaming up the gorgeous angel that has landed in my cockpit."

His brilliant brown eyes had a reckless, wild look to them, and a lock of dark hair fell over his forehead. He was clean-shaven, but the shadow of a day's growth darkened his jaw.

"A dream. Yes, definitely a dream. Now go back to sleep and pretend you never saw me."

Climbing out of the wooden fuselage, trying not to expose too much leg, she stepped down the ladder hurriedly. Her high heels crunched as she reached the gravel floor. She backed away from him, carefully keeping out of reach.

"Forgive my haste," she said, "but I do believe I'll be going."

She turned and started walking briskly, trying not to wobble on the uneven ground. There was always a chance it would work. Then she had to go and trip.

"Now hold on a minute." He clamped a hand strong as a vise around her arm and steadied her before she fell.

Damnit. She was caught.

"It's not safe for a lady like you to wander around an empty racetrack in the dark. Tell me what you're doing here, and I'll take you back where you belong."

He let her go slowly, making sure she was steady, then pulled a flashlight from his pocket and turned it on her. Frozen in place, she watched him take her in—the shimmering golden gown that hugged her curves and barely covered her knees; the dripping diamonds that flashed and sparked in the light; the blonde curls, tied back in a careful chignon. She looked every inch the tipsy socialite that she was, damn it all.

His smoldering coffee-colored eyes sparked with dangerous interest for a moment. Then he shook his head as if to clear it. "You look familiar. Do I know you from somewhere?"

Oh hell. He recognized her. It was only a matter of time until he realized who she was.

"Don't be ridiculous," she said, heart pounding a mile a minute. "Just let me go, and pretend you never saw me. It's all a dream. I'm not really here." Sweat trickled down the back of her neck as she waited to see how he would respond.

He put the flashlight down on the bottom wing of a nearby biplane and stepped close. Their shadows stretched larger than life against the far wall of the hangar.

"You know a high-class girl like you really shouldn't spend time in an empty hangar at midnight with a guy like me."

She stayed still and silent, praying he would let her go, though some part of her relished the danger. The heart-pounding rush of courting peril had always held an undeniable appeal for her.

"So why is a nice girl like you sneaking around here like a burglar?"

"Who said I was a nice girl?" The words came out before she could stop them. God, she must have lost her mind to blurt out something like that to a stranger in the night.

"Hmm," he said with an appreciative smile. "You do look like sin wrapped in silk." He leaned in, and his breath tickled her neck. Something electric crackled between them, and she could hardly breathe. Then he took a step back, holding his hands up again. "But on the off chance I'm not dreaming, I'm going to keep my hands off you and behave like a gentleman."

She wasn't sure whether to flee or lean in. This was all so unreal, and her head was so addled by the heady mix of hazard, attraction, and champagne. "Thank you. I'm having a very bad night, and I would greatly appreciate it if you would let me go."

His gaze softened. "You're free to go any time you like, but I really would prefer to take you back to wherever it is you came from. It isn't safe for a girl in diamonds to wander around at night like this. Where did you come from, anyway? Gorgeous socialites don't exactly come wandering into my hangar every day."

She raised an eyebrow. "*Your* hangar? I thought it was the Belmont family's hangar." Oh dear. She shouldn't have said that.

"Shit."

And there it was. His eyes widened with realization, and his body froze. She was no longer his mystery angel in the night.

"You're Aurora Belmont."

"I prefer 'Rory.' Only my father calls me Aurora," she said, struggling to keep her composure.

"You're the daughter of August Belmont Jr., the financier who owns the land we're standing on, not to mention half of New York City. You're *that* Aurora Belmont."

He backed up several steps and stared.

"Yes, I'm *that* Aurora Belmont."

"Worse yet, he's an army major now, from what I've heard, which makes him my superior officer."

She should have been relieved that he was backing away like he'd seen a ghost. Why was she disappointed by his sudden distance? "Are you going to let me go back to my party at the Turf and Field Club?"

He looked like a man enthralled by a cobra.

"Yes, Miss Belmont."

"Call me Rory."

"No, thank you, Miss Belmont. I'd prefer not to be overly familiar with a woman whose father could have me hanged for looking at her wrong."

She rolled her eyes.

"That's absurd. My father has never hanged anyone. Shot, yes. He's serving in the war, after all." She backed away and started heading for the barn doors without him, determined to make her escape.

"On the other hand, anything could happen to you out there alone in the night. I'd better see you safely back to your party even if it does mean risking my neck." He jogged after her.

"I assure you it's not necessary." She picked up the pace.

"And I assure you, it is," he said, easily catching up with her. "What kind of gentleman would I be if I didn't look out for a damsel in distress?"

"I am *not* a damsel in distress." She walked a bit faster, even if his concern was rather touching. It wouldn't do to be seen with a strange man. People would certainly assume the worst, especially after Archie.

"Oh, then you're happy to be going back to whatever fancy party you ran away from?"

No, she wasn't, but she could hardly tell him that. "My fiancé won't be pleased if I come back to our engagement party with a strange man."

"You ran away from your own engagement party? Are they trying to marry you off to some old geezer or something, Miss Belmont?"

She stopped in her tracks and turned on him. His guesses were a little bit too close to the mark.

"He's not that old."

He raised an eyebrow.

Damn. She shouldn't have included the "that." "For your information, he's only forty-three, not old at all." Not like some of the prospective husbands her father tried to foist on her before he landed on Edward. Uninspiring as Edward was, he was the best of the lot.

"Still twice your age, I'd wager." Hank's eyes were filled with insufferable pity as he reached out to touch her but stopped short.

"For a man so terrified of my father, you're awfully forward.

Why don't you keep your opinions to yourself?" She scowled as her pulse quickened.

"Yes, Miss Belmont," he said, but he held her gaze. For a moment, it was as if he could see into her soul—all the pain and vulnerability she hid from the world laid bare. She braced herself for his disdain. After all, there was nothing the men in her life despised more than displays of feminine weakness. But instead, his expression was filled with kindness and compassion, and something inside her broke.

Swallowing hard, she turned away and began walking again with him trailing several feet behind.

"I'll be leaving now," she said, spotting the door to the club. "Or are you going to follow me in there and ruin my reputation all over again?"

To her infinite relief, he stopped. "Good luck, princess."

Pausing, she felt scorched by a pair of soulful brown eyes. She turned her head one last time, glancing at his silhouette.

"Goodbye, Hank."

Heart pounding, she walked back into the club.

2

Well, that was a terrible night's sleep.

Hank poured himself a crap cup of coffee in the lunchroom, staring out over the whitewashed picnic tables and squinting at the sunlight through the windows. It was only seven-thirty in the morning, and already it was hot as Hades. The new cadets would be here soon, poor sods. He supposed he should make some attempt to look like a heroic pilot instead of someone dead twice over from exhaustion, smelling as hot and swampy as he felt. He really needed to change his shirt. Good grief.

He choked down the caustic brew and headed to the locker room. A shave, a shower, and clean clothes would do wonders for him. Making a beeline for his cubby, he pushed past the full-body leather flying suit that hung there and grabbed a towel and some soap from his ditty bag. The room still smelled of fresh paint, having been built only a month before. Only half of the cubbies were in use, but that would change soon enough.

As he gathered his things, his thoughts turned to the previous night.

Aurora Belmont. Aurora fucking Belmont. Not that he ever

slept well on guard in the hangar, but Jesus Christ. *Rory*, she wanted him to call her. Princess Rory.

Over and over the nightmare replayed as he dozed after she left. It started pleasantly enough. She came back despite his warnings, a mischievous look in those sparkling blue eyes, and he peeled that sinful dress off her luscious body and…Papa Belmont materialized from thin air, took aim, and unmanned him.

As a pilot, Hank had no great attachment to his life, but by God while he lived, he wanted his cock and balls safe from harm. And now, he found himself peeking around every corner to make sure Major Belmont wasn't standing there with a shotgun, ready to blow them off.

Even getting into the white-tiled shower stall, he looked twice before closing the flimsy tan curtain behind him. No, it was just a bad dream. He shook himself and lathered up. She had every reason to keep their little meeting secret. He was in no danger, was he? Thank God he was never going to see her again.

Of course, in attempting to ban her from his thoughts, he brought her front and center. His cock began to stir, and he gave it a withering look. Instead of retreating, it grew unapologetically rampant. "Fine," he grumbled aloud. "I'll ring up Dorothy and see if she's up for a visit." At the word "Dorothy," it deflated. "Oh, come on. Now you don't like Dorothy?"

"Hawley, are you conversing with your willy again?" asked a familiar voice with a slight Irish brogue that made him jump a mile.

"Go to hell, O'Donnell."

Two men's laughter rang out after that.

Hank groaned. "Not you too, Pritchard. I thought I was alone in here. Can't a man lecture his wayward prick in peace?"

More laughter, but this time he joined them. After all, he was a grown man talking to his willy.

"You've got fifteen minutes until the new cadets get here, Hawley," said Lieutenant Pritchard. "You might want to hurry things along. You know the major will be miffed if you're late again."

"I'll be there."

He shut off the faucet, toweled off, wrapped his towel around his waist, and headed to the sinks for a shave.

"Who's got you lecturing your willy this time, Hawley?" Lieutenant O'Donnell called out. "Apparently, it isn't Dorothy."

"No, not Dorothy. A society girl I met by accident. Completely gorgeous and completely untouchable. Don't know what I was thinking even speaking to her."

He really should stick to girls like Dorothy, who wanted nothing more than an occasional good time, no strings attached.

"Oho! Nice going, Hawley," said Pritchard. "Get yourself one of those Upper East Side Knickerbocker girls, and you are set for life."

He lathered his face and began to shave. "Not likely to marry me, seeing how she already has a fiancé."

"They say forbidden fruit tastes the sweetest," Pritchard wheedled.

"What did she look like?" O'Donnell asked. "Blonde or brunette?"

"Blonde."

Hank nicked himself and cursed.

"Blue eyes or brown?" O'Donnell persisted.

"Blue."

"Thin or…nicely rounded?"

"O'Donnell," he warned, and he rinsed off his face and put a bit of tissue on the spot he nicked.

But apparently, O'Donnell wasn't done. While Hank was getting dressed, he asked, "To which fruits would you compare her various assets? For example—"

"Shut up, O'Donnell, before you say something you will regret."

"Oo, she really got under your skin, didn't she?" His friend was grinning from ear to ear.

"I said, shut your trap."

Hank ran a comb through his hair and hurried out to the lunchroom, grabbing himself another cup of heinous coffee, and arrived in the hangar just in time to greet the major and the new cadets. He came to attention.

"At ease, Hawley," Major Fleet said. They both stood by the chalkboard at the front of the room and watched the cadets seat themselves at lunchroom tables. "Am I imagining things, or is this batch even younger than the last?"

"With all due respect, I don't think they got younger. I think we got older, sir."

Major Fleet smiled. "And thank God for that, eh? Another day older. Another day wiser."

"Can't complain, sir," Hank said, taking another drink and wondering if someone swapped the coffee with gasoline.

O'Donnell and Pritchard came in with their own steaming mugs and saluted.

"Time to get started, don't you think, gentlemen?" Major Fleet asked the three of them, then made his way to the front of the room. "Cadets, welcome to the U.S. Postal Service."

As usual, there were a couple of quiet snickers. "It's true that no one is shooting at you here, but make no mistake, this is dangerous work. Every day, we push the limits of what is possible with these airplanes. New York to Philadelphia and Philadelphia to Washington, D.C.: both routes push our Jennies to their maximum range. Lieutenant Hawley, about how often would you say you run out of fuel before you land?"

"One out of every four trips, sir."

Hank watched as the more fearful among them swallowed and gripped their seats.

"Lieutenant O'Donnell, what happens if there's thick cloud cover and you veer off course?"

"You run out of fuel, sir."

More gripped their seats.

"Lieutenant Pritchard, what happens if the weather is against you, and you face unexpected headwinds?"

"You run out of fuel, sir."

Now the entire cadet class sat wide-eyed.

"And Lieutenant Hawley, what happens if you let your mind wander and you do a piss poor job of navigating?"

Hank turned to the cadets. "Cadets, what do you think happens?"

"You run out of fuel, sir," they answered as one from the worn wooden benches.

"That's right, boys," said Major Fleet, pacing back and forth in front of his audience with his hands behind his back. "And we haven't even talked about mechanical failures. Every time you take to the skies, you are taking a risk. Mistakes in the air are deadly." He stopped his pacing and turned to face the cadets. "Now, our military leaders think you need some extra practice with navigation before you face the Germans."

A skinny cadet with huge eyes and plentiful freckles raised his hand in the first row. "How does this help us against the Germans, sir?"

"Your name, cadet?" the major asked with a smile. Someone always asked this question without fail.

"Brown, sir."

"Well, Cadet Brown, do you know what the number one cause of death for Allied pilots is?"

Frowning, the cadet said, "Enemy fire, sir?"

"You would think so, wouldn't you?" Major Fleet answered. "But no, it isn't enemy fire." He perused all the young, eager faces, giving them a significant look. "It's navigation errors. Green pilots follow their leaders into combat, get separated from the group in the fog of battle, and then can't find their way home. That, gentlemen, is why you are here.

"Lieutenant Hawley here is going to demonstrate to you this morning how to land with the engines off."

Beautiful. He was this morning's sacrificial lamb. He absolutely didn't get enough sleep for this, but, of course, he could never say no.

"Death or glory," he murmured to O'Donnell, who raised his cup of joe in a mock toast.

"Death or glory, you crazy bastard," O'Donnell replied. "Your society girl doesn't know what she's missing!"

Hank led the way out to the hangar, deliberately choosing a different Jenny than the one where Princess Belmont was perched last night. The last thing he needed was the distraction of imagining her lovely legs splayed across the fuselage right in front of him. He narrated his pre-flight checks for the benefit of the cadets. Mechanical failures were all too common with the Jennies. A man had to check every inch of the plane with a mechanic's precision to ensure it was safe to fly.

Satisfied at last that the plane was ready, he signaled to O'Donnell to swing the propeller. O'Donnell gave it a good shove and backed out of the way. Hank opened the throttle and taxied out to the runway.

It was a bright, sunny day out, with not a cloud in the sky to obscure the punishing sun. The air rippled with heat, and his soaked shirt was sticking to him. Sweat stung his eyes beneath his goggles, and he couldn't wipe it away. Blinking and squinting, he picked up speed on the runway. The wings lifted as if pulled by some invisible hand and left the ground behind.

Suddenly, his exhaustion disappeared, replaced by the familiar exhilaration of flight. The roar of the engine vibrated the whole plane. A breeze, nonexistent moments before, blew the sweat from his face. The ground dropped away, and he was a bird in the sky, flying toward the unreachable heavens. Maybe someday mankind would build a plane that could reach the stars, but for now, he was content to know he flew as high as any man ever had.

There was nothing like the freedom of flight. Every time he took off, he was gambling with death, but there was a peace in knowing the dice had been rolled already. He was in the air and he would either land safe or not. His skill could only take him so far. Fate held his life in the balance. One day, he would lose this gamble, but nothing made him feel more alive than cheating death time and again.

Turning back toward the runway, he said a silent prayer and cut the engine. No matter how many times he did this, it was a white-knuckle ride. It should have been peaceful, quietly gliding, the only sound the whistle of air through the wires on the wings. But death was coming toward him fast. If he didn't maneuver the plane just so, he would crash, giving the cadets a lesson they would never forget and follow his brother, Benny, into the hereafter.

"Not today, Death, you son of a bitch." He adjusted the angle of approach. Closer, closer. Benny's face came to mind, as it so often did when he was in danger. Taking a deep breath, he pushed away the memory. He needed all his concentration for the task at hand.

Pulling up at the last moment, the wheels made contact with solid ground—a clean, gentle landing. The skid dragged against the runway, slowing the plane to a halt, and he said another silent prayer of thanks. He wasn't a churchgoer, but no man who did what he did could live long without someone to pray to. Facing the thin line between today and eternity again and again did that to a man.

It wasn't wise to tempt fate like that over and over, but the thought of finishing his engineering degree and taking a desk job filled him with dread. He wasn't ready yet. The rush was addictive, and he couldn't let it go.

As he came to a halt, the cadets cheered and ran over to the plane, almost distracting him from an expensive black car that drove up and stopped in the distance. A chauffer discharged two passengers, one a man, one a woman. Some sixth sense prickled the hair on the back of his neck. Who were they, and why did they make him so damned nervous?

He went through his landing checks mechanically, describing aloud what he was doing, then he climbed down to rejoin the group of starry-eyed recruits who insisted on slapping him on the back and shaking his hand.

Behind the cadets was a stranger in uniform—a major in the Army Air Service, judging from the man's epaulets. He had a thick mustache and dark, piercing eyes. His posture and bearing were unmistakably aristocratic. Beside him was a blonde with a suspiciously familiar silhouette, wearing a powder-blue confection that matched her eyes. No. It couldn't be.

"Ah, there you are, Lieutenant Hawley," said Major Fleet. "Major Belmont here arrived just in time to see your performance." Hank jumped to attention, surreptitiously checking Major Belmont for a gun. Sweat trickled down his back. He forced himself to smile. *Simply delighted to meet you, sir. Never mind that your daughter and I had a little rendezvous last night in this very hangar.*

Major Belmont smiled back. "I brought my daughter, Aurora, with me. She's fascinated by airplanes and insisted I bring her along."

She smiled and nodded at Hank with cool distance, as if he was a stranger. Well, what did he expect? A kiss?

"Hawley here is the best pilot we have," said Major Fleet. "He served under me in France. I brought him home to the States when we launched airmail service back in May. He's been with us from the start."

Princess Rory was looking around at anything but him. He would do well to watch the two majors instead of her, he reminded himself. As he dragged his eyes away, she met his gaze for a split second. Something crackled and sparked within him in that moment, just as it had last night. Did she feel it too? Whatever this was, it was too dangerous to indulge.

Fortunately, her father seemed not to have noticed.

"Major Belmont, I have to ask," said Fleet, "what brings you out here today? It's always a pleasure to see you, but we weren't expecting you."

Major Belmont shrugged. "I had a free morning and wanted to see how this airmail experiment was going. By the way, how much longer do you think you'll be using my racetrack as an airstrip? I'm happy to support the cause and all, but the noise of the airplanes scares the horses."

"I don't know, Major. We're working as quickly as possible on an alternative. If the postmaster general had only given us a chance to prepare properly before starting service—"

"No need to explain, Major. I still don't know how you got this operation up and running on such short notice. It's nothing short of a miracle if you ask me. When the war is over, you come look me up. A man like you could go far."

Major Fleet smiled. "Thank you. I'll keep that in mind."

As if Major Fleet needed a millionaire to give him a leg up. As if he hadn't climbed the ranks and earned the same rank that Belmont bought. The condescension was astonishing!

"Papa?" Princess Rory said, putting her hand on her father's arm. "Do you suppose that nice gentleman over there—" she pointed at Hank, and his heart stopped, "—might be willing to show me one of the planes? You know how I love to see them up close."

Major Fleet answered by calling out, "Lieutenant Hawley. The young lady wants to see one of our Jennies. Can you show her while the major and I catch up? O'Donnell, Pritchard, take the cadets and walk them through the steps for landing with engines cut."

She sauntered over and took his arm, as if she were strolling through the park with her beau. The intoxicating scent of magnolias wafted over to him. He did his best not to flinch at her touch.

Clearing his throat, he led her over to the nearest Jenny. "Miss Belmont—"

"Rory," she corrected quietly.

"Not on your life," he murmured for her ears only. "Your father's standing right there."

She smiled. "Show me the airplane, Lieutenant Hawley," she said aloud.

"Of course, Miss Belmont," he answered in a loud enough voice to carry to the majors.

She dug her nails into his arm. Lovely fingers. Flawless manicure. Her nails were the palest of pinks.

"This model of plane is called—"

"A Jenny, short for Curtiss JN-4, manufactured up in Buffalo by Curtiss Aeroplane and Motor Company based on a design by Glenn Curtiss and B. Douglas Thomas. It has a Hispano-Suiza 8 V-8 engine with one hundred-fifty horsepower and a maximum speed of seventy-five miles per hour. It has a wingspan of forty-three feet seven inches and a length of twenty-seven feet four inches. It's nine feet eleven inches high and weighs just over a ton empty."

He swallowed hard.

She trailed her fingers along the fuselage, and it took all his concentration to avoid imagining those fingers on his own flesh. *Dorothy. Focus on Dorothy. Poor Dorothy. I'll have to let her down easy.*

"I want to learn to fly, you see, but Father won't let me." She looked at the plane with the same hungry reverence he felt the first time he was close to one. If man could fly, then he had to try it. From the moment he set eyes on the rickety contraption, he was lost. If only Benny hadn't been bitten by the same bug.

Turning to look him in the eye, Princess Belmont said, "Take me up? I want to feel the wind on my face."

What?

"I don't think your father would approve, Miss Belmont."

"Papa!" she called out. He was still standing with Major Fleet beside the hangar.

"Yes, dear?"

"I'd like to go for a short flight. May I? This nice young man has offered to fly me."

"*I did not*," Hank whispered furiously at her.

"I'm afraid not, my dear. We must be going. Another time," her father said.

Hank watched her jaw and fists clench, but she said nothing. "Another time," she said as she stroked the fuselage one last time. Turning to him, she said, "Until next time, Hank," and sauntered off.

As he watched their car drive off, he took a deep, shuddering breath. He could only pray there wouldn't be a next time. The woman was a danger to his health. Thank heavens she was completely out of his reach.

3

On the ride back to the city, Papa ignored Rory as usual, making notes in his ever-present little black notebook. After all these years, it shouldn't have needled her, but it did. His accounts had always taken precedence over her. But ever since her scandal, he seemed determined to pretend she was part of the scenery.

She stared out the window in stony silence, trying not to let the distance between them get under her skin. To distract herself, she let her mind wander to airplanes, the magic of flight, and…a certain pilot. She couldn't shake the memory of his muscular arms surrounding her—that deep voice, that smoky scent, those penetrating eyes. What would it be like if she was someone else, someone who was free to see where their flirtatious encounter led?

Alas, she would never find out. Her fate was sealed. Her wedding had been announced, and her father had already signed the marriage contract on her behalf. From a legal standpoint, she as good as belonged to Edward already. Her gilded cage awaited. A bleak, loveless life stretched out before her, and she shivered despite the heat.

It was a relief to arrive home to find Aunt Alva waiting for her. If she couldn't have love, at least she could find purpose.

Rory looked at her stout and imposing aunt decked out in blue serge despite the heat, her face as hard and determined as any army veteran. If Rory was something of a hoyden, Aunt Alva was Her Majesty Queen of Hoydendom. A notorious blue-stocking from her early days, her aunt had been attending rallies, chaining herself to things, and getting arrested for several decades. Every time she saw Aunt Alva, she had to resist the ridiculous temptation to salute.

"Rory, my dear," Aunt Alva said with the cadence of a general, "are you prepared for battle this afternoon? We march on city hall, August," she said, turning to Rory's father. "We'll show that Mayor Hylan the power that women hold in this town. And then we're headed down to Wall Street. Those stock-market hooligans are overdue for a lesson in women's equality."

"For the love of God, be careful, Alva. You know I don't want Rory to end up in jail. It would reflect poorly on the senator," her father said. "None of us want a scandal so close to the wedding."

Aunt Alva waved her hand, brushing his concerns away. "He should consider it a privilege to be marrying a young lady so dedicated to the cause. But don't you worry, August. You know I always look out for her." Peering over his shoulder toward Rory, she called out, "Don't forget water. We can't have you passing out. And bring an apple too in case you're hungry. And a hand-kerchief. And don't forget a parasol—dual purpose. It protects you from the sun and you can whack people with it."

Rory rushed around collecting supplies and provisions for the afternoon. In no time, she was packed and ready to go.

She waved goodbye to her father, who didn't even look up, and headed out, taking a deep breath and grinning at the after-noon sun. "Thank heavens for you," she said as she stepped into the back of her aunt's chauffeured car. "Papa was such a trial this morning. I went all that way out to Belmont Park with him, and he wouldn't let me fly."

Aunt Alva tutted. "Your father is enlightened about many things, but he doesn't believe women can face the same dangers as men. And your stepmother is no help. She wholeheartedly agrees. Someday I'll succeed in convincing them both the only way to make you safe is to let you take risks and harden yourself through adversity."

Rory yearned for the chance to do exactly that. Her life was altogether too coddled, and she longed to test herself against real and meaningful challenges.

"If only your mother had lived," Aunt Alva continued, "she would have set him straight. She was a formidable woman, your mother. It's a shame you never got to know her. I may have only married into the Belmont family, but I knew your mother for many years. She was always a fiercely loyal friend. When things fell apart with my swine of a first husband, she stood by me even as many of my other society friends suddenly stopped calling. Did you know she was my matron of honor when I married Oliver?"

Rory did know. She'd heard the story many times. Stories were all she had of her mother. Aunt Alva always made her sound so heroic…and so different in every way from Rory's stepmother Eleanor.

"I wish I'd known her," Rory said because she knew her aunt expected her to say something, though she never really knew what to say when Aunt Alva talked like this.

"She was so happy when I joined the family, and we got to be sisters. It broke my heart to lose her just two years later. I was almost as devastated as when my Oliver died. I cried for months! You become more like her with every passing day, did you know that?"

Rory swallowed hard, heat rising in her throat. What would it have been like to grow up with two loving parents instead of one who seemed to resent her very existence?

"She would have been so proud of you, my dear."

Shifting in her seat, Rory looked out the window and clenched her fists, nails digging into the palms of her hands. It would have been so lovely to believe her aunt's kind words, but she knew exactly where she stood with her only surviving parent. *Would Mother have been any more understanding of my dramatic fall from grace had she lived?*

But such thoughts served no purpose. She had to be practical. After all, how could she complain about a life of leisure and comfort when so many in the world struggled for their daily bread?

"Look at the crowd," she said, changing the subject as New York City Hall came into view. "This may be our biggest rally yet." Her heart swelled at the sight of so many women gathered to fight for their rights, displacing the hollow ache from thoughts of her long-deceased mother. The energy of the crowd was infectious, and she could hardly wait to join them and lose herself in the energy of the protest.

When the car stopped, a swarm of friends surrounded them, anxious to welcome them and get access to the signs Aunt Alva always had stashed in the trunk. Rory allowed her spirits to be buoyed up by their infectious enthusiasm.

"Evelyn," Rory cried, climbing out of the car. "I'm so happy to see you!" She rushed to her friend's side. "How is Clyde?" she whispered.

"Shh! Not here." Evelyn blushed.

Rory laughed. "No one can hear us, dear. I swear your secret is safe with me. After all, you already know all my secrets."

"Speaking of… Have you seen your pilot again?"

As soon as Rory returned to the engagement party after visiting the hangar, she dragged Evelyn into a quiet corner and told her everything, much to her friend's delight. There was nothing Evelyn loved more than a juicy secret, not that she would ever tell a soul. Rory trusted her completely. It was because of Evelyn's encouragement that she'd gone to the airfield in the morning.

"Maybe I have," Rory said with a wink. "But you go first. How is that artist of yours? I haven't seen him in ages."

Evelyn leaned closer. "We've been keeping a low profile. Mama got suspicious, but maybe you'll see him tonight if—"

"Uh oh. Aunt Alva is signaling us. We'd better get in place. I'll catch up with you later." Disappointed at the interruption, Rory wove her way to the front of the crowd beside her aunt, but her spirits soon lifted as the energy of the crowd infected her.

During marches like this, the collective power of thousands of protesters filled her with hope for a better future that she hardly dared imagine. Nothing would change her engagement with Edward, but perhaps life would be more tolerable with him if women won the vote and could fight for fairer laws. Once she married, Edward would own her property and her person in every meaningful sense. The only way to buy herself a modicum of freedom and autonomy was to change the laws of the land.

Holding up their signs, the crowd of suffragettes began to march. "*Shout, shout up with your song! Cry with the wind for the dawn is breaking,*" they sang in a remarkably civilized chorus. They practically sounded like a church choir. Rory floated on a wave of hope and exhilaration at the sound.

Police closed in around them as they marched. That only prompted Rory to sing all the louder, even if she wasn't the most tuneful of the bunch. She linked arms with Alva and Evelyn, bracing herself for a confrontation.

As they marched past the doors of city hall, Rory belted her favorite line of the song, "*Life, strife, these two are one, naught can be done but with faith and daring.*" She had both faith and daring and was determined to win the day. The country might have founding fathers, but after the suffrage movement won the day, it would have founding mothers too. And she was determined to be one of them.

As the march turned south on Broadway toward the southern tip of Manhattan, the police formed a human barricade to stop them from proceeding. Rory's heart beat faster as they approached. She, Evelyn, and Aunt Alva were at the center of a human chain that pressed closer and closer to the police, forcing them to edge back to avoid direct conflict. The police knew exactly who the three of them were and knew better than to push back, but the women behind them were more vulnerable. It was an honor to be part of this powerful group of angry women and to lend her name to their defense. This must have been how George Washington felt, vanquishing the British at long last at the Battle of Yorktown.

Rory yelled the final words of the song instead of singing them. "March, march, many as one! Shoulder to shoulder, and friend to friend!" A particularly burly looking policeman locked eyes with the working-class woman behind her, leering and smacking his baton in his hand. Rory stepped forward to shield the woman. She might not have a bayonet, but she had an umbrella and knew how to use it.

He made a move toward them, baton swinging.

"Don't you touch her," Rory said, positioning herself directly in front of the officer.

He narrowed his eyes and smirked without slowing his advance. "You're a troublemaker, ain't ya, princess?"

"I'm exercising my right as a citizen to protest unjust laws." She grasped her umbrella, ready to raise it in defense, as her heart pounded so loudly she could hardly hear the crowd around her.

All her accumulated anger at her father, Edward, and her circumstances focused to a point as the world fell away and she stared the officer down. She refused to let another man try to put her in her place, and she certainly wasn't going to allow him to touch a hair on the heads of any of the women behind her. If he was foolish enough to cross her, he would learn just how much fight she had left in her, despite the world's attempts to put her down.

Aunt Alva pulled her back and stepped forward. "Come to the other side of me, right now," she said, hauling Rory with a force that belied her age. "I promised your father you wouldn't get in trouble, and I'll thank you not to tempt fate."

Rory kept her eyes locked on the officer.

For a long, tense moment, they stared each other down.

"If you touch one hair on the head of these women, I swear you will live to regret it." Rory knew she shouldn't goad the man, but she refused to be silenced.

"Let it go, Ernie. These birds ain't worth it," said the officer beside him, pulling him back. The man backed away slowly. "Go take a walk and cool off before you do something stupid."

With one last resentful look, the man turned and disappeared.

A little burst of triumph welled in Rory's heart. She had won. At least for now.

She let out her breath slowly, relaxing the death grip she had on her umbrella. Her pent-up fury receded slowly, leaving her on edge and spent. The sun beat down on her, and she gritted her teeth, grim determination replacing her earlier buoyancy.

As the march circled back to City Hall, she chanted until her voice grew hoarse, praying that their words didn't fall on deaf ears. But whether they changed any minds or not, the march stiffened her resolve to fight on. For another hour, they sang and chanted in the heat, and Rory lost herself in the energy of the crowd, letting it inspire her and ignoring her aching feet and raw throat.

She thought about Hank's daring landing earlier today and the way the cadets celebrated his safe return. Nothing worth having was without risk. If he could face down death, then surely, she could fight on with these amazing women around her. The struggle made her feel alive and connected to others in a way that nothing else did, even if the progress of the suffrage movement was agonizingly slow.

As Aunt Alva gave the call to disperse, and the women around her went their separate ways, Evelyn caught her arm. "You look like a woman in need of tea."

Rory knew "tea" meant Manhattans and dancing at a secret club they both frequented. It sounded like heaven. "I wish I could, but I'm afraid I can't. I'm supposed to accompany Edward to the opera."

It was a grim prospect after the exhilaration of the march. How was one supposed to go back to playing the socialite after the elation of freedom, even if it was only for a few hours? And yet that was exactly what she would have to do. After touching the sky, she had to set foot on the mundane ground once again.

"Too bad. Next time?" asked Evelyn.

"Definitely."

Their conversation was interrupted by Aunt Alva, who had just finished announcing the details of the next march to a small group crowded around her. "Come now, Rory, my dear." She gestured toward the car.

Rory kissed Evelyn on the cheek and said her goodbyes, then joined her aunt for the drive home.

When the car rolled up to the curb outside her mansion, Rory's stomach clenched as she looked up at the gray stone.

Aunt Alva reached over and squeezed her hand. "You'll be out of that house and away from your father soon enough, my dear."

If only that gave her comfort.

Rory put on a smile and squeezed her aunt's hand. "See you soon, Aunt Alva."

Hurrying through the door, she was stopped by the butler. "Edward is in the drawing room, Miss, and wishes to see you."

With a little sigh, she headed down the hall to see her fiancé. The last thing she wanted at that moment was to spend time with him.

Her father was talking in low tones with Edward as she entered the wood-paneled room, padding along the thick, hunter-green rug.

"There you are at last, Aurora," Edward said, looking up from his conversation with her father with a pinched smile. "I've been waiting a rather long time." The edge in his voice made Rory want to turn around and walk back out of the room.

She let out her breath slowly, forcing herself to smile. He was in a mood. That didn't bode well for the rest of the evening.

"I only just got back. I need time to change into my dress for this evening," she said, sweeping in and kissing him chastely on the cheek.

"I'll leave you two alone," her father said, looking between them with narrowed eyes and a touch of a smile. "Think about what I said, Edward. I'm counting on your vote to stop this nonsense," he added as he left the room.

"You can count on me," Edward called out as the door shut. "I wanted to speak to you, Aurora."

She looked her fiancé up and down, trying to remind herself of all the reasons she had agreed to marry him. From the outside, they looked like a match made in heaven. He was handsome. She would give him that. The man had an athletic build and thick silver hair, and he filled out his finely tailored suit rather well. She might have found him attractive if only he were better behaved. But this was hardly a love match. She was marrying him for practical reasons, and he was doing likewise. Still, it rankled that he couldn't be bothered to remember her preferred name.

"We're engaged. Please call me Rory."

He rolled his eyes. "Rory, Aurora—I really don't care. I need you to come to Washington, D.C. tomorrow. There's a fundraiser at the Wilkinson's that I need you to accompany me to."

"I have plans already." Did he really expect her to drop everything and head to D.C. on no notice?

"Then cancel them."

Apparently, he did. How could she get out of this? "Don't you think it's a bit improper for me to travel alone to D.C. and attend events with you before we're wed?"

It was a stretch, but maybe it would work.

"What are you worried about? It's not as if you have a reputation to protect."

Her jaw dropped as fifty retorts spun through her head. *Would he dare say such a thing in front of Papa? Not to mention the hypocrisy, given his own behavior.* She forced herself to take a deep breath. *Now, now. Be a practical girl, Rory. It's not as if you don't know exactly where you stand with him.*

"How is the wedding planning going?" he asked lightly, as if he hadn't just gravely insulted her.

She cleared her throat, struggling to maintain composure. "It would be going just fine if my stepmother didn't interfere so much. You'd think it was her wedding, the way she orders me around. I wish we could keep things simple and small. I don't even know half the people on the guest list."

"Small would defeat the purpose."

Breathe, Rory. She plastered a false smile on her face. "How so? I thought the purpose was to get married."

"Of course, but the other purpose is the spectacle. I want my rivals to shake in their shoes, knowing I have the wealth and influence of August Belmont behind me."

And there it was, stated in no uncertain terms. "I hope you and my father's money live happily ever after."

She shouldn't have said it, but it was too late to take back.

"That's not how I meant it, and you know it." He looked at her as if she was an obstinate three-year-old. *God, how insulting.*

"Do I?"

Why was this bothering her so much today? Usually, she managed to be sensible.

"Don't be ridiculous, sweetheart. You know I'm not just marrying you for your money."

No, you're also marrying me to have a pretty ornament for your arm, someone attractive to bear your children, someone to impress your peers and put your past scandals with women to rest. I knew what I was signing up for.

She shivered despite the heat in the room.

"Don't worry, Edward," she said, resolutely pulling her gaze back to her fiancé. "I haven't suddenly developed any silly romantic notions. I'm a practical girl. But even practical girls like to think they are valued for more than their papa's bank account."

"Ah, so you're fishing for compliments," he said with a dismissive smirk. "How tiresome."

She was about to explode and tell Edward exactly what she thought of him when they were interrupted by a noise at the door. Her father walked in. "I forgot my notebook," he said, glancing around the room without looking at them.

"I should really go get ready for this evening," she said, taking advantage of the momentary distraction to make her escape. It was best if she left before she said anything irrevocable.

She hurried to her room. As soon as the door closed behind her, she heaved a sigh of relief. There were solid, rational reasons for marrying Edward. But she couldn't help but wish she could have flown away in one of the airplanes she visited the night before. If only she knew how to fly! More than once she'd thought about simply running away, impossible though that would be, given her fame in the society pages. But what would it have been like if she could have left her old life behind and simply become someone else? What would it have been like to marry a man who cared for her wellbeing?

As she dressed, her imagination wandered once again to her

mysterious pilot. He'd shown her more kindness in one evening than her fiancé had in their entire acquaintance. She smiled to herself and shook her head. Some things were not meant to be.

Putting the finishing touches on her makeup and pulling on a deep plum satin gown that fell to her calves, she headed downstairs back to Edward, dreading the night ahead.

4

———

*B*ack to work. It was another sweltering day. Sweat trickled down the back of Hank's neck as he parked his Model T and headed toward the hangar at Belmont Park.

He spotted the Turf and Field Club in the distance with its ridiculous turrets. For a moment, he was a knight in shining armor, riding on a horse to rescue a princess with blonde curls and mischievous blue eyes from an evil prince who wanted to steal her away.

What the hell is wrong with you, Hawley? He shook his head to clear it.

Coffee. That was what he needed.

Heading straight to the lunchroom, he poured himself a cup, took a drink, and winced. Yup. That woke him up all right.

After a few more acidic gulps, he sauntered out to his Jenny and yawned. Would he ever get the hang of mornings?

At least he wasn't thinking about Rory Belmont.

He didn't think about her as he went through the motions of his pre-flight checks. He definitely didn't picture her perched on the fuselage of his plane, her mischievous eyes following his every move.

As he took off, there was no feminine voice whispering, "Oh, Hank, I've never had such a smooth takeoff. Show me how you do it."

Because he *wasn't* thinking about her, damnit.

But despite his best intentions, the fantasy his mind had created slipped into the cockpit with him, straddling him and saying, "Take me higher, Hank. Take me soaring through the clouds." She moved against him, her taut nipples brushing against his chest through her thin, silk blouse.

No. Absolutely not. Hank had a plane to fly.

Michigan. Think of your family back in Michigan.

That just brought him back to this week's conversation with his sister. Another sore topic.

"Are you taking care of yourself, Hank?" Kate asked.

He wasn't, but he couldn't very well tell her that.

"Yes, Kate. You can tell Ma I'm taking good care of myself," he said into the phone. "Early to bed, early to rise. Apple a day and all that, I promise. Is *she* taking care of herself?"

"She's doing what she's always done—up at dawn milking cows and feeding chickens and then puttering around the farm all day. Lately, she's been canning up a storm. The house smelled like tomatoes for a week. And we had a bumper crop of zucchini. I can't tell you when I last had a zucchini-free meal."

Hank laughed. "What I wouldn't give for some of Ma's cooking, zucchini and all," he said.

"You should come home for a visit. Ma misses you."

"I will. I just don't know when," Hank sighed.

"It's been a rough year for her, losing Pops…and Benny. It would mean so much to her if you would come."

Hank winced at the catch in his sister's voice as she said Benny's name. "I will. I promise I'll try to figure out a time. Listen, I've got to go. I'll call you again same time next week. Give my love to Ma."

"Will do. Fly safe."

"I always do."

Another lie. He took unnecessary risks, and he knew it. Benny was the good son, the one who always did the right thing. If anyone was going to survive the war, it should have been him. Pneumonia took down Pops in the same year. It was just too much.

Hank adjusted his goggles and checked his navigation. Still on course, thank heavens.

But Michigan was still on his mind.

He was the man of the family now, even if he couldn't think of anyone less suited. He'd never wanted to stay on the farm. With a healthy father and a big brother who was eager to take it on, he never thought he'd have to.

Now he was prolonging the inevitable, putting off his return again and again because he knew if he went back, he'd never escape. Seeing Ma and Kate all alone on that farm with just Jeremiah and the farm hands to help would break his heart. He couldn't leave them to fend for themselves. But as long as he didn't go back, he could pretend everything was fine. He could avoid thinking about the enormous holes Pops and Benny left in their lives. It wasn't real. He didn't have to face it. Every week, he told himself just one more week, but it had been over a year now since Pops' funeral.

It was time to go. No more excuses. He should go buy those train tickets to Michigan right now. Except he couldn't. Because he was in the air, halfway to Philadelphia. And there wouldn't be time when he landed. He was supposed to change planes and fly to D.C. He wouldn't be back in the city with free time until Thursday. Hell, he'd waited this long, he could wait a few more days, couldn't he?

He checked his fuel levels and made a slight course adjustment.

As he looked up, a dark stripe appeared in the far distance, and he swore. The storm clouds moved fast, roiling where the coastal breeze hit the inland heat. He tried to find a nice field to land in to wait out the storm, but there were no good options. Before he knew it, he was flying into the storm. Thunder rumbled around him, and lightning flashed. The sky darkened, and rain began pouring down. The mail was safe beneath an oilcloth, but he was exposed, protected only by his goggles, leather jacket, and aviator cap.

Rain spattered his face and streamed down his neck, soaking his shirt and pants. *I just need to get to the other side.* A pocket of turbulence jolted him and made his heart skip a beat. *Stay with me, Jenny. Stay with me.*

These summer storms never lasted long. Fifteen, twenty minutes of violent drenching, then they disappeared.

He gripped the stick for dear life, praying this didn't knock him too far off course. Thunder cracked, and lightning struck right in front of him. The sizzle echoed in his ears as he prayed as hard as he'd ever prayed in his life.

The plane seemed to be trying to buck him out. He fumbled for the safety strap he usually didn't bother with and fastened it across his lap. Maybe today was the day he'd lose the fight. Who would miss him if he didn't make it out? His family? A few friends in the Postal Service? Hank didn't have much to show for himself aside from a few medals during the war. If only there was someone special, someone who loved him, a reason to return home.

Hank shook himself as the plane bucked again. This was the whole reason he'd avoided getting close. This right here. What right did he have to someone's heart when he did this for a living?

No. If he made it out of this, and that was a big if, he was going to keep his promise to himself to remain a bachelor. Because it was only a matter of time before this job killed him. If he fell in love, he'd only end up breaking hearts. It wouldn't be fair.

As if to prove his point, the plane began to spin out of control. He was losing altitude fast. Instinct and training kicked in and moved him through the motions of recovering. *Idle the engine. Ailerons neutral. Rudder opposite the spin. Elevator forward.*

A ray of sunshine pierced the clouds ahead. Was he coming out the other side? As he flew forward, the wind died down. The rain turned to a drizzle and then stopped. And as suddenly as it had started, it was over.

Breathing hard, Hank forced himself to relax, loosening the death grip he had on the stick and moving around as if to prove to himself he was still all there.

His brother's face hovered in his mind's eye. *Was this how Benny died? A spot of bad weather? Or was it enemy fire? Or an engine malfunction?* All Hank knew was the debris of Benny's plane was found near the town of Cantigny. How his brother died, Hank would never know. It ate at him. How long would it be before he followed his brother to the same fate?

But it was no good thinking like that. Hank shook his head to clear it and tried to focus on the present.

Examining the landscape, Hank cursed. He'd veered inland and had to get back on course and pray his fuel would get him to Philadelphia. Adjusting his trajectory, he made a beeline for his destination, letting the hot sun dry his soaked clothes. Just as Philadelphia came into view, the engine began to sputter. He wasn't going to make it. Desperately, he scanned for a field where he could set down and found one in the nick of time—a wheat field by the look of it. They'd have to compensate the farmer, but it was a small price to pay to keep the Jenny intact, not to mention saving his neck.

It was a bumpy descent that made him think fondly of his landing without power just the other day. At least then he'd had a beautifully clear runway. At the moment, he was praying that the stalks of wheat wouldn't damage his delicate wooden wings as they whipped against the plane with terrifying cracking sounds.

There was no socialite in powder blue waiting for him at the end of this rough and jarring ride, but thank God, he made it on one piece.

No sooner did he grind to a shuddering halt than the farmer came running at him wielding a pitchfork.

"What do you think you're doing to my field, you young whippersnapper?" the man demanded.

"I'm with the Postal Service, sir. My airplane ran out of fuel before I could land. Can you take me to the nearest telephone? I'd be happy to pay you," he said, knowing he'd be reimbursed. Because this was a common occurrence, they had a standard operating procedure for it.

The man narrowed his eyes, but he lowered his pitchfork. "I'll take you for fifty cents, even if you do look like something the cat dragged in."

It was highway robbery, but Hank had no choice. "Done." He handed over the money.

After the man dropped him off, he called the airfield and asked for a cadet to come out and bring fuel. The cadet could make the hop to the airfield with the Jenny while Hank drove the truck back.

Before long, he was at the airfield, taking a shower and putting on clean, dry clothes. It made him feel human again. He ate some lunch and smoked a cigar before heading off to D.C. in a different Jenny.

Everything went exactly according to plan on the second leg of his journey, and he landed in D.C. by suppertime. Lieutenant O'Donnell was there when he landed, as was Lieutenant Thompson, who he hadn't seen in about a month. "You got tomorrow off, Hawley?" Thompson asked.

"I do."

"Thought so. We're going out on the town tonight. Join us?"

"With pleasure." A night out with the boys. That was what he needed to keep his mind off things.

"Oh good," O'Donnell said, rubbing his hands together. "Maybe we'll finally pry out of you who this mystery woman was."

"Mystery woman?" Thompson asked. "Tell me everything."

"I thought you were engaged, Thompson." Hank shook his head.

"Engaged isn't dead, Hank. Spill the beans."

"He won't say where he met her or who she is. All we know is that she's a rich blonde with blue eyes." O'Donnell stopped in his tracks. "Saaaayyyyy, that Belmont girl who came to the airstrip the other day fits the description. It isn't her, is it?" O'Donnell's eyes sparkled with mischief.

Hank lit a cigar to hide his alarm. "As if a girl like that would even deign to speak to me."

"That's not a 'no,'" said Thompson, nudging Hank in the ribs.

"You two are worse than a sewing circle, you know that?" Hank said, waving his friend off with his cigar. "Now let's go find some nice girls that think we're goddamn heroes and show them a good time, shall we?"

Thompson led the way to a waiting cab. "I heard about this place from Ericson. He says the jazz is hot and the ladies are hotter. It's on Massachusetts Avenue by Dupont Circle."

They rode the short distance to the bar and got out of the taxi. Hank could hear the ragtime piano spilling out of the High Flyer from the sidewalk. As they walked inside, the scent of beer and hot pretzels permeated his nostrils. Peanut shells littered the floor, and a wooden propeller hung on the back wall with a sign claiming it was from the Wright Flyer.

Hank chuckled. Fat chance of that. Everyone knew the Wright brothers were more secretive than the Military Intelligence Division when it came to their planes. But it was fitting somehow for a pilot bar. What pilot didn't make a tall claim from time to time?

The place was hopping even though dinner hour had only just begun. A group of young women out for some fun settled into the table beside them. Before long, they were all on the dance floor together doing the turkey trot.

Hank found himself with a brunette named Sarah. "I work at a flower shop, and everyone says I have very discerning taste!" she yelled to him above the din.

He smiled indulgently. Normally, he would be turning on the charm, but for some reason he wasn't feeling it this evening. He listened politely and danced politely, and when she said it was time for her to go, he didn't try to stop her.

"What's with you?" O'Donnell asked when the brunette he'd been entwined with all evening went to the powder room. "She was cute. You're not still pining for your heiress, are you?"

"'Course not," he said quickly, attempting a nonchalant laugh. How could it possibly have anything to do with Rory? That would be ridiculous. "She just didn't interest me that much."

"Ha! Sure. You know, there's a cute blonde over there alone by the bar. Maybe she can take your mind off a certain other blonde who remains nameless?"

With limited enthusiasm, Hank made his way to the buxom blonde by the bar and introduced himself. She had kind, warm brown eyes that made him feel instantly at ease. He asked her for a dance, and she obliged. Then she let him buy her a drink. She told him about her job as a telephone operator, and he listened attentively, wondering why he felt no spark with her. Normally, a girl like her would light him up like a Christmas tree, but if he was being honest with himself, he was going through the motions.

He leaned in and kissed her, willing himself to muster some heat, but the kiss was as tepid as bathwater, at least for him. She seemed enthusiastic enough. He tried to imagine making love to her as he nuzzled her neck and ran his hands up and down her back. It was appealing in theory, but he felt numb, detached. Maybe he'd had too much to drink?

At that moment, the door opened, and in walked a silver-haired man oozing power. This guy had to be a politician or a business executive, someone who was accustomed to bending others to his will with a rakish smile and daunting eyes the color of ice. His perfectly tailored gray suit looked like it cost more than Hank's annual salary. And on his arm was…

Oh *no*.

5

The moment Rory walked in, she spotted him. Her pilot. What were the odds? Seeing him draped over some blonde at the bar, something inside her caught and burned wild. Even though it was *none* of her business. Who was he to her? Just an idle daydream.

The bartender waved at Edward. That was odd. Surely, Edward didn't know the bartender. Edward didn't respond, so it must have been a case of mistaken identity. This was definitely not the sort of place Edward usually frequented. For heaven's sake, there were peanut shells on the floor, and there was a propeller on the wall.

Edward steered her to a table. "They're all watching us. I like that dress you're wearing. Very attention catching."

She gave him a half smile. Yes, she looked good. Her dress was the latest fashion from Paris, made of dusky pink silk with a low square neckline and the merest whisper of transparent fabric hinting at sleeves. The skirt draped like the robes on a Greek statue, asymmetrical folds clinging to her shape. It fell to mid-calf, as short as propriety would allow. A long string of pearls dripped to her waist, and her hair was in a chignon, with ornately beaded ribbon in a band around her head.

Edward looked dapper as usual this evening in his gray, worsted wool suit with a midnight-blue silk tie. To all the world, they looked like a match made in heaven. Only she seemed to care that his eye wandered constantly. He ordered them drinks and an assortment of bar snacks.

She glanced at Hank, who was not looking in her direction at all. Good. That was as it should be.

"Are you all right? You seem a bit distracted," Edward asked, settling back in his chair.

"Hmm?" she said. "Oh, I'm fine. I thought I saw someone that looked familiar, but I was wrong."

"Familiar? At a place like this? Not likely," he said with a laugh.

The sense that he was withholding something grew, but she did her best to ignore it.

Their drinks arrived, and he raised his glass. "To the Belmonts."

She sighed inwardly. He was toasting her father, not her, but she would take what she could get.

"Well, I can't argue with that. To me." She clinked her glass against his and took a sip. Mmm. *Thank heavens for Manhattans.*

At that moment, a new singer took the stage, an oddly familiar redhead in a gown even more clinging than her own. Edward's expression suddenly turned into an appreciative leer, and the singer looked straight at him, then glanced at Rory and looked away.

Rory's stomach lurched. Her nails bit into her palms as something within her clicked. She could see Edward's hands on the perfectly round red silk-encased buttocks on stage. The singer from the engagement party. The absolute nerve of this man…

"Edward?" she said as lightly as she could manage.

"Hmm?" he said still staring at the stage.

"Edward," she hissed. He turned at last, blinking rapidly.

"What is *she* doing here?" she demanded.

He shrugged and took a drink. "What is who doing here?"

"The singer. She's one of your paramours, isn't she?" Her insides turned to ice. Enough was enough.

"Rory, now let's not jump to conclusions—"

"*Now*, you're calling me Rory? Admit the truth. She is, isn't she?"

He was silent.

She fought the urge to throw her drink in his face. "I shouldn't be surprised. I just wouldn't have expected you to flaunt it like this."

"I'm not flaunting—"

"Oh? What would you call this?" she hissed more vehemently than she intended.

You're a practical girl, remember?

She kept her gaze on Edward, trying not to notice that now Hank was looking at her. He wasn't the only one looking either. She and Edward were making a scene, no matter how quiet they tried to be.

"I thought it was for the best," Edward said quietly. "She spends a lot of time at my house. I thought it was better for you to meet her now than after we're married."

What?

"'After we're married'? You weren't planning to keep bringing her home, were you? If not for decency's sake, what about the marriage contract you signed with Papa?"

His face fell. His brow furrowed. She'd foolishly hoped the fidelity clause would keep Edward's more flagrant indiscretions in check once they were wed, but apparently she was wrong.

"You said you were a practical girl. Your father would never enforce the fidelity clause unless you complained. I thought you'd understand. What am I supposed to do while you're off with those termagants you call friends fighting for the vote? This is supposed to be a modern marriage. I thought you understood what that meant. I like you fine, but committing to you and only you for the rest of my life… What man could keep a promise like that?"

"Every married man worth his salt. That's who," she fumed, failing to keep her voice down. "Not to mention any senator who wants to keep his job. What do you think your constituents would think of our 'modern marriage'? And exactly how modern is it? Would I be free to behave just as badly as you?"

"People are looking, Rory," he whispered. "Let's go back to my place and we can finish this discussion in private."

"If you think I'm coming back to your place after this, you have another think coming," she whispered back.

"What are you going to do? Stay in a hotel?" he laughed.

"Yes, that's exactly what I'm going to do. You know Papa's secretary always reserves me a room when I come down to visit, and I intend to use it. Go home, Edward. I need some time to myself."

"Fine," he said aloud, throwing down his napkin and several bills to cover their tab. "We'll talk about this later when you're less hysterical." With that, he stormed out of the club, leaving her alone.

Just keep breathing.

She downed the remnants of her drink and ordered another. The singer caught her eye and gave her a triumphant look. She had to get out of here.

"Rory?"

That voice. She looked up. Hank finally used her name.

"Are you all right?" he asked. The blonde, she noticed, stood abandoned back at the bar, looking bereft.

"Of course, I'm all right." But a tear rolled down her cheek. "Damn it all," she said, furiously wiping it away. She wasn't supposed to feel like this. Her arrangement with Edward *was* a practical one, not a romantic one, so why was she crying?

"Of course, you are, princess," Hank said, taking a seat

without being invited. "Looks to me like you need to get out of here before that asshole you came in with comes back."

"Watch your tongue. He's my fiancé," she shot back reflexively.

"And he doesn't deserve you." Somewhat to her disappointment, he kept a respectful distance.

"And you do?" She eyed him with suspicion.

"Oh, I definitely don't deserve you. Listen, let me see you safely to wherever it is you're going. You look like you need a friend."

She chuckled through her tears. "And now you're a friend?"

"I am if you'll let me be." His face was earnest, but his eyes sparked with something more.

Rory exhaled. Of all the reasons to find herself alone with him, why did it have to be this?

"I don't know what's gotten into me," she said, straightening her shoulders and patting her skirt and hair. Edward could rot in hell for all she cared.

"Come on, princess," he said, standing and offering his hand. "I solemnly swear I won't lay a hand on you." There was that penetrating look again, as if he understood her all too well. She wanted to look away, but she was hooked, caught.

Draining her glass, she dug out some change from her purse to pay for her drink.

"Aw, princess, let me get that for you," he said, frowning at the money she just laid on the table and reaching for his wallet.

"No, no. That's quite all right. Look! I've already taken care of it." The waiter whisked by and picked up the payment. Rory sighed with relief. While she wanted to trust Hank, she didn't know what his expectations might be if she let him pay. It was probably best if she kept a bit of distance, even if a wayward part of her craved just the opposite.

Nonetheless, she let him take her hand and lead her out without resistance while he flagged down a cab.

"Hotel Monaco," she directed the driver.

Sitting in the back of the cab, she could feel the heat radiating from Hank. His arm just barely brushed against her own.

"You really aren't going to lay a hand on me?" she said, trying to ignore the coiling warmth at her core caused by his proximity.

His eyes smoldered. "You're angry at someone else. Distracted. It wouldn't be right."

But he wanted her. She was sure of it. At least someone did.

The magnetic pull of his proximity drew her closer, closer… Her eyes flicked to his lips. He held her gaze but kept his distance, placing a gentle hand on hers and shaking his head slowly.

She must look a fright after crying. He must be horrified.

"I'm sorry you're seeing me like this," she said, unable to pull away from his penetrating gaze.

"I'm glad I was there to help. No one deserves to be treated like that. If he can't see what he has in you, then he's a fool."

What would it be like to be loved and cherished by someone like Hank? Not that she should engage in such a maudlin train of thought. But there was something about him that made her want to crawl into his protective embrace and never come out. Whoever won his heart would be a very lucky woman indeed.

Sadly, that woman would never be her.

Looking away, she laughed ruefully. "No, I'm the fool for thinking I could go through with this marriage without tears. Edward is a pig, and I shouldn't have expected anything better."

"Of course, you should expect better."

She shook her head and laughed ruefully. "Nice men don't want to marry fallen women." She caught his gaze and held it, wondering how he would react. "I'm sure you've heard about my scandal. Everyone else in New York has."

He smiled and shrugged. "You're not fallen for doing what men and women have done together from the beginning of time."

What a dear he was! If only more men took that perspective, her life might not have been so miserable at the moment.

"You should see what the gossip rags write about me. 'Fallen' is the least of it. Did you know my father didn't think he'd ever be able to marry off a misfit like me? It's truly stunning the amount of money he offered Edward to take me off his hands." She caught Hank's eye again and leaned in. "You should stay away from me, you know. I'm nothing but trouble. Everyone says so."

The corner of his mouth twitched up into a mischievous half smile. "And what if I like trouble?"

My God, this man and the things he makes me want to do.

Of course, that was the moment the cab ground to a halt in front of her hotel. How did they get there so quickly? As she was about to say good night and open the door, he took her hand. She sat there frozen and gaping as he raised it to his lips and kissed her fingers. It was so polite and yet so intimate. She'd never felt so much from such a subtle touch.

"Are you busy tomorrow morning?" she found herself asking. What was she doing? No good could come of seeing more of this man, especially here in D.C. with Edward so nearby. There was a decent chance Edward would come back to find her and talk things out in the morning. Though maybe that was why she was asking. If she had to face Edward, she wanted backup.

"No. Why?"

"Come back tomorrow morning at eight and have breakfast with me."

He smiled. "With pleasure. Goodnight, Rory."

"Goodnight, Hank."

The cab door closed, and he drove off into the night, leaving her alone with her newly shattered future. There would be consequences for spurning Edward. She knew that. But that was a problem for later.

6

---

hat am I doing with Rory Belmont? Hank grazed the straight razor along his jaw in the communal bathroom at the Roadside Inn where he always stayed when in D.C. Pritchard was still snoring away back in their room. He'd hardly slept a wink.

And yet, here Hank was, getting cleaned up for breakfast with Her Highness as if he had any hope of...of what? Did he think he was going to charm her into bed? Did he think he was going to woo her? Ridiculous. He shouldn't get anywhere near her, but for some reason, she kept showing up, and he couldn't bring himself to stay away. Something about seeing her shaken and vulnerable last night made it all the worse. Her veneer slipped, and he caught a glimpse of the woman beneath. The sight made him ache in ways he didn't think possible.

And so, he kept flying toward her flame, knowing full well he would burn in the end.

Showered, shaved, and as ready as he could be, he donned his uniform jacket despite the heat. It was the most formal garment he had with him, and that hotel he dropped her off at last night looked all kinds of hoity-toity.

He just hoped that fiancé of hers stayed away. There was no telling what Hank would do if the senator made an appearance.

Why would a man ever want to cheat on Rory Belmont? It was clear enough what they were arguing about without hearing the words, given the way Edward had been looking at the singer. Even after a good night's sleep, Hank was still simmering with outrage on her behalf.

He'd had to straighten out more than one of his sister, Kate's, beaus when they didn't treat her with the proper respect. He couldn't punch a senator, but last night he'd been sorely tempted. No wonder she was sneaking into hangars in the middle of the night, seducing unsuspecting pilots if this was how her fiancé treated her. She deserved someone that worshiped the ground she walked on, someone who would never even think of straying.

Already sweating beneath his jacket, he caught a cab to the Hotel Monaco. In the darkness last night, he hadn't fully appreciated its grandeur. This morning, as he walked up the red-carpeted steps, glimpsing the ornate columns, he wondered yet again what he'd gotten himself into.

A concierge intercepted him as he walked in. "Excuse me, sir. May I be of assistance?" The man seemed to be quite adept at blocking Hank's progress while appearing polite and solicitous. Uniform or no, he stuck out like a sore thumb in this swanky joint.

"Yes, I'm meeting Miss Aurora Belmont for breakfast."

The man's eyes widened.

"I see. May I have your name?"

"Hank Hawley."

"If you would wait right here," the concierge said as he whisked off to parts unknown. Hank stood to the side and looked around at the understated opulence of the hotel lobby—all dark wood and hunter-green walls with matching drapes in neat, scalloped folds.

He got a few sideways glances from the well-dressed hotel

patrons and ignored them. He had as much right to be here as anyone.

The concierge returned with Rory trailing after. "Hank, I'm so glad you came," she enthused as the concierge looked abashed. "You mustn't blame him for being cautious," she said, gesturing toward the concierge. "I asked him to warn me if anyone came looking for me in case Edward decided he needed to cure my hysteria sooner rather than later."

"Good. I didn't care for how he treated you yesterday." In fact, he'd gotten quite a bit of satisfaction imagining running the man through with a sword. Sadly, the days of sword duels were long gone, but a man could dream.

"Come. Sit. I'd rather not talk where everyone in the lobby can hear," she said quietly, directing him to an elegant table at the hotel's restaurant laid out with a wide assortment of baked goods. He pulled out her chair, then went around to his own.

As soon as they were seated, a waiter came by. "Would you prefer coffee or tea, sir?"

"Coffee, please."

"Do you take anything with your coffee?"

Hank tried not to laugh, thinking of the sad coffee pots at the hangars with no cream or sugar. "No, thank you. Black is fine for me."

As soon as the waiter was gone, Rory said, "I knew you'd be a coffee man."

"Tea tastes like water. Dark and bitter suits me better." He ate a raspberry scone in three bites.

"Oh? Are you dark and bitter?" she asked with a mocking smile.

"I'm not weak tea."

Her smile spread. By God, she was gorgeous.

"So," he said, picking up the coffee that just arrived and taking a sip. "You asked me to come, and here I am. Why am I here?"

"Because I like you, Hank. You don't bore me."

He took another sip of coffee and watched her. Damn good coffee. Not a hint of gasoline. "I like you too. And you are anything but boring. But I'll ask you again. Why am I here? A woman like you has no business spending time with a man like me. And you still have a fiancé, a senator no less. Whatever it is you want, I can't help thinking it will end poorly for me."

"Really, Hank," she said, waving a croissant. "You make it sound like I'm plotting your demise when all I really want is to—"

She was interrupted by a commotion at the door. The senator came barging in, shoving past a very flustered concierge. He stopped abruptly on seeing Hank.

"Jesus, Aurora," Edward whispered harshly. "I came here to apologize, but here you are with your lover, having breakfast for the whole world to see. Did you just pick up the first man at the bar to offer you a drink? Is this your idea of revenge? Last night, you sure as hell seemed to disapprove of this sort of thing, but here you are, sitting with this trash like he belongs here. Do you have no sense of decency?"

Hank turned to Rory and raised an eyebrow. This was exactly what he feared. Shaking his head, he exhaled. He walked right into this like an idiot.

"He's not my *lover*, Edward. You're making a scene," she said under her breath.

"He was at the club last night, and now he's eating breakfast with you in your hotel. You expect me to believe you didn't spend the night with him?" The senator leaned on the back of an empty chair, looming over them both.

"Yes, I expect you to believe it. Ask the hotel staff if you don't believe me. He arrived fifteen minutes ago. He works at my father's airfield. I spoke with him briefly after you left the club last night, and I asked him to meet me here this morning."

Heads were starting to turn. The dozen or so other patrons nibbling on their morning croissants couldn't help but be drawn into the drama. People were alike that way. No one could resist ogling a train wreck.

Turning on Hank, the senator said in an undertone, "Leave. I don't ever want to see your face again."

Rory's hand shot out to restrain Hank. It was unnecessary. He had no intention of leaving her alone with him.

"I'm not the uninvited guest," Hank countered calmly, meeting the senator's gaze. "If anyone should be leaving, it's you, sir."

The senator's eyes narrowed. "If we weren't in public, I'd punch your smug face."

"And I'd make you regret it." He smiled. The senator was fit for his age, but he was no match for Hank in a fight, and they both knew it. "I'll thank you to leave Miss Belmont alone and leave us to our breakfast, Senator." He popped a bite-sized pastry in his mouth.

If he didn't know what trouble he was getting himself into, Hank would be enjoying himself. Maybe he was, despite the trouble.

The middle-aged woman at the next table stopped pretending to drink her tea and propped her chin on her hand, leaning in.

Turning back to Rory, the senator said, "For God's sake, we're supposed to be getting married in a month."

"Obviously, that's not going to happen."

The senator's eyes went wide. "No. You can't do that. The wedding has to go forward. If you won't let me talk some sense into you, I'll go see your father. He'll know what to do to get you to behave. He won't think much of the company you're keeping," he said, glancing at Hank.

"Don't treat me like a child," Rory answered. "If this is you apologizing, you need to review the definition of the word."

"I'm sorry, Aurora. I handled last night poorly."

"Have you broken things off with her?"

Hank watched the senator closely. His face turned bright red, and his mouth opened and closed several times before he said. "You're completely missing the point. I'm saying I'm sorry."

"Leave, Edward," she said. "Go speak to my father if you wish. We're done here." She slid the sparkling diamond engagement ring off and put it down on the table in front of the senator.

The woman at the next table's eyes went wide, and she pressed her hand to her mouth.

The senator stood and loomed over Rory. "Now see here, I—"

Hank stood and wedged himself between Rory and the senator. "She asked you to leave."

Standing tall, Hank had several inches on Edward and was considerably more muscular.

The senator huffed. "I don't know who you are, you scurf, but I intend to find out. And I will make you sorry you ever came within a mile of Miss Belmont." Grabbing the ring, he turned and left.

Hank sat down again and looked at Rory. She shuddered, and something inside him clenched at the sight. He hated seeing her hurt like this, even if it was none of his business.

She sat silently, looking in the direction the senator departed, then turned her attention back on Hank. "I'm so sorry. I admit I wanted you here for moral support in case he showed up, and maybe I wanted to make him a little jealous. But I never thought he would jump to such absurd conclusions. Now I'm worried he really will make trouble for you."

"Princess, you let me worry about me. What's the worst he could do?"

"He's smart and powerful. I'm sure he'll come up with something."

Hank shrugged. "I have nothing to lose, as he'll find out if he comes after me."

"That can't be true." Rory's brows furrowed adorably.

Averting his gaze to his plate, he said, "I have a job that's trying to kill me and a patch of dirt back home in Michigan nobody in their right mind would want. He wants to take away either of those, he'd be doing me a favor."

"But you love flying," she said, putting her hand on his. He forced himself to think of icy locales. The Arctic. The Himalayas. Siberia. Lord, this woman. He let out his breath slowly, glad that a tablecloth hid his reaction to her touch.

"He can't stop me from flying. Worst he could do is send me back to the front, and I'd rather be there fighting than here delivering birthday cards anyway."

She squeezed his hand. He was going to need some time to compose himself before standing up from this table.

"Well, I'm glad you're here. And I'm sorry about him."

"What will your father do?" An image of Major Belmont with a shotgun flashed through his mind yet again. *Damn that dream.*

"He'll lecture me, possibly threaten to disown me if I don't go through with the wedding."

"Would he really disown you?"

She shrugged. "Possibly. He's threatened it before. When I got caught kissing a gardener at the Astor's, he nearly disowned me on the spot. Had Mrs. Astor not promised to hush the whole thing up, he probably would have. There's a part of me that wouldn't mind if he did. I could get a job as a teacher or a shop girl and live on my own for the first time in my life. It could be quite liberating."

Hank laughed. *Imagine Rory Belmont working as a shop girl.* Even he could offer her a better life than that. If he was the marrying sort, that was. But no woman in her right mind would want to hitch herself to a man that took the risks he did. And besides, high-society ladies didn't marry nobodies like him.

"Really, it would!" She could probably see the skepticism written on his face.

"The day you become a shop girl is the day I become the king of England." He popped another tiny pastry in his mouth.

"Very funny. Now let's get back to the other reason why I

asked you here," she said, a devious look on her face. "You still owe me a flight."

He chuckled. "How do you figure?"

"You didn't give me one last week at the airfield." She leaned forward, her eyes full of enthusiasm. It was all he could do not to claim her lips right then and there.

"No, I did not. Nor did I offer to."

"Details," she said brushing his statement away with an elegant hand. "Take me today. It would cheer me up."

"Not on your life, princess. Do you know how dangerous airplanes are? It's not for nothing they've nicknamed the airmail operation 'Uncle Sam's Suicide Club.'"

She leaned back, folding her arms. "Don't be a bore, Hank. I'm only asking for a short flight. Just up and then down again, a taste of freedom above the clouds and then we come back to earth safe and sound. I've ridden in an airplane once before and nothing terrible happened, and I've seen what a skilled and capable pilot you are. I'm certain you'll bring me back in one piece. Please?" She touched his arm again.

It was a bad idea, a terrible idea, but with her hand on his arm, his resistance was crumbling. That senator was really a piece of work, and Hank wanted to do *something* to cheer her up. Nobody deserved to be treated like that. The urge to whisk her away from all her troubles and do whatever it took to drive away the sadness behind her smile was almost irresistible. And he knew better than anyone what a tonic it was to leave the world behind and soar up in the clouds.

"All right. One quick flight. Just up and down, like you said. I'm only agreeing because you had a very bad morning, and I feel sorry for you."

She clapped her hands together and grinned.

"Meet me at the airstrip at Polo Field in an hour, and I'll take you up," he said, brushing himself off and putting down his napkin. Fortunately, the prospect of being responsible for her safety in his aircraft deflated any other thoughts that had been stirring.

Kissing her hand, he took his leave and headed straight to the airstrip to get a plane ready. He'd have to repair one of the broken ones. Delaying the mail for her entertainment was not an option. Fortunately, he knew how to take apart a Jenny and put her back together in his sleep. He'd have one up and running in no time.

She never did answer his question, he realized as he paid the cab driver. He still had no idea what she might want from him. He only knew what he wanted from her, and that was as impossible as flying to the moon.

Speed and danger. That was what Rory needed to forget her troubles. Thank heavens for Hank Hawley. This flight was just the thing to sooth her soul.

She took a cab to Polo Field, which until recently had been a park. The hastily constructed hangar gleamed with fresh whitewash, looking like a newly built barn. The runway was merely a long, open stretch of grass, and the trees had been cleared from one end to allow for safe departures and arrivals. Was there even enough room for an airplane to take off? It looked rather short.

Speed and danger? What a wonderful, terrible idea. Her father would be apoplectic if he found out, but at the moment, she couldn't bring herself to care. She needed to feel free of her cage even if she knew, deep down, she wasn't.

It didn't take long to find Hank. He was underneath a Jenny, jacket off, sleeves rolled up, grease streaking both arms, as he did something with a wrench.

She stood there appreciating the way his corded arm muscles flexed beneath his tanned skin before saying, "Hello, Hank."

He jumped at the sound of her voice and hit his head,

muttering a string of curses under his breath. It was delightful fun unnerving him.

"I'm almost done, princess. Give me a minute," he said, going back to tightening something. With a grunt, he gave it a final twist, put down the wrench in his tool box, and brushed off his hands, which made no difference to the grease. She could see his tattoo clearly now. It was a Jenny on his left forearm that rippled like it was flying through the air when he flexed. Fitting.

"Give me a moment to wash up, and we'll be on our way," he said, heading over to a small building nearby.

She stayed with the plane. It was such a sleek and alluring machine with its dual wings and its curving fuselage—sculpted perfection hiding a snarling beast of an engine within. The fabric that stretched taut across the wooden frames of the wings was painted with round medallions bearing stars, reminding her of a crisp dress uniform, bedecked with medals and perfectly tailored to display the machine's tantalizing curves. She ran her hand along the fuselage until she reached the prominent arc of the rudder and examined it at length. Then she walked to the front and traced the powerful petal-shaped propeller blades.

As she contemplated the crisscross of wires holding the wings together like a suspension bridge, she felt his presence behind her. He drew close. If she backed up a few inches, they would be touching.

"She's beautiful," she said.

"Yes, she is."

She could feel his eyes on her, smell his masculine scent. The temptation to lean back and sink into him was almost over-whelming.

"They say seventy-five miles per hour is a Jenny's maximum speed, but I've pushed them faster. Would you like to see?" he murmured right next to her ear.

Oh yes, she would. Turning to face him, eyes wide, she smiled mischievously. "Show me. I like to go fast."

"Yes, you do," he said, returning her grin with a slow, devilish one of his own.

"How did you get permission to take me up?" Surely, he couldn't simply take a government plane up for pleasure.

"I promised the mechanics a round of beer this evening to turn a blind eye. Don't worry. They won't tell tales." He gestured toward the front cockpit. "Would you like to get in?"

Were her undergarments on fire? It certainly felt as if they were.

Climbing the ladder resting against the fuselage, she slid into the cockpit. She was glad she remembered to wear divided skirts for this outing. Today, she was dressed all in white, a fitted cotton shirtwaist on top and linen on the bottom with brown suede kitten-heel pumps. Hank handed her goggles and a cap that fastened under the chin. Putting them on gave her a little shiver.

"You've been up in an airplane before, I assume?" Hank pulled the ladder away and climbed into the rear cockpit.

"Only once. Papa worries too much." She didn't feel that Hank needed to know how apoplectic her father was when she paid a pilot to take her up after an aeronautics display on Long Island. He definitely didn't need to know that Papa tried to have the man arrested for kidnapping. Fortunately, the police refused when she explained it had been entirely her idea.

"As he should. Are you sure you want to do this?"

"Absolutely sure," she said, hardly able to contain her excitement.

He shook his head. "All right then. Here we go."

He took a few minutes to check everything, and she recited her own mental checklist as he went, recalling the names and functions of each component of the plane with loving detail. When he finished, he signaled to a nearby mechanic, who gave the propeller a good swing and backed away. Hank opened the throttle.

It was a bright, clear day, not a cloud in the sky. They taxied into position and started down the runway going faster and faster… She felt the lift as the plane left the ground and let out a whoop of glee. The wind whipped in her face as they cleared the end of the runway and soared up into the sky so high it was dizzying. She looked down, and the world below hardly looked real. This was every bit as good as she remembered.

Her heart jolted with adrenaline as they passed a flock of birds, and landmarks slipped beneath them like so many pebbles in a stream. Their speed was breathtaking. Her father's car only went thirty miles per hour. They were going more than double that.

Hank flew past the White House and the Capitol Building. He soared out over the Potomac into Virginia, quickly leaving the city behind. They flew over farmland, a patchwork quilt below them in shades of green and gold. It was glorious. She felt more alive than she'd ever felt on land.

Up in the air like this, she had not a worry in the world. There was no Edward, no father, no expectations. Who she was didn't matter. She was a leaf on the wind, and the world below was irrelevant. She threw her head back and yelped once again, not caring if Hank thought she was a madwoman. This was living. She couldn't get enough of it.

Then the engine choked.

There was a jolt. It sputtered.

She gulped hard.

It died.

Her heart was in her mouth. She turned to look at Hank.

He cursed a blue streak as he tried to restart the engine. They began to lose altitude. Her stomach lurched. For a mad moment, she was sure this was the end and braced herself with all her strength, clenching her eyes shut. Waves of terror washed through her as she attempted to breathe. In and out. In and out. She opened one eye and then the other. They were still in the air. All was quiet except the whistling of wind past the wires.

"Hank," she yelled, daring a glance backward. "What's happening?"

"The engine died. Don't worry, princess. I'll get you down safe. I've done this before. You saw me do this the day we met, remember?"

She nodded slowly. "Right. Of course." That morning, his airplane glided down out of the sky silent and graceful as a bird. This was nothing new to him. He would get her down safe. She hoped.

Turning back around to avoid further distraction, she closed her eyes again and tried to calm herself. This was a lot of peril, even for her, though some perverse part of her was enjoying it even now. Confronted with her own mortality, she felt a strange clarity and freedom. In this moment, all that mattered were the people she loved, and Edward was notably absent from that list. She could never go back to him, no matter the cost. So much for being a practical girl.

Opening her eyes, she watched as time slowed. Every second felt like an eternity as they drifted toward the ground. At peace, she put her arms out and felt the quiet buffeting of the wind, as if she herself were floating down like a bird. Wind was such a strange thing, soft enough to caress her face but strong enough to hold them up.

The ground came closer and closer. Rory could see that Hank was making for a fallow field. The world no longer felt so far away and unreal. It was whizzing by, dangerously close. She clutched the sides of the cockpit and breathed deeply. Every second that she wasn't dead was a miracle. And still some part of her reveled in the risk. This was so much more dangerous than anything else she'd done, like staring down a line of police times ten. The feelings coursing through her were equal parts terror and euphoria. Most of all, she felt so very alive.

The moment of truth. The plane touched down with a jolt and then floated back up again for a moment before settling back down with a bone-jarring rattle in the midst of grasses as tall as her waist. After grinding to a bumpy halt, she took a deep, shuddering breath. Intense elation flooded her like a drug. He did it! The urge to move overpowered her. She unstrapped herself and slid down from the cockpit, ran to the middle of the field and let out a barbaric howl, venting all the feelings flowing through her in that moment.

"Princess, are you okay?"

She ran back to the plane where Hank stood watching her and jumped into his waiting arms. Her momentum slammed them against the fuselage, as their lips met in a desperate kiss.

Nothing had prepared her for the sensation of that kiss, the intensity, the heat. She felt as if her whole body was aflame from the mere touching of lips and tongue. They devoured each other with a ferocity and intensity that could only be the result of their brush with death.

With a few quick steps, Hank turned them so that she was the one pinned against the fuselage. His hands caressed every curve of her as she climbed him like a cat until she was perched on him, legs around his hips and nails digging into his back. His hard length pressed against her, right where she wanted him, separated from her by only a few layers of cloth.

She'd kissed her fair share of men, but never had they felt so right or tasted so good. He was exactly what she needed, her equal in passion and fierceness. His tongue was firm and demanding, coaxing her to be bolder with her own. She nipped at his lower lip, and his moan reverberated against her. The sound went straight to her core.

"Rory, we have to stop, or I'm going to lose control," he said in a rasping voice right next to her ear.

"Then lose control." She kissed him again, but he pulled away.

"We're stranded in a field in the middle of nowhere."

"What better place? Who knows if we'll ever find ourselves

alone together like this again?" She kissed his neck and ran her hands down his chest. Her reward was a desperate groan.

"I know I'm going to regret saying this, but much as I want you, I have to try to fix the plane. If I can't get it running again, I have to figure out how to get you back to D.C. And leaving all of that aside, I wouldn't feel right making love to you in a weedy field."

Shaking her head in the curve of his neck, she said, "What about in the cockpit? I've always wanted to canoodle in a Jenny."

"Christ, woman." He throbbed at the suggestion. There was no denying what his cock wanted.

"I want you, Hank, and we may never have this chance again."

He kissed her softly, gently, and everything inside her melted.

"Not today, princess." With that he pulled away and climbed into the cockpit, coming back down moments later with a tool kit.

She remained leaning against the fuselage, panting and not entirely sure her legs would support her yet. Closing her eyes, she squeezed her fists and tried to calm the fever he'd left her with. Her whole body was aflame. Didn't he feel the same? How could he walk away?

Because he respected her. He put her wellbeing above his gratification, unlike every other man she'd ever met. It wasn't any easier for him than it was for her, she was certain. That was not a dispassionate kiss. For a glorious moment, he had lost control and unleashed his full, animal need, and she had savored every second of it. But somehow, it wound her up even more that he had stopped short. No one did that. She should know. She'd been fending off unwanted advances ever since she grew breasts.

Damn his chivalry. Couldn't he see she was a woman in need?

She shoved off from the plane, deliberately not looking at him, and walked to the opposite end of the field. There was a patch of purple wildflowers. She picked a dozen or so and started to weave them together into a flower crown, like she used to do when she was a little girl on outings with her nanny. If she was Hank's princess, she might as well play the part.

Deliberately turning her thoughts away from the man beneath the airplane, she contemplated what she would face when she returned to New York, and the invisible bars of her life closed in around her. The remaining tingles of warmth fled, and her stomach clenched.

Her father would be furious. There was no question. But she couldn't go forward with marrying Edward now. Everything in her rebelled against the thought of spending her life with him.

It wasn't just his mistress. It was his lack of interest in her as a person, his obsession with power and money, the fact that he called her hysterical for objecting to what any self-respecting woman would find intolerable. At first, she thought he would give her a modicum of freedom, respectability, but now she saw that he only offered a different kind of cage.

Edward was just like her father, too consumed by his own schemes to value her as she deserved. He offered what she wanted only to placate her so that he could gain access to her father's money. He didn't truly appreciate her in her own right.

Even if it meant Papa disowned her, the engagement was over. She could teach. After all, she had a B.A. in history from Smith College. She spoke fluent French and could read Latin. Her knowledge of American and European history was exceptional. Surely someone would be willing to hire her. If teaching didn't work out, she could become a shop girl. She was certain she could get work at a makeup counter. They always looked for pretty faces to sell their product. Or perhaps she could sell flowers?

It wouldn't be easy. She'd spoken to enough working-class suffragettes to know the struggles they faced. And she herself had never struggled a day in her life, surrounded by servants who took care of her every need. But the freedom of such a life called to her—freedom to live as she chose, freedom to love as she chose. Her gaze strayed to Hank, and she shook her head. It was silly to think there was anything for them but these few stolen hours.

She put the finishing touches on her floral crown and donned it before going to check on him.

"Hank," she said, leaning down so he could see her face. "How is it going? Is there anything I can do to help?"

He gave her an odd look that lasted a little too long. "When my sister was little, she always wanted to play princess, but my brother and I would only cooperate if we got to be knights and fight with swords. She'd get bored while we whacked at each other with sticks and so she'd start weaving flowers together like you're wearing now. I never would have admitted it to her at the time, but I always thought she looked so pretty in her flower crowns."

She laughed. "Believe me, I know all about being the only sister with brothers. I have three of them you know—not that any of them will speak to me after my scandal. Where are your siblings now?"

"Kate's back in Michigan with her husband Jeremiah. They help Ma with the farm." He paused. "My brother died in the war."

The grief in his eyes made her heart ache.

"I'm so sorry. That must have been a terrible loss."

He turned back to his work without a word.

She wanted to ask him more about his brother, but it was clear he wasn't feeling forthcoming. "Do you go back to Michigan often to see your family?"

He wrenched something loose with unnecessary force. "Twice last year, but I haven't been yet this year. I owe them a visit."

"Do you fly when you visit?"

He laughed. "Do I look rich enough to own my own or even rent a plane? I take the train same as everyone else."

"Be glad you're not rich. It's a curse. Everyone wants your

money, and no one cares about you." She was feeling the sting more than usual this morning.

"I care about you, and I don't want your money," he said, pausing in his work.

"That's unexpectedly sweet of you to say." She didn't think he was after her money, but she also didn't expect him to care about her beyond the animal attraction they shared.

"What? You think I can't be sweet?" He wiped his greasy hands on a rag then put them in his pockets as he leaned in to claim her lips. He didn't want to muss her outfit, she realized. It was a gentle kiss, soft and beguiling, filling her with a hungry ache. And then he stopped. Again.

"I'm finished, by the way," he said, stepping back. "We can leave as soon as you're ready."

"It's safe?" She gave the machine a dubious look. Much as she enjoyed the thrill of their landing, she had reservations about subjecting herself to a repeat.

"It's never safe, as this morning should have made clear. But she's as safe as she can be. I'm going to need your help to get her started. At my signal, I need you to start the engine."

Accepting his hand up into the cockpit, she tried to tamp down her trepidation about flying again, not to mention about returning to deal with Edward and her father. He climbed up on the wing and stood beside her, instructing her on what she needed to do. Her hand shook slightly as she carried out his instructions to open the throttle from her cockpit while he got the propeller started, but everything went smoothly. The engine started, and he climbed into the rear cockpit quickly. They taxied and took off.

8

On the trip back, Hank watched Rory closely. She hardly moved. Gone was the exuberant woman who whooped with glee as they flew into the sky. A melancholy seemed to have settled on her, and he ached to chase it away. It pained him to see her like this. He knew exactly how he'd chase it away too. Preferably in the cockpit of a Jenny. But some madness had possessed him in that field, and he turned her down. What was he thinking?

He no longer wondered what she wanted from him. She'd made her interest abundantly clear. She wanted the same thing he wanted of her. Except that wasn't quite right. Something made him hesitate when faced with the possibility of a tryst with her. Making love to her once and then never seeing her again felt all wrong, though he couldn't say why. He couldn't expect an ongoing relationship with her, nor was he the sort of man who engaged in relationships.

She had him all mixed up. There was no two ways about it. He no longer knew what he wanted from her aside from continuing to be near her. The only thing he was certain of was that this was not the end. Not yet. Somehow, they would see each other again.

She couldn't stay away any more than he could. Something kept bringing them back together. They couldn't escape each other's orbits until something knocked them free of their gravitational attraction.

The return journey was uneventful and surprisingly brief. Before he knew it, he was coming in for a landing at Polo Field as if the last three hours hadn't happened. When they came to a stop, he walked around to her and caught her as she slid down instead of getting the ladder—anything for a bit more contact. Her breath hitched as he held her for a moment too long when she landed on the ground.

She stepped away, avoiding his gaze. They were back in public now. Appearances mattered once again. The distance between them grew staggering as they stood facing each other, trying not to kiss.

"You should go," he said at last, unable to force his feet to walk away.

"Yes, I should," she said, meeting his gaze at last.

They stood looking at each other for far too long. It took the lanky silhouette of O'Donnell walking his way to snap him out of his reverie.

"You should go now. O'Donnell already suspects. If he tells Major Fleet, I'll lose my job," he said, nodding in the direction of his friend who seemed not to have noticed them yet.

She nodded and turned to go, looking back one last time as she walked off. He swallowed hard and forced himself to turn away.

O'Donnell sauntered over, glancing at her retreating figure. "Was that Miss Belmont?"

"None of your business, O'Donnell," Hank snapped.

"Oh my! I'm right. It was Miss Belmont. Well done. I was wondering why you didn't show a bit more enthusiasm at the club last night. By the way, when did you leave? I missed you.

Thompson said you went off with some blonde whose boyfriend jilted her."

Thank God O'Donnell didn't know he'd left with Rory. The last thing he needed was O'Donnell spreading the rumor they spent the night together. It was bad enough that the senator thought that.

It could have been true, he thought with growing regret. If he'd kissed her in the cab, he was sure she would have invited him up. And then this morning in the field… Something was wrong with him. He never turned down a good time, nor did he find risk daunting. He thrived on it. So what was holding him back? Aside from common sense and self-preservation.

"Nothing came of it. She was too upset," he said honestly.

O'Donnell shrugged. "You should have stuck with the blonde at the bar with the tremendous knockers. She was heartbroken when you left. I had to buy her a drink and call you a cad to cheer her up."

"How selfless of you," Hank grumbled.

"I found a sweet little brunette named Patty looking for a good time. We got a room together and kept each other awake 'til dawn. I tell you I am dog-tired today."

Hank tried not to roll his eyes.

"Then what brings you out to the field?"

"Checking tomorrow's schedule. I wanted to see whether I could enjoy Patty's company for another night and catch up on sleep in the morning before I fly. I'm in luck. I'm not scheduled to leave until 1 p.m.," O'Donnell said with a wide grin. "Care to join me in some calisthenics? I'm hoping it will help clear the cobwebs from the old cranium."

Hank said, "Sure," without really thinking about it. His mind was still on Rory. As he went through the motions of pushups, squats, sit-ups, and then jogging with O'Donnell, he turned over the moments when he said "no" again and again in his mind. He wanted her. There was no question. The mere thought of her sent blood rushing to places where he didn't need it right this moment. It wasn't lack of desire or fear of risk. And then it hit him.

Oh no, Hank, you idiot. You're falling for her. You won't sleep with her because you want something more.

Of all the stupid, ridiculous, impossible, irresponsible… Christ. This was a disaster. He was falling for Rory Belmont, princess of New York. Never mind that she was totally unreachable. Never mind that he didn't want entanglements. And neither did she. To her, he was only a bit of fun. Hadn't she said so? But with Rory Belmont, his heart completely ignored his head, not to mention his cock.

He wanted to spend time with her, hear what she had to say. He wanted to defend her from all the people trying to use her. And yes, he wanted to sleep with her, but apparently he couldn't bring himself to follow through until they shared a deeper, more meaningful connection—a connection she wouldn't, couldn't welcome. Hell and damnation, this was a pretty fix.

"Rory Belmont, you will be the death of me," he mumbled to himself as he jogged.

"What was that?" asked O'Donnell, running beside him.

"Nothing," he said with a shrug and a nonchalant smile.

"No, it was something. I thought I heard the word 'Belmont' in there. You may as well tell me. I'll winkle it out of you one way or another. You know I will."

Hank sighed. "Have you ever had feelings for a woman you couldn't ever be with?"

"'Feelings' did you say? I must have misheard. The Hank Hawley I know doesn't have feelings. He has his fun and moves on. Clean and simple."

"Not this time, apparently," Hank said, gritting his teeth. "She's gotten under my skin."

"Saints preserve us! Are you telling me you have a heart under all that useless muscle?"

Hank laughed. He couldn't help it. "Don't tell a soul."

"Oh, I won't. Except Thompson. And maybe Pritchard. I can't keep something this juicy completely to myself, you know. But aside from them, I swear your secret is safe with me."

"Christ. Leave it to me to spill the beans to the biggest gossip west of the Mississippi. Look, O'Donnell, it isn't safe for her if this gets out. She has a fiancé." Or had. But somehow, Hank didn't believe that particular drama was over. "Not to mention her father—"

"I'm not going to tell Major Belmont. Who do you think I am? He'd shoot your balls off for looking at her the wrong way."

Hank cleared his throat, not at all grateful for the reminder. "You see my point about keeping this secret."

"At least let me tell Thompson. I'll swear him to secrecy."

"No one," Hank said forcefully. "Or I'll forget to keep secret what happened with that girl from Poughkeepsie when you took her on a ferry ride."

"It's not my fault she got seasick right after kissing me."

"If you don't want Thompson and Pritchard warning every girl you meet that your kisses make girls puke, you're going to keep my secret." Hank wasn't entirely sure this would work. O'Donnell might decide it was worth a few months of ribbing to spill about Rory Belmont.

"Fine, fine. You have my word."

Hank heaved a sigh of relief.

"But I still get to tease you about it in private," O'Donnell added.

Looking up to heaven, Hank said a silent prayer for patience.

Two hours later, Hank was sitting on a bench in the park next to the runway, eating a sandwich, lost in thought, when an unpleasant voice interrupted him.

"I found out who you are," said the senator, approaching from behind and making him jump. How the hell did the senator find him in the middle of a park? "Hank Hawley. Airmail pilot. I should have known. She has a weakness for pilots."

The senator sat down on the bench beside him, looking out at the trees. The man was lucky to live in the twentieth century, or Hank might have lopped off the man's head with a broadsword for his audacity.

"I could take your job, send you back to the front."

Hank smiled. "There's nothing I'd like better. You think I dreamed of being a pilot so that I could ferry birthday cards back and forth?"

"It would take you away from Aurora."

With a shrug, he said, "There's nothing between Rory and me. How could there be? She's the princess of New York and I'm a nobody. By all means, send me back to the front."

The senator exhaled with force. "Stay away from her. Do you hear?"

"Hard not to. You're yelling in my face." Hank smiled his chilliest smile.

"She may not forgive me any time soon, but I'll be damned if I'm going to lose her to a piece of shit like you." The man looked almost rabid.

"Good luck, Senator. If you're worried about a shmuck like me, you need it."

The senator got up and walked away without another word. Asshole. He had no idea how badly he'd lost already. No wonder Rory was starved for affection.

And you'd like to give it to her, wouldn't you? Hank, you idiot, walk away and let this go.

But he couldn't. Ridiculous schemes to see her again began

floating through his head, each more outrageous than the last. It was a terrible idea, absurdly dangerous for both of them. But when had danger ever stopped him?

The trick was how to get to her. So far, their meetings had largely been a matter of chance. How could he see her intentionally?

Looking down at the insignia embroidered on the jacket draped over his arm, the answer clicked into place. The mail. He'd have to make the letter look innocent enough that it would get to her but still make it clear who it was from and what he was asking.

He got up and went to a five and dime where he bought stationery, envelopes, and a pen. Then he stopped at the post office and bought a roll of stamps with a Jenny printed on them. He came back to the park, found a picnic bench, and sat down to write.

For several minutes, he stared at the blank page, unable to write a word. Then he set pen to paper and wrote, in his best penmanship.

> *"Dear Miss Belmont,*
>
> *The Pilots' Benevolent Association cordially invites you to a silent auction fundraiser to be held at the Flatiron Building the evening of Tuesday, June 25th at 8 p.m. All proceeds will be given to the widows and children of pilots lost during the war. RSVP to 218 Garfield Ave, Mineola, NY 11501.*
>
> *Sincerely,*
> *Hank Hawley*
> *Chairman of the Board"*

Hank looked it over, nodded, and folded it up. He put it in an envelope, wrote his return address, listing the Pilots' Benevolent Association as the sender, and added a stamp. Now he needed to find out her address so that he could post it. Everyone knew where Belmont Mansion was, but he had no idea what the street address was. He'd have to go for a stroll along Park Avenue to check the building number, something he could do as soon as he got back to New York.

He tucked the letter carefully into his pocket. This was madness. He'd clearly lost his mind. He had no business doing this, but he had to see her again. That was all this was, he decided. He would see her one more time and get her out of his system.

9

———

"I'm not going to marry him, Papa. Nothing you're going to say will change my mind." Rory fought to keep her voice even and hold back the tears that prickled the corners of her eyes.

She paced on the lush floral carpet of the drawing room. Deep reds and golds, in a modern style, showcased the latest furniture imported from Paris. A gentleman named Ruhlmann designed them all, and her stepmother, Eleanor, thought he was a genius. Everything had clean angles and sleek lines, a bold aesthetic that spoke of progress and innovation. Though her stepmother wasn't exactly young anymore, she insisted on keeping up with the latest trends as if she was still in her twenties.

Eleanor lounged on the sofa, her irritatingly pretty face filled with feigned concern. Her dark hair was swept into a loose, elegant bun, a long string of pearls dripping down her front. Her father stood and lectured, twisting his mustache every so often, as he always did when worked up.

"Be reasonable," he said. "The man made a mistake. I don't approve of his activities any more than you do, and I gave him a piece of my mind. But you must understand it isn't uncommon.

Men have… Well, they have…needs. And Edward was a widower for many years before he met you. It's hardly surprising he found a way to have his needs met prior to you."

"This wasn't prior to me, Papa. He's still seeing her and planned to continue seeing her after we were married. He talked about her being a regular guest in our home."

Her father put a placating hand on her shoulder, and she shook him off.

"Darling, I know you're angry," Eleanor said. "And you have every right to be. You've lived a very sheltered life, and this must all be very shocking."

Rory laughed bitterly. Suggesting she was naïve in these matters was absurd.

"All we're asking is that you give him another chance," her father said. "He's sworn to me that he is parting ways with the singer and that he will be faithful to you. I told him I would cut off all financial support if I ever found out he strayed."

"So you see, my dear, you have nothing to fear," her stepmother said, her eyes full of reassurance.

Rory shook her head slowly. "And you think I should marry a man that requires a bribe to uphold his vows?"

"I insist you give him a chance. Let him demonstrate his change of heart to you. This match would benefit both of our families tremendously. You know we need friends in Congress to keep the regulators in check. I always thought you were a practical girl, that you understood these things. I'd rather not force the issue, but I will if I must."

Her stomach plummeted. She'd been bracing herself for this, but hearing her father say it aloud destroyed her last, slender hope that he would see reason. Nonetheless, she wasn't giving up. "I am a practical girl, and I do understand. But there are limits. And even if he has had a change of heart, I still don't want to marry him. He doesn't care about me. All he wants is your money. At best, he's putting up with me. He made that clear."

Her father began pacing. "That's not what he told me. He swears he's in love with you."

"Of course, he would tell you that. It's in his interest to tell you whatever you want to hear. Papa, I don't love him, and I'm not going to marry him."

Her father stopped his pacing and pinned her with a look that made her shiver. "Is there someone else? Edward said he thought there was, but I didn't believe it."

Was there someone else? She thought of yesterday morning with Hank. Though the kisses were delicious, he refused her in the end.

"No, there's no one else. Edward saw me with an acquaintance and misunderstood the situation. I think his guilty conscience led him to jump to conclusions."

"Good," he said, clenching his fist by his side. "Because if I ever find out you've been sneaking around behind his back, then I will disown you."

She looked at her shoes, unable to withstand the intensity of his glare. "I understand."

Her stepmother's gaze was all concern. Rory had to resist the urge to yank on her hair. "We're only trying to do what's best for you, dear."

"I honestly can't see how this is what's best for me. And frankly, it's insulting to be told by the two of you I don't know my own mind and heart." Her father's decision to marry a stage actress had been widely considered unwise when they wed. Some of his former friends refused to do business with him anymore. The Vanderbilts tried to freeze him out of society entirely, though they came around eventually. They might never have done so if it hadn't been for Aunt Alva.

Rory, for her part, had been appalled to learn at age twelve that she was going to have a "new mother." She didn't begrudge her father the right to remarry after over a decade as a widower, but the disruption Eleanor had caused in Rory's young life was immense. After years of being teased by her school mates for having a "floozy" for a stepmother, Rory didn't care to be lectured on the virtues of a proper society marriage by either of them.

"Aurora June Belmont," her father said. "I will have none of your lip. We're done with this conversation until you're ready to discuss this like an adult instead of an obstinate child. Go." He pointed to the door.

She left with all the dignity she could summon, but as soon as she was out of the room, she ran.

Up in her room, she collapsed on her Louis XV canopy bed, whose curtains and coverlet matched the blue rococo wallpaper. Taking a deep breath, she composed herself and went over to her ornately gilded and inlaid desk, taking out a silver fountain pen and thick, ivory paper. She was a practical girl, and she had a practical problem. What could she say to Edward that would convince him to give up? There had to be some way to end this once and for all.

> *"Dear Edward,*
> ~~*I have been infected with rabies.*~~
> ~~*I have recently learned I am barren.*~~
> ~~*My father's money is a myth.*~~
> ~~*The President ordered*~~
> *I do not wish to marry you."*

It was no use. There was no magic formula that would make him beg off. She threw away the paper.

Her mind wandered momentarily to Hank, to the way he'd kissed her right after they landed in that field. Oh Lord, she wanted him so badly. Why didn't he give in? He was clearly attracted to her. She would swear he wanted her as ferociously as she wanted him. But then why would he stop short?

Hank Hawley was not her current problem, however. Edward

Windham needed to be out of the picture before she could entertain any thoughts of Hank. Her father was quite serious about disowning her, she was certain. While she was willing to face those consequences if all else failed, she didn't want to invite them.

She pulled out a clean sheet of paper. Time to end this once and for all.

"Dear Edward,

I know that you have been in touch with Papa about our engagement. He has taken your side and tried to convince me to relent. I want you to know I am certain that I will not change my mind, no matter what either of you threatens. Please consider our engagement terminated.

Sincerely,

Rory"

Thank heavens she never let that marriage contract go out, not that she would have gone through with it even with a signed contract. Papa would have been furious about paying the penalties for a broken engagement, though, not to mention the scandal. As it was, the only damage was to her reputation, and she hardly cared about that.

There was a knock on her door. "Just a moment," she called out.

"Miss, I just wanted to let you know that Evelyn is here. She wanted me to ask if you wanted to go for a drive," her maid, Kelly, said through the door.

"You can come in."

Kelly tucked a wisp of red hair behind her ear as she entered and closed the door behind her. Rory had a special place in her heart for her maid. The two of them were nearly the same age, and on more than one occasion, Kelly had helped her out of sticky situations. It was good to have a friend in this big, cold household.

Offering a sympathetic smile, Kelly said, "I heard you and your father had words."

"I'm afraid so," Rory admitted. "I refuse to marry Edward after what he did to me, but Father refuses to take no for an answer. It's put me in quite a foul mood."

Kelly patted her shoulder. "You know, you always feel better after spending time with your friends."

It was true. A drive with Evelyn would be just the thing. "Tell her I'll be down in a minute," she said. She finished addressing her letter and put a Jenny stamp on it. "Would you mind posting this?"

"Of course, Miss."

"Thank you, Kelly. You're a doll."

There. Now she was free.

Kelly hurried off with the letter, and Rory checked herself briefly in the mirror, powdering her face and putting on fresh lipstick. Even with her friend, she wanted to put on a brave face.

Downstairs, she found Evelyn in the front parlor, staring out the window.

"Come to take me for a drive?" Rory put her hand on Evelyn's shoulder, and her friend turned and folded her in a hug.

"I heard through the grapevine how things have gone off with Edward. I thought you could use some cheering up."

"Smashing," she said, a wide grin on her face.

"I was thinking we could drive out to the racetrack and put a few of the horses through their paces. What do you say?"

Even better. Riding meant going out to Belmont Park. Maybe she would see Hank. Her heart sped at the thought. Not that she could do so much as say hello with Evelyn in tow. Much as she trusted her friend, she wasn't ready to share the secret of Hank with anyone yet.

"You are my favorite person in the whole wide world. Did you know that? I'm not dressed for riding. Give me a moment."

Upstairs, she put on khaki pants with a buttoned front panel and ballooning fabric at the thighs, tapering to a slim fit for her calf. On top, she wore a collared white shirt with a red and brown striped silk tie. Donning calf-hugging riding boots, a knee-length flared khaki jacket, and a camel-colored cloche hat, she was ready.

Out front, she found Evelyn standing beside her Le Zebre sports car, cheerfully telling curious passersby about its horse-power and top speed. It drew the eye, distracting even from the imposing façade of the mansion.

"You want to drive?" Evelyn asked her with a sideways smile.

"Ooh! Thank you," she said with glee, catching the keys Evelyn tossed.

She climbed into the leather-upholstered driver's seat, she turned the ignition key, and a doorman turned the crank in front. The engine caught, and the long, polished, burgundy snout of the car roared to life. She loved this sound almost as much as the engine of a Jenny.

Pulling out into the street, she floored it, and they barreled down Park Avenue, terrifying pedestrians and motorists alike. Turning on Fifty-ninth Street, she sped toward the Queensboro Bridge, then zoomed over the soaring steel cantilever structure into the smoky wilds of Queens. Free of the city's traffic, she sped up, pushing forty miles per hour. She whooped with glee, and her friend joined her.

They arrived at Belmont Park in thirty-eight minutes, their shortest time yet. She absolutely hadn't been thinking about Hank the whole way there. He barely crossed her mind. He defi-nitely wouldn't be in that hangar she was staring at avidly, heart thundering.

Shaking herself, she got out of the car and said, "Thank you so much. That was exactly what I needed."

"Thank heavens. I find so many problems can be solved by irresponsibly fast driving."

"So do I. Let's go find some horses to ride until we've forgotten all of our cares."

As they passed the enormous barn doors of the hangar, she lingered for a moment, looking at the airplanes and surreptitiously checking for a certain pilot with dark hair and sinful eyes. All she saw was a couple of mechanics going about their business. One of them waved to her as she passed. A Jenny flew overhead, coming in for a landing on the main racetrack. Her stomach clenched for a moment at the thought that it might be Hank.

She hurried to catch up to her friend. As they waited in the stable for their horses to be saddled, she tried to ignore the sounds of the plane landing outside. She was tempted to run out to see if it was him, but she stayed put, joking absently with Evelyn.

Two grooms brought out their horses. "Let's race." Evelyn grinned widely.

They mounted and rode to the starting line on the track. Since everything was closed during the week because of the airplanes, they had the racetrack to themselves. The grooms all knew the flight schedules, and it was easy to avoid being on the track when it was in use.

Evelyn gave the signal, and they took off. Riding a galloping horse felt like flying but more predictable. A horse, unlike a plane, had a mind of its own and a sense of self-preservation. There was a unity of intention when riding a fine racehorse like this. Together, they could do anything, but if her mind wandered even for a moment, she lost the connection and the advantage.

As they rounded the corner of the training track, she caught a glimpse of a Jenny taxiing into the hangar. She couldn't quite make out the pilot. In that moment, Evelyn pulled ahead. Cursing, she urged her horse on and tore after her friend, only a length behind. Pounding along the straightaway, she gained until they were neck and neck.

She felt the finely tuned muscle and determination of the creature beneath her, so responsive and spirited. This horse loved speed as much as she did, and as the finish line came into view, a final burst of energy took them into the lead by a nose, and she yelled triumphantly as Evelyn cursed her defeat.

Catching her friend's eye, they both burst out laughing. "Good race, Rory. As usual, you take the cup. I bow to your superior skill, My Lady Demoness of Speed." She dismounted and bowed mockingly. "Rest the horses and have another go?"

"Of course," Rory said, dismounting herself.

"Did you notice we had an audience?" Evelyn pointed to the stands.

There she saw a familiar profile beside a tall, thin one. She swallowed hard. He was here, watching her. Wasn't this what she secretly hoped for? But it was dangerous for him to be here. She couldn't go over and say hello. Nonetheless, she could feel his eyes on her like a caress, even at this distance.

Evelyn nudged her with her elbow. "That's not that pilot you told me about, is it?"

Rory's cheeks heated, and she coughed to disguise her reaction. Fortunately, Evelyn didn't do anything but smile like a Cheshire Cat. Clearing her throat, she asked, "Ready to lose another race?"

"Not on your life. I'm going to win this one."

Mounting once again, they rode to the starting line. At Evelyn's signal, they both tore out onto the track once again. Only this time, a piece of her attention was on the man in the stands.

Rory fell behind. She picked up the pace, almost catching up. Her friend pulled ahead, and try as she might, she couldn't gain the lead. Evelyn was a nose ahead of her when they crossed the finish line.

Evelyn hopped down from her horse and did a very undignified victory dance.

"Fine. You can be My Lady Demoness of Speed just this once," she said with mock resignation. "Best of three?"

"You're on once this beauty has had a chance to catch his breath." Evelyn led her horse to water. "You know, you should enlist Aunt Alva's help with your father. He seems to be terrified of her."

Rory shook her head, smiling. "I'll speak to her. You're right. She can help."

In the third race, Rory put her head down and poured all her focus into the ride. She was damned well not going to lose to Evelyn again with Hank looking on. Keeping her eyes on the track ahead and ignoring everything else, she sped around the track, the wind whipping her face. She hardly even noticed where Evelyn was. As she crossed the finish line, she crowed in triumph, her friend an entire length behind her.

"I let you win because you're distressed," Evelyn said, sidling up.

"Pish-tosh. Do I look distressed to you?"

Evelyn's face turned suddenly serious. "You do a bit, actually. It feels like you're trying too hard to convince me everything is fine. I hope this little distraction helped."

"It did. And I love you for it. Let's head back. I have plans with this evening."

They dismounted and handed the horses over to the grooms. "What was this one's name again?" she asked. "I'd like to ride her again next time I come out."

"Epona, Miss."

Her brow furrowed. "That's an unusual name."

"Goddess of horses, Miss."

She smiled. "Appropriate."

Taking a glance at the stands, she saw they were empty. Hank was gone. It was for the best.

"Excuse me for a moment while I powder my nose," she said to Evelyn.

She walked over to the building with the bathrooms, which were some distance from the stables, and attended to her needs. As she walked out again, a strong hand grasped her elbow.

"Rory." That voice.

"Hank." She grinned.

"You didn't come all the way out here to see little old me, did you?" His smile melted every bone in her body.

"Of course not," she lied. "I'm here to race horses with Evelyn."

"Oh really?"

He took her in his arms and bent her backwards. His lips consumed hers with a desperation and fury that left her breathless. It was a kiss unlike any other she had experienced, sending lightning bolts all through her body but especially to the core of her desire. She wished he could lower her to the ground and have her right there. Their tongues twined in a carnal dance until she saw stars. Then, as suddenly as he'd embraced her, he released her. She glanced around and saw two grooms walking their way.

Breathless and flushed, she stepped back to a safe distance and cleared her throat.

"I sent you an invitation, princess. I hope you'll accept." There was a mischievous twinkle in his eye.

"An invitation? To what?" Lord, she wanted to see him again, but did she dare go out in public with him after that run-in with Edward? Her father would have a fit.

"No one will suspect a thing. I promise," he said as if reading her mind.

She nodded and smiled, anticipation thrumming in her veins.

"Until next time, Hank."

He tipped his hat at her and disappeared.

She licked her lips, relishing the taste of him. Until next time indeed. But how soon would that be?

10

On June twenty-fifth, Hank stood outside the Flatiron Building in his best suit, chatting with his army friend Walter Amboy as he waited for Rory. The modern lines of the triangular skyscraper jutted into Madison Square, parting streams of pedestrians like the prow of an enormous ship.

"Thanks for doing this, Amboy."

"Yeah, well, I owe ya. If you hadn't taken Marge to the hospital that day, God knows what would have happened. Be careful, though. This could cost me my job if you get caught."

Hank put a reassuring hand on his shoulder. "I promise we won't get you in trouble."

Walter straightened his doorman's uniform. "That her?"

Hank's head whipped around, and he stopped breathing. There she was, getting out of a cab. Her dress was cream silk draped with black chiffon, the square neckline revealing her décolletage. Her blonde curls were pinned up, and she wore a wide black ribbon in a band around her head. The bow dripped down her back, inviting him to unwrap her like a present.

Walter whistled low. "Jesus, Hank. Where'd you meet a lady like that?" he murmured under his breath.

"Belmont Park," Hank answered absently, unable to tear his eyes away from Rory.

"I've been to Belmont Park," Walter said in an awed whisper. "I ain't seen nothing like her."

Finding his feet at last, Hank walked up and offered her his arm. Even her light touch on his arm made him ravenous.

"Welcome to the Pilots' Benevolent Association fundraiser," he said with a sly smile. "You look ravishing."

"Thank you. Your invitation was quite creative, you know. My family didn't suspect a thing."

Her scent of magnolias wafted his way. He wanted to bury his face in her neck and breathe deep.

"So what are we doing? Something more fun than a boring old fundraiser, I hope."

"How would you feel about a bit of trespassing?"

Her eyes widened in obvious delight. "Oh, that sounds perfect. What's the plan?"

"Allow me to introduce my friend, Walter. Walter, this is Rory. Rory, this is Walter. He's going to be our guide this evening."

Walter turned bright red and looked ready to fall over if a breeze hit him wrong.

"Very nice to meet you, Walter."

"You too, my lady… I mean miss… I mean…"

"Call me Rory," she said with a smile.

Rory turned to look at Hank, her eyes filled with amusement. It was all Hank could do to refrain from kissing her senseless on the spot. He picked up his satchel, filled with provisions for the evening.

"Walter, will you lead the way?"

Showing them into the building, Walter took them up the elevators. On the twenty-second floor, Walter opened the door to a warren of offices with a sign that said, "U.S. Realty." He led them over to an office on the side and opened a window, putting a wooden chair just beneath it.

"Climb out through here," Walter whispered, even though there was no one around to hear them. "I'll be back in two hours to escort you back out. Don't touch anything in here or I'll lose my job. Bathrooms are just off the stairs one floor down if you need them. Stairs are over there," he said pointing. With that, he departed.

"Let me climb out first, and I'll help you," Hank said, stepping onto the chair and out through the window. There was a bit of a drop, as he landed on the thin strip of roof between the outer wall and the parapet. He turned just in time to catch Rory as she climbed out the window with remarkable grace. He stifled a groan as her body slid against his.

Unable to contain himself anymore, he kissed her hungrily, and she responded with equal fervor. Her kiss was all sweetness and sin, her lips parting to invite him in, then sucking gently on his tongue, causing other parts of his anatomy to jump to life. Some distant part of his mind reminded him how impossible this all was, how she lived in an entirely different world than him. Just as quickly, he dismissed it.

He couldn't stand this torture for very long. He needed more of her, and tonight, he intended to have it—not everything, but enough for them to slake their thirst for each other. After that, they would go back to their separate lives, and she would marry some wealthy scion of a venerable family. And he, if he survived his job, would marry someone like Dorothy. This was one time, and it would have to last a lifetime.

Breaking their embrace, he gestured toward a metal ladder attached to the side of the building. "How would you like to stand on the roof of the tallest building north of Fourteenth Street?"

He was rewarded with a wide grin that made his cock stand even taller. As she climbed the ladder ahead of him, he had a glorious view of her long, elegantly tapered legs, even catching a glimpse of her garters. He shook himself and blinked several times, willing himself to remember he was on a ladder twenty-two stories up. When he reached the top, she was already at the front or prow—as he thought of it—watching the river of car lights stream up and down Broadway and Fifth Avenue. The view was as breathtaking as he remembered from the time Walter brought him up here, made all the more stunning by her irresistible silhouette. The light summer breeze did nothing to cool the fire blazing within him.

Forcing himself to go slowly, he opened his satchel and laid out a picnic blanket, a bottle of champagne, two glasses, and a basket of perfectly ripe strawberries. If this was his last night with her, everything had to be perfect. When everything was in place, he stood and walked over to her.

Taking care not to startle her, he came up behind her, put his hands on her hips, and nuzzled her neck. She let out an appreciative, "Mmm."

"Do you like it?" he murmured in her ear.

"Standing up here feels like flying," she said. "The whole world is at my feet, pulsing with light and life. I might as well be floating on a cloud."

Needing more of her, he nibbled on her ear, and his hand moved up to cup the delicious swell of one breast, his fingers finding and teasing her nipple through the fabric. He held her firmly to ensure she didn't lose her balance. Despite the parapet one floor below, up here it felt like nothing stood between them and the street twenty-two floors down.

She melted back against him, making the most arousing little noises as his hands grew bolder. Tonight, he was going to have his way with Princess Belmont despite the dangers to them both. Even the mental image of Major Belmont with a shotgun was insufficient to keep him from touching her. It would be worth bodily harm to feel her softness and vitality beneath his calloused hands tonight.

Reaching beneath the neckline of her dress, he caressed her silky-smooth skin until he found her taut nipple again and rolled it between his fingers, loving the gasp it elicited. He could hardly believe this was real, but her fluttering heart beneath his hand was no fantasy. She wanted this as much as he did, leaning into him and moving against him. She was driving him out of his mind, and he needed more. His other hand travelled down her abdomen, brushing across the joining of her thighs, and beginning to gather up her skirt.

"I want to touch you, Rory. If at any time you want me to stop, tell me, and I will. But I want to touch you. Here." Once again, he brushed his hand against the intersection of her legs.

She gasped. "Then touch me, Hank. I want you to."

White hot desire shot through him at her words. It was too much. The untouchable princess wanted *him*, plain old Hank Hawley. How had he gotten so lucky?

Her beautiful buttocks pressed against his arousal, driving him to distraction as he continued to gather her skirts. When he arrived at the hem, he reached beneath and found the divide in her bloomers, easing his finger between her folds.

Oh God. She's so wet for me.

Something between a growl and a purr rumbled in his chest as he began to stroke. She shivered against him as he teased and tantalized.

"The whole city is yours, princess. Every twinkling light, every dark corner. The moon and stars too. It's just you and me and the universe up here."

She shuddered as he increased his pace, putting a finger inside her. He groaned as she pulsed around him. They were hidden in plain sight up here. As always, she thrived on the risk, showing no hesitation about being so exposed.

"Oh, Hank. I'm going to..." He added another finger, and she rocked against him. The throbbing waves of her release began to clench around his fingers, and he held her tight, determined to keep her steady and safe. She trembled against him, making his own arousal so intense he thought he was going to burst like a green boy.

He ached to strip off her dress and slide into her, feeling her heat and slick wetness on his cock. But he promised himself he wouldn't. She wasn't his and never could be. It would be too much to ask. There couldn't be any unwanted consequences from tonight. They couldn't risk it.

As her climax subsided, she turned slightly and looked over her shoulder at him. He was sure he'd never seen anything as erotic as her face in that moment—her kiss-stung lips, bedroom eyes, and afterglow.

He turned her and claimed her lips, kissing her softly even as he strained to keep himself from climbing on top of her and making her his in every sense.

Panting between kisses, she said, "I've never felt anything like that. I didn't know it was possible to feel like that."

Did she have any idea what she was doing to him? He was trying to keep control, but everything she said and did pushed him closer to the edge.

They stumbled together back to the blanket where they collapsed in a tangle of limbs. He kissed her deeply, struggling to hold back and take things slowly. She was so languid and dreamy after her release, stretching beneath him like a cat.

Determined to keep his head, he rolled off of her and simply held her for a long moment as they gazed at the stars together.

As some modicum of sanity returned, he murmured in her ear, "Champagne?"

She grinned and traced a finger down his cheek. "That would be lovely."

Sitting up, he pulled the champagne from his satchel, opened it, and poured two glasses. The cost of the champagne was extravagant, but the store said it was the best they had. He wanted to do this right.

She held up the glass. "To surprises," she said. "This might be the best surprise I've ever had."

He clinked his glass against hers and took a sip. The champagne was worth the price, he decided. It tasted like sparkling stars on a summer's night. He picked up a strawberry and held it to her lips. She half bit, half sucked it off its stem, and said, "Mmm," upon tasting it. He had no choice but to kiss her. The strawberry and champagne lingered on her lips.

"You taste like heaven," he said.

"You taste like temptation," she answered, placing a strawberry against his lips. He sucked it from its stem, letting the flavor explode in his mouth. It was perfect. She was perfect. He had no business falling for her, but he absolutely was.

"I should stay away from you, you know," she said, taking another drink and looking off into the night. "My father is going to disown me if he finds out I'm with anyone other than Edward, not to mention what he would do to you."

While he suspected that was the case, his stomach tightened at hearing it stated so baldly. It was too much of a risk for her to take for him. And while he told the senator he didn't care if he was sent back to the front, the truth was he was rather attached to the job he had now, and her father would almost certainly see to it that Hank was assigned to something he wouldn't return from. There was a difference between risking death and walking into it, eyes wide open.

"We can't ever do this again," he said. "There's too much at stake."

She nodded without looking at him. "Let's forget about all of that for now, though. We're here and the rest of the world can go hang for all I care." Taking a long drink, she put her hand on his leg.

Her touch, so close to where he needed it, made him close his eyes and bite his lip.

"You want me," she said. "I want you. Let's make each other feel very, very good, shall we?"

11

Rory wanted Hank naked, though she didn't suppose she could get her wish up here. He took off his jacket, but it wasn't nearly enough. He was still wearing a vest, a shirt, and socks, as well as a union suit beneath. His shoes, like her own, were discarded beside the blanket.

Climbing into his lap, she straddled him, and he groaned. "Rory, you're playing with fire. I only have so much self-control."

She wished she had a phonograph record of him saying, "Rory, you're playing with fire," over and over. That voice did things to her.

So did his cock, the bulge of which she could feel nestled between her legs, right where she wanted it. Such a shame there was so much fabric in the way. It was past time to get rid of some clothing.

She started with his vest, unbuttoning it, and sliding it off his round, muscular shoulders. Then she began to work her way down the buttons of his shirt, one by one, listening to his ragged, uneven breathing as she progressed. He inhaled sharply when she pulled the shirt from his waistband but didn't stop her.

As she peeled off his shirt, she finally got an unobstructed view of his powerful arms. His sleeveless union suit still hid his chest, but she could see its contours clearly beneath the thin, summer fabric. She kissed down his neck and nipped at his shoulder. Good Lord, he was lovely to look at. If she had all the time in the world, she would trace each muscle with lips and tongue, tasting his shape. But tonight, there was not the time for that. No, she had other things in mind.

When she started to unbutton his union suit, he brushed her hand away. "My turn now," he said. Wrapping his arms around her, he began unbuttoning her dress. Before long, the dress loosened and gaped, revealing the top of her chemise and corset. He slid her sleeves and the straps of her chemise off her shoulders and feasted on the newly revealed skin. Then he reached in to free her breasts, teasing her nipples with his rough fingers. He gasped at the sight of her. "So perfect. Even more beautiful than I imagined."

She had always been indifferent to her breasts. They weren't small, but they weren't large either. They filled out a dress nicely, she supposed. But the way he looked at her with worshipful awe gave her a new appreciation of her own form.

"I've been dying to do this," he said, bowing his head and sucking a nipple into his mouth. She arched backward, giving him greater access as his mouth did devilish things that sent her spinning off into the outer stratosphere. This was so much more than she expected. Edward liked to grab her breasts and squeeze them, but he never made tender love to them like Hank was doing. She never knew her breasts could feel so much.

As he licked, suckled, and grazed her nipples with his teeth, her arousal intensified until she could hardly stand it. She needed more, and she needed it now.

Reaching down, she grasped him through his trousers, and he let out a strangled sound. Suddenly, he flipped her on her back, hovering over her, panting hard, pressing his length against her.

"Oh, Rory. The things I'd like to do to you..."

She writhed suggestively beneath him, desperate for more. He sat back on his knees, and she waited, expecting him to unbutton his trousers. Instead, he pressed her legs apart and lowered his head. What was he doing? Edward certainly had never done this.

When she felt the first lick, she thought she might climb out of her own skin. It was a sensation unlike any she'd ever experienced, so much more intense than mere touch. He licked her again, and she thrashed, but he held her tight. She could not escape.

From time to time, Edward asked her to pleasure him with her mouth, but she'd never heard of a man doing the same for a woman. "Wait," she rasped as his tongue touched her again.

He froze. "I can stop if you want me to," he said, looking up at her, breathing hard.

"No," she said at last. "It's only that I never knew you could…" The words to describe what was happening eluded her.

"Lick your beautiful pussy until you fall to pieces?"

She nodded slowly, reveling in the erotic thrill of having him say such bold, obscene things to her. Edward never said anything like that.

"Now that I know," she said, "I think you should continue immediately."

With a moan of pleasure, he buried his face between her legs and began licking her sensitive nub as if she were a ripe strawberry, lapping at the tender fruit, sucking on it until she cried out. Then his tongue found her entrance and thrust into her again and again as lips and teeth continued to graze the bundle of nerves above. Her hips bucked wildly, but he held her in place.

The stars above her seemed to pulsate in time with her own bursts of sensation, the sky itself joining in their sensual dance. Her hands twined in his dark, silky hair as he drove her mad. Her whole body began to tremble. Darkness crept into the edges of her vision, winking out the stars. A gentle breeze caressed her bare breasts, making her nipples taut as the night enveloped her, and she shuddered in the most powerful release she'd ever experienced.

Looking up from between her legs, Hank said, "I wish I had a thousand years to make you come like that again and again. That was beyond my wildest dreams." He kissed and nipped at her inner thigh, as warmth and contentedness suffused her body.

She fully expected him to unbutton himself, thrust into her, and take his pleasure, but he didn't. Instead, he kissed her gently, letting her taste her own salty essence on his lips. So delightfully wicked! They kissed and kissed, and still, he didn't make a move. Finally, she pulled back.

"Now, it's your turn," she said, raking her nails up the fabric that tented tightly over his arousal. His whole body tensed at her touch.

"You don't have to worry about me, princess. Tonight was for you." Nonetheless, his eyes were filled with fire, and the way his flesh jumped beneath her hand spoke to the intensity of his need.

"You aren't the only one that's been dreaming about this, Hank. I want you inside me." She squeezed, making him moan. "You don't have to worry about consequences. I'm wearing a diaphragm."

"No. It's too risky. Even with protection, things can go wrong. Much as I want to, it isn't worth the risk."

He wasn't going to take her? But she wanted to see his ecstasy every bit as much as he'd wanted to see hers. She wanted to feel him inside her, filling her, thrusting into her.

"You're disappointed," he said.

"A bit," she admitted. "I want all of you. I *want* you inside me." She stroked his rigid flesh, and his head dropped back.

"Sweet Jesus," he said to the moon.

"But I suppose I could settle for tasting you." She began to unfasten his pants with a sly smile.

"Oh my God."

Finishing with his pants, she unbuttoned his union suit, top to bottom so that she could see and touch his chest as well as his cock. As he sprang free, her eyes widened, and she smiled.

"Gorgeous," she said, grazing her fingers up the length of him and using her finger to spread the pearl of moisture over his tip. He made an animal noise through gritted teeth.

She took him in her mouth, running her tongue over his velvety tip.

"Oh fuck," he exclaimed, running his fingers through her hair. By God, he was delicious. Teasing and tantalizing, she took him deeper and deeper, enjoying each moan and jerk she elicited. Unlike Edward, he didn't grab her head and thrust into her throat. He let her take him at her own pace. It was a pleasure to test his control. Every time his hips bucked, a little thrill went through her.

"Please, Rory. I need—"

She sucked him deep, relaxing her throat to take him in all the way, and he cried out, "Oh, fuck! Yes!"

Her pilot was completely at her mercy, right where she wanted him. Cupping his balls in her hand, she licked and sucked him into a frenzy. He was clearly on the cusp. It was only moments before he cried out, and she felt a hot spurt of salty liquid dripping down her throat.

He collapsed back on the blanket and lay there catching his breath for a long moment. "I'm sorry for losing control. I shouldn't have come in your mouth, but I couldn't help it."

"No need to apologize. You were delicious. Better than champagne." And she meant it. He intoxicated her, and his seed was his quintessence.

He opened his arms, inviting her to join him. Snuggling against him, she rested her head against his heart, listening to its steady beat.

"You're very good at that," he said, kissing the top of her head and hugging her close. "That was... I have no words."

"Well, I have had practice," she said quietly and then immediately regretted it. Why would she bring up Archie at a time like this?

Hank's muscles tensed.

"That bastard who ran out on you? I knew he didn't deserve you, but now I'm questioning his sanity. How could he walk away when you…? Jesus Christ."

She chuckled grimly. What could she possibly say? It was charming how loyal her pilot was. It was such a shame that this evening was all they could ever have together. But she intended to enjoy every minute of his attention and affection for as long as it lasted.

"You've got some luck with men, you know that?" He pulled her close and kissed the top of her head, filling her with warm languor. "I don't know which is worse—Archie or Edward."

"Let's not talk about them. We were having such a nice time."

"All right, but just promise me you won't marry that skunk Edward," Hank murmured into her hair. "I know you can't be with me, but please don't spend your life with him."

"I won't. Papa is demanding I reconsider, but I won't relent. Edward Windham and I are finished." She would rather be disinherited than go back to him.

"Good," he said giving her a squeeze. "You deserve so much more."

A lump formed in her throat, and she swallowed it down. It wouldn't do to get maudlin or sentimental about Hank. She had to guard her feelings before she got her heart broken. After all, he was just a man, and men, in her experience, had very short attention spans.

Pulling away from his embrace, she sat up and poured herself some more champagne.

He joined her, buttoning the bottom of his union suit and fastening his pants before he got himself a drink.

He took a long sip of champagne. "Why did you agree to marry Edward in the first place?" The question startled her. It must have shown on her face. "I'm sorry. I said I wouldn't talk about him anymore, and it's none of my business."

She sighed. It wasn't surprising that he was curious, and he deserved an answer after all he'd done for her. "At first, I thought Edward was my knight in shining armor, rescuing me from my damaged reputation, and offering to let me take flying lessons after we wed. Obviously, I was mistaken. It didn't take me long to realize how much more he cared about my father's money than about me, and as time went on, he took less and less trouble to hide his affairs from me. I misjudged him, but at least I've gotten rid of him before it was too late."

Hank nodded and stayed silent. She took a sip.

"How is it that a man like you is still single? Surely, the ladies must have been knocking down your door."

He chuckled and took a drink. "I've always been a bit reckless. If I ever commit myself to a woman, I want to give her my whole self. I don't want to drive her crazy with worry by continuing to fly. But I have yet to meet a woman I like better than danger, so I stick to women who want a little companionship with no strings attached."

"What if you met a woman who likes danger?"

"You mean like you?"

She smiled. *Yes, exactly like me.*

"I've never met anyone like you. And, as we've discussed, you are out of the question."

Alas, she was. She might be able to escape Edward Windham, but her father would never agree to let her marry a pilot. Not that she was looking to marry Hank. She hardly knew anything about him. What she truly wanted was the freedom to be his "companion with no strings attached" until she was ready to move on. It sounded like an ideal arrangement. Very modern. It was the most she could hope for within the constraints of her life —a furtive affair that gave her a taste of what it might have been like if she was truly free to fly from the cage of society's expectations.

"I envy you your freedom," she said. "You can be with who you choose."

He laughed. "Not always."

"Oh?"

By way of answer, he leaned in and kissed her. "If it was up to me, this wouldn't be the last time I saw you."

"Maybe I can find a way."

What was she thinking? This was madness. If they got caught, it would cost her everything, not to mention what it would likely cost him.

"No. It's too dangerous for you. You shouldn't risk everything to see me. I know you love danger, but this is too much. This is goodbye, princess."

Even as he said it, the rush of the risk hit her, and she realized she was going to do it because of the danger, not despite it. Nonetheless, she kept quiet. Before she spoke, she needed a plan.

"What time is it? We'll need a few minutes to pull ourselves together before your friend comes for us."

Hank checked his watch. "Good point. We have fifteen minutes."

"I should visit the powder room to fix my hair and makeup. Can you button me up?"

He did so slowly, kissing her neck as he went. "I don't want this to end," he said with a sigh.

"Neither do I."

As she repaired her appearance, a plan began to form. She knew the exact excuse she would use to see him once again.

Too soon, Hank's friend Walter returned to escort them downstairs. They rode down in the ornate elevators in silence, Hank holding her hand. And then it was time to hail a cab and say goodbye.

"So long, princess. I'll remember tonight for the rest of my life." Hank gave her one last sweet and gentle kiss before helping her into the cab. "I know I'll never see you again, so I wish you all the love and happiness in the world."

"Oh, Hank," she said with a sly smile. "Never say never." She blew him a kiss, closed the door, and gave directions to the cabbie.

As the lights of the city flew by in a blur, her mind was spinning with ideas. This most certainly was not the last time she would see Hank Hawley, not after a night like tonight. Breathing in, she could still smell his manly scent mingling with her magnolia perfume. It made her smile. She had to see this man again, and her birthday gave her the perfect excuse.

12

Hank's head felt as if someone was chiseling it apart. He opened an eye to find the morning light blinding him through his bedroom window. Looking down, he realized he was fully dressed, including his shoes. He was going to kill O'Donnell next time he saw him.

Why did they drink so much whiskey?

Rory Belmont. That was why.

He squeezed his eyes shut. There wasn't enough whiskey in the world.

Rolling over, he picked up the milky white card on his bedside table with gold print inviting him to Aurora Belmont's birthday gala, a benefit for the Pilots' Benevolent Association to be held at the Waldorf on July twenty-first. Major Fleet handed out the invitations himself, saying he received them from Major Belmont. He told them he expected every one of them to attend.

Hank didn't know whether to laugh or cry, not that he could do either in front of Major Fleet. It had only been a week since he last saw her. Despite his determination to let her go, the woman had arranged a goddamn gala in honor of an organization he invented, all to get his attention. As if she didn't already have it.

As if he could think of anything else after that night on the roof of the Flatiron building. It was unbelievably reckless and more than a little flattering that she would go to such lengths, but the risks were too great. What did she hope to accomplish by inviting him to a grand affair where everyone would be watching?

Yesterday, after the invitations were handed out, O'Donnell immediately turned to him and waggled his eyebrows. The moment they were dismissed, O'Donnell's onslaught began and didn't end until Hank spilled everything to him in a bar over far too much whiskey. Well not everything. He refused to provide details of what happened that night at the Flatiron, but O'Donnell drew his own conclusions.

Christ. He'd gone and told the biggest gossip he knew his biggest secret.

Sure, O'Donnell had sworn he wouldn't tell a soul. "I'm your friend, you big oaf," he said. "I'm not going to let you or her get in trouble because of me. Besides, you're going to need my help if you want time alone with her at this shindig."

"How do you figure?" Hank asked, already dreading the response.

"You'll need an alibi when you sneak away, someone who can swear you left for reasons wholly unrelated to Miss Belmont. You wouldn't want people drawing conclusions when the two of you sneak away at the same time."

It was a fair point but not one Hank was ready to concede. "There will be no sneaking away. It's too dangerous. There will be no gossip because nothing will happen."

"Really? She's throwing this whole party for you, and you're going to turn her down? On her birthday?"

Hank had a momentary vision of sneaking away from the party to a quiet hotel room, stripping off her evening gown, and making love to her until dawn. And it would be making love, not fucking. He felt altogether too much for her, which made it all the more important that he stay away.

"I'm not going to let her get disowned on her birthday." He emptied his glass.

Signaling the bartender for another round, O'Donnell said, "And you don't think she'll have a plan to avoid getting caught? Besides which, do you really think she'll let you refuse?"

And that was why he drank an ocean of whiskey last night. He wanted her and couldn't have her and couldn't say no.

With a groan, he put down the invitation and sat up. His mouth tasted like a distillery. Still. He had to pull himself together. At 1 p.m., he had to fly the mail to Philadelphia. It was already—he grabbed his alarm clock and squinted at it—eleven thirty.

He got up and stumbled into his pristine kitchen, filling the percolator with water and coffee, turning on the gas range.

As he fried up some eggs and bacon, he thought about how well his bachelor's life suited him. He was quite capable of keeping house, gardening, and cooking his own simple meals without assistance. It was a good thing, too, because as he told Rory, he had no plans to settle down.

If only it wasn't such a lonely life. Not that he couldn't find female companionship when he wanted it, but what would it be like to be with someone who truly understood him—someone like Rory?

He shook his throbbing head. If he was having thoughts like that, he must not have been entirely sober yet.

Five minutes later, he sat down at his compact kitchen table with his coffee and giant plate of hangover food. The caffeine, grease, and salt did their magic, and he was able to look out the front window at his blooming pink roses without wincing.

But try as he might to focus on his food, he couldn't stop thinking of Rory. What would it be like if she was a nobody like him and they could be together? Instead of waking up late and hung over, he would have woken up early with her in his arms. He'd cook her breakfast because he couldn't imagine Rory being domestically inclined in any universe. She'd kiss him goodbye as he went off to a responsible job that paid him well and didn't require him to risk his life. If she wanted to work, she could, but she didn't have to.

He'd come home in the evening to her abysmal attempt to make dinner. They'd laugh over it, and he'd cook up some simple steak and potatoes, maybe with some home-grown carrots on the side. After dinner, he would take her to bed and make furious love to her until they were sated and exhausted.

On weekends when the weather was nice, they would go to the airfield and rent a plane, enjoying the thrill without the risk and discomfort of going up in all weather, year-round. Maybe she would get her pilot's license, though the thought of Rory terrorizing the airspace above Long Island was somewhat frightening.

Children would come eventually. The thought of a tiny Rory running amok around the neighborhood made his heart ache—a little daredevil, just like her mama, jumping off ledges, climbing tall trees.

Maybe he would finally finish his engineering degree and start his own aeronautics business like a responsible family man. Who knew airplanes better than him? He could build something of his own instead of working for others. The kids would be proud of their Pops. Rory's face would shine with pride.

It was an idyllic picture, he thought to himself, scooping up the last of his breakfast with a piece of toast. It was also impossible. Her father would never allow it, and even if he did, she wasn't interested in anything more than a bit of fun. She said so. Not that it mattered, because he was perfectly content as a bachelor.

He looked at his kitchen clock. Time to call Kate. He walked over to the living room and picked up the phone. It was lucky the house was wired already when he moved in. Most of the other houses weren't yet. Kate was standing at a pay phone, he knew, so he had to be precise about what time he called. The farm was unlikely to get wired anytime soon.

"Hello, operator?"

"What number, please?"

"I'm placing a long-distance call to Michigan. It's Grand Rapids 5-9354."

"Just a moment. Let me connect you."

He heard a crackling noise and then ringing. "Hello, Hank. Is that you?"

It was always a relief to hear Kate's voice on the other end. "Hi Kate. It's me."

"It's so good to hear your voice." That was always the first thing she said, but he felt the same way.

"You too. How are the boys?" The last time he saw them, they were three and five. Now they were four and six and he was willing to bet, inches taller than the last time he saw them.

"They're making me pull my hair out, as usual. Pete says he wants to be a pilot, just like his Uncle Hank. He climbed onto the roof with cardboard wings. Jeremiah—that's my husband—had to go up there and get him down."

Hank laughed. "He's just like me. I'm so sorry, Kate."

"He'd love to see you."

Hank ran his hand through his hair. "I know. I'll come out. I promise."

"Soon?" He could hear a touch of hope and a lot of disappointment in that single word.

"Soon." He really did need to buy those tickets. "How's Ma?"

"She twisted her ankle out in the barn and now she's laid up. She's driving us all nuts. You know she's never been one to sit still."

"I'm sorry to hear that. I hope she heals soon. For all of your sakes." He fiddled with the cord, not sure what to say.

"How have you been, Hank? Have you been staying safe?"

He thought about what he had been up to and lied once again.

"Always," he said softly. "Things have been good for me. The weather has been cooperating, so the flights have been easy. I'm looking forward to some nice fall breezes when summer comes to an end."

"Met anybody special?"

So they were going to have that conversation today. Kate always was persistent when she wanted information out of him.

"What makes you think I'd tell you if I did?" he asked with a smirk.

"Oh, so there is someone? When there isn't, you just say 'no one.'"

Damnit.

"Yes. Fine. There's someone, but it's hopeless." It felt good to unburden himself, even if he couldn't share details.

"She doesn't like you?"

"She likes me just fine. Her parents don't like me." *That's an understatement.*

"Ah. Tricky. But I'm sure you'll find a way to win them over. Who can withstand a Hank Hawley charm campaign? Speaking of which, Suzie Green still asks about you."

"If she's waiting on me, she's going to wait a very long time." Suzie Green. There was a name he hadn't heard in ages. They dated for two months in high school, and she left him for George Simpson. It seemed she might have regretted her choice. Well, it was too late now.

"I'll let her know you're taken. Does this mystery woman have a name?"

What harm was there in telling? "Her name is Rory, and she likes danger as much as I do. Maybe even more."

"Oh my. Then it's serious between you?"

How to answer that... "I'm not sure."

"Because of the parents?"

She was too perceptive by half. "Mostly."

"What does that mean?"

It means she's throwing me a gala at the Waldorf, but I still don't know if she wants anything more than a fling.

"It means I'm not sure."

"Well, Hank, you'd better work on getting sure. You'll never convince the parents if you don't convince yourself."

This conversation was not helpful. "How's Jeremiah doing?"

"Don't change the subject."

"How is Pete doing in school?"

"Hank." There was a long pause. "Fine. Don't tell me. I'll find out when you call me up to say you're married."

"Katherine, if I ever get married, and that's a big 'if,' you will be at the wedding. And don't get your hopes up about me marrying Rory. It's not going to happen."

"We'll see."

"Listen, Kate, I have to go, or I'll be late for my flight."

"Fine. Same time next week?"

"Yup."

"Goodbye, Hank. And good luck."

"Thanks. I need it."

He hung up and drove to the airfield, wondering exactly how charming he'd have to be to convince Major Belmont to let him court his only daughter.

13

Rory absently added a flourish to the "W" in "Women" on the pro-suffrage signs she was painting with her aunt.

"My dear, you seem distracted," said Aunt Alva.

"I'm sorry. It's the party planning. I can hardly think of anything else," she said, looking up.

"I applaud you for using your birthday to serve a good cause. Not many girls your age would think to do something like that." Aunt Alva beamed at Rory, who blushed thinking of her ulterior motives. "That beastly Edward doesn't deserve you, as I've told your father."

"Has he relented at all?" she asked, rinsing a brush and opening a bottle of blue paint.

"Not yet. But don't lose hope, dearest. We may not have won the day, but the campaign has hardly begun. I won't have my favorite niece wedded to a philanderer." She spread glue liberally on a stick and attached it to a sign. "Has Edward tried to contact you at all?"

No, which was surprising. "He's been oddly silent. It worries me. I feel like he's plotting against me, though of course that's absurd."

Aunt Alva shook her head. "It's for the best, my dear. It's always better to make a clean break and stay away from each other until tempers have cooled."

Rory switched to the red paint to add flourishes to the word "vote."

"Papa has threatened to disown me if I don't give Edward a chance. He refuses to believe it's over."

Aunt Alva sighed. "Yes, he told me. Have no fear. If he disowns you, which I doubt he would actually do, you can always come and live with me."

Something inside Rory unclenched at her aunt's words. It was a relief to know she had options on the off chance that her father followed through on his threat.

"Thank you, Aunt Alva. That's very generous of you."

The thought of living with her aunt had a certain appeal. While she suspected Aunt Alva would be less oblivious to her sneaking out than her father, it would be nice to live with someone who respected her as a person and didn't view her merely as a means of advancing the family's interests. The tricky part would be figuring out how to see Hank. Aunt Alva wasn't any more likely than her father to approve of her involving herself with a pilot.

It didn't matter anyway because her father hadn't done anything yet.

"I should get going," Rory said. "I have an appointment to meet with a pilot's widow in twenty minutes."

Rory headed out and got into the back of her chauffeured car, ready to cross town to meet another war widow. This had all started as a way to see Hank again, but she couldn't bring herself to raise funds for an organization that didn't exist. With Evelyn's help, and some strategic dropping of her father's name, she had created the Pilot's Benevolent Association from whole cloth in two weeks. It was exhausting, but never in her life had she felt so filled with purpose.

The driver pulled to a stop in front of a neat brick townhouse on the Upper West Side with flowering window boxes. She got out and rang the doorbell for apartment number two.

The woman who opened the door didn't look much older than Rory. She had thick, shining auburn hair and soulful green eyes. She was dressed in a cotton dress that had obviously been dyed black. The tiny flowers of the original print peeked through in places. In her arms, she held a sleeping infant. "Miss Belmont?" the woman said quietly.

"Yes, that's me. And I assume you are Mrs. Prince?" Rory whispered.

"Call me Ann," she said, opening the door and leading her up a narrow flight of stairs to the second floor.

"And you can call me Rory."

Ann led her into a small and tidy parlor with a large bay window overlooking the street. An elaborate, crocheted runner hung over the upright piano across the room from where they sat. The piano bench cushion was covered in needlepoint roses. A vase of silk flowers sat on top of the piano beside a large, framed picture of Mrs. Prince and her husband on their wedding day. Rory sat in a tall green wingback chair, and Ann sat in a rocking chair.

"Can I get you anything? Tea? Coffee?" Ann asked in a quiet voice.

"Don't bother yourself. I wouldn't want to wake the baby."

Ann's face showed obvious relief. "That's very considerate. He kept me up all night. I only just got him to sleep."

"I'm sorry if I caught you at a bad time. Should I come back another day?" Rory started to stand, and Ann shook her head with a furrowed brow.

"No, please stay. I've had so few visitors since the baby

arrived, and I understand you may be able to help me with my predicament. Please stay."

The baby stirred, and they both held their breath. Then he settled back down, and they sighed in relief.

"I'd love to learn how the Pilots' Benevolent Association could be of assistance," Rory said, taking out a small notebook to record Ann's request.

"Well, I lost Roger six months ago. I was five months pregnant at the time." Her eyes shone with unshed tears that she blinked away. "I lost my teaching job when I got pregnant, so we were living on his salary alone. I got a lump sum from the military, but it only takes me so far. I was hoping to go back to work after the baby was born. My mother was going to care for him, but a fever took her last month." She could no longer hold the tears back. They trickled down her cheeks as she furiously wiped them away.

"I promised myself I wouldn't cry," Ann said.

"I'm so sorry for your losses. I can't begin to imagine how hard things must be for you right now."

This woman pulled on Rory's heartstrings even more than the others she'd met. God. What must it be like to lose a husband while expecting a child?

Ann sniffed and nodded. "I can't afford to stay here. I have a small house on Long Island that I inherited when my mother passed, but it's badly in need of repair. It needs a new roof, and there's water damage that needs fixing to make it fit for the baby and me. I was hoping your organization might help me pay for the repairs. I'll pay you back as soon as I'm working again. I'm not asking for a handout. I just need help to get settled."

Rory nodded. "You are under no obligation to pay back the money, but if you wish to contribute so that others like you can receive assistance, that would be most welcome. How much do you need?"

"Eight hundred dollars for the roof and repairs. I've spoken to half a dozen contractors, and that's the lowest cost I could find."

Smiling, Rory said, "I think we can manage that. We're having a gala on the twenty-first to raise funds. Would you be willing to come and tell your story? I've arranged for childcare for the mothers that need it in order to attend, so you don't need to worry about the baby."

"Of course, I'll go. But I don't have anything suitable to wear."

Rory smiled. "Don't worry about that. No one is expecting war widows to be wearing finery. If the evening is successful, which I fully expect it will be, I should be able to get you your money at the beginning of October. Does that work for you?"

The tears started flowing again. "Thank you so much. You are a life saver. If Roger was here, he would have fixed it himself. He was always so handy. But then if Roger was here, there would be no need to move at all."

"You must miss him terribly."

"I do," Ann said with a sniffle. "We were high school sweethearts. He was the love of my life. We'd only been married six months when his plane went down in France near the German border. So foolish of me to fall for a pilot. There's something about them, though. They're so bold and fearless. They make you feel like anything is possible. Roger was always like that, even before he learned to fly. I couldn't resist him, even knowing the dangers."

Rory thought of Hank. That was exactly how she felt around him—as if anything was possible. She understood the pull of a pilot all too well. "Pilots are a special breed. It takes someone with a strong heart to love one." She would have to guard her heart, or she was all too likely to find herself in the very same position as this widow.

Ann smiled through her tears. "I suppose it does."

"I shouldn't take up any more of your time," Rory said, getting up to go. "Thank you for agreeing to come to the gala. Here's an invitation," she said, pulling it out of her purse.

"Thank *you* for the money. It truly is a life saver."

"Of course. That's why we're here. Take care, and I'll see you in a few weeks."

As she descended the stairs, Rory wondered what it would be like to be married to Hank and then lose him like that. It made her stomach clench, and a lump formed in her throat at the thought of anything happening to Hank. She shook herself and squared her shoulders as she got into the car for the drive home. Hank would be fine. Hadn't he demonstrated that he could get through even the direst emergencies? She'd gotten herself worked up talking to Ann Prince. That was all.

And yet she couldn't help imagining what it would be like to marry Hank with her family's blessing. He wouldn't need to work as a pilot anymore. Perhaps he could work in her father's company or start his own. Maybe he could start an airplane business and give Glenn Curtiss a run for his money. They would buy a plane, of course, and he would let her get her pilot's license. Her father would insist they live on the Upper East Side, though perhaps they could keep his place in Mineola as a vacation bungalow.

Why was she spending time on daydreams? She couldn't afford to get attached to Hank for so many reasons. He wasn't a man looking to be tied down, and given the dangers of his job, the chances that this would all end in grief and heartbreak were high. Not to mention that her father would disown her. And yet something within her warned that her heart was in more danger than she wanted to admit. She could only hope that seeing him one last time, she would be able to get him out of her system once and for all.

14

At last, Hank was satisfied that he had ironed every last wrinkle out of his dress uniform and polished his shoes to a mirror shine. He sat on his bed in his union suit staring at it. Would Rory approve? Ladies always liked a man in dress uniform, so starched and formal. But tonight, he'd be competing with men in full black-tie formal wear, men like Edward who could buy everything Hank owned many times over. That said, the uniform was a great equalizer. Scions of wealthy families who joined the armed forces wore the same uniforms as nobodies from Michigan.

Would the senator be there? For Rory's sake, he hoped not. But her father might have overridden her objections. If that smug son-of-a-bitch had the nerve to show his face, Hank would make him regret it. If he wasn't there, though, Hank hoped to find a quiet moment with the birthday girl to say goodbye.

Earlier, he went to the barber for a haircut and shave so that he would look as debonaire as he could manage. His chances of kissing her goodbye were less than zero, but he wanted to be perfectly smooth for her, nonetheless. The time had come. He dabbed the merest hint of cologne on himself and dressed.

Looking in the mirror, he couldn't help but be pleased with the results. He might not be a fancy industrialist or financier, but the olive uniform with the wide leather belt had a heroism to it that no formalwear could convey, no matter how expensive.

On the drive to the Waldorf, his determination to keep his distance after the party grew. They were from two different worlds and didn't belong together, not to mention that his job was too dangerous to contemplate a committed relationship with anyone, let alone her. How could he have let her get under his skin like that? This had to be the end. The game had gone too far. They were not meant to be together, and if he had to be the strong one and resist temptation, so be it.

He walked up the steps, firm in his conviction, striding with purpose toward the ballroom where he'd been directed. This hotel was one swanky joint with its thick, lush carpet and electric fixtures lighting his way. Determination filled him as he walked through the ballroom doors and took in the crowd, keeping an eye out for Edward just in case.

All his good intentions fell away when he saw her. Christ, she was gorgeous! That pale blue gown she was wearing perfectly matched her eyes. Her arms were bare to the shoulder where beaded straps were all that held up her gown. All that creamy skin was just begging for his caress. He wanted to pluck those little straps right off and watch the whole gown slide down over her soft curves until it puddled on the floor.

Speaking of curves, that neckline was damned near indecent. The swell of her breasts was barely covered by draping fabric that looked as if it might slip at any moment to reveal the pink of her nipples. And the back was even worse, leaving her bare to the waist. He wanted to trace her spine with his fingers and watch her nipples tighten in response. It would take so little to run his hand beneath the slinky fabric to cup her gorgeous ass.

No, that was not what he was there for. *Hold it together, Hawley.*

The skirt seemed safe enough, all swoops and drapes down to her ankles, but then she moved, revealing decadent glimpses of calf and shin as she glided around the room.

For a moment, everything else disappeared, and all he could do was stare.

A nudge from O'Donnell brought him out of his reverie. "If you want your secret to stay secret, you'd better stop staring at her like a piece of cake you're about to devour."

"Hmm?" He looked at his lanky friend. O'Donnell cleaned up nice when he tried.

"Fortunately, you aren't the only man drooling over her this evening. Half of them seem to be able to look at nothing else. Your gaping doesn't seem to have drawn attention. Yet."

Word must have gotten around about her rift with Edward because O'Donnell was right. The urge to swoop in and steal her away almost overwhelmed his good sense. Those other men didn't deserve to see her like this. Every last one of them was imagining her naked, he was certain, and the thought made him see red.

O'Donnell steered him over to the bar and got him a whiskey.

Hank deliberately turned his gaze to his friend and away from Rory and her many admirers. He almost would have preferred Edward's presence to this. At least then he could have concentrated all his loathing in one place. It would be a small miracle if he made it through the night without starting a brawl. Hank forced himself to breathe and smile. *Thank God for whiskey!*

"Quite the swanky shindig, eh?" O'Donnell said, clinking glasses with Hank. "I've never seen the like, nor do I expect to again. Did you see the ice sculptures in the shape of a Jenny?"

Looking over where O'Donnell was pointing, he saw a buffet table dripping with fresh fruit and little bite-sized baked things he didn't know the name of, flanked by two formidable sculptures of airplanes. At the center of the table was a five-tiered cake covered with fanciful frosting flowers. Waiters circulated with glasses of champagne, offering them to guests seated at round tables arranged around a central dance floor. A live band was setting up at the front.

Had her engagement party been this ritzy? He'd wondered more than once what it would have been like if he had stayed with her the night that they met instead of letting her go back on her own. What if he'd sauntered into the middle of that party, dressed in his oil-stained uniform with her on his arm, a humble knight to defend her honor? All hell would have broken loose. That was what. But now every time he passed the Turf and Field Club, he imagined the scene and wondered what it was like inside. He'd probably never find out, but he imagined it was something like this.

The room they were in looked like a wedding cake with marble pillars and decorative plasterwork on the ceiling. Electric chandeliers hung down, turned just high enough to sparkle and provide a bit of ambient light to complement the candles on the tables. It was only slightly brighter than a nightclub, but still, Rory was bright as the moon as she traversed the room. Even as he tried not to look, he sensed her, following her in his mind when he couldn't with his eyes.

Had she seen him yet? He didn't think so. He was hiding in a corner with O'Donnell who was perusing the other ladies in attendance, looking for potential dance partners.

"Oh, I like that one over there in the black dress with the auburn hair. She doesn't look as hoity-toity as the rest. I bet I could get her to dance with me."

Hank looked over at the woman in question. She had lovely green eyes, a dress that was several years out of fashion, and seemed as out of place as they were in this party. "Be careful. She might be a war widow and may not be in the mood for dancing," Hank said, putting two and two together.

"Pshaw," said O'Donnell, taking a drink. "All the more reason to get her to dance. She needs a little fun in her life, and I'm just the man to give it to her."

At that moment, a spotlight turned on a podium, and Major Belmont stepped up. "Ladies and gentlemen, I think we all know why we're gathered here this evening. We're here to raise funds for a very worthy cause: the Pilots' Benevolent Association."

Hank had to stifle a snort of laughter at that. The major must not be aware the organization was invented less than a month ago. There was applause all around. Hank's gaze traveled to Rory, and his laughter died. Her lovely lips turned down in a frown. And then it hit him. The major made no mention of Rory even though it was her own damned birthday party.

"It's a pleasure to see so many of my friends here tonight, showing their support. I, myself, plan to make a generous dona-tion," Major Belmont continued. "I've met several young ladies here this evening that will be beneficiaries of our gifts. Their stories are tragic and moving. We've lost too many brave young men in this war, and our pilots are amongst the bravest of the bunch. Let's make sure these young women get the support they deserve after the tremendous sacrifice their families have made for our country."

There was more applause. And still not one mention of Rory.

"And now I would like to introduce the head of this wonderful charitable effort, Evelyn Carnegie."

The major stepped aside, and Rory pressed her lips together in a thin line. *What a way to treat your own daughter on her birthday!*

A petite brunette took the stage, piercing the crowd with fiery brown eyes. Despite her size, she had every bit as much poise and presence as Major Belmont.

"Good evening, ladies and gentlemen," Evelyn said in a clear, ringing voice. "Thank you for gathering this evening to support this wonderful cause. And a special thank you to the young women that agreed to come this evening to share their stories with you. I encourage you to speak with them and hear their stories of bravery in adversity. I am proud to support such strong, upright women who have lost so much in supporting our cause overseas. They are truly inspiring."

Hank was impressed. Somehow, Rory and her friend had turned his imaginary organization into a real charity in less than a month. It was quite a feat.

"But there's another special woman I would like to celebrate tonight. Rory Belmont." At last, someone remembered Rory! There was an uproar of applause and cheering. "She has been a tireless advocate for the cause, going out and meeting with widows to learn their stories and hear their needs, and she is the inspiration behind this evening, choosing to use her birthday celebration to raise money for the cause. Please join me in a toast to the birthday girl," Evelyn said, raising a glass. Waiters magically appeared all over the room with more champagne for those that needed it. "To Rory. Her kind heart and tireless work ethic put us all to shame. To her health and happiness!"

Hank raised a glass and drank along with everyone else in the room. The birthday girl was finally getting her due.

Evelyn beckoned Rory up to the podium. "And now, I give you the birthday girl."

Hank clapped as hard as he could, wishing he could somehow make up for her father's cold performance. Applause came from every corner of the room. At least her friends appreciated her properly. Her father was off in a corner, talking with some pompous old windbag and ignoring the festivities.

"Good evening, everyone, and thank you for coming." Most people wouldn't see the hint of strain beneath her dazzling grin, but Hank knew she was hurting. He wanted to wrap her in his arms, carry her away, and kiss her until she forgot all her troubles. But he couldn't. Not tonight with everyone watching.

"I would like to thank my dear friend Evelyn for all the tremendous work she has done in support of the cause." Genuine warmth emanated from Rory as she looked at Evelyn. It was good to know she had at least one true friend to stand by her. "This is a truly worthy effort, and I owe a great debt of thanks to her. To Evelyn," Rory said, raising a glass. Everyone drank.

"It's no secret," she continued, "how much I love everything related to airplanes and flying. But my work with the Pilots' Benevolent Association has taught me about the dangers of flight as well, not just physical danger but dangers to the heart. It takes a brave man to fly up into the sky like a bird, and it takes a strong woman to love and marry such a man."

Her eyes met Hank's for the briefest of moments, and his heart skipped a beat. Her words made his heart ache. He knew too well the risk a woman took falling for a man like him, and now she knew too. She'd sat with the widows, heard their stories, and seen the pain in their eyes. The risk was no longer theoretical for her. If she fell for him, she knew very well what could happen, and it filled him with guilt. But she still went through with all of this, even with what she'd learned, so what did that mean? It almost made him hope this was only a fling for her, despite his own feelings. It would be for the best.

"The sacrifices these women have made put us all to shame. Please join me in supporting these brave women who have lost so much. To the pilots' wives," she said, raising her glass and her audience followed suit.

He reveled in this moment of being able to look unabashed at her instead of pretending he was occupied by other things. As if he could pay attention to anything else when she was in the room. She was so vibrant, so alive, so good. She took his joke organization and built something truly admirable from it. Rory Belmont did nothing by half measures. And this incredible woman wanted him.

O'Donnell was right. It was going to be next to impossible to deny her tonight. The madness he felt in her presence had only grown in intensity. If she was willing to risk so much to see him, how could he refuse the risk of seeing her? But it wasn't his own risk that concerned him. It was hers. Getting caught with him would mean she'd lose everything, including what she'd worked so hard to build tonight. And if Edward made an appearance, he'd recognize Hank and tell Major Belmont. Another reason to be grateful that good-for-nothing stuffed suit didn't show up.

"Time to stop staring like a slavering idiot," said O'Donnell, nudging him in the side with his elbow. "It seems you were right about Miss Auburn Hair. But even if she's a widow, she deserves a little fun in her life. What do you say to a wager? I bet you five dollars I can get her on the dance floor."

Hank smiled, happy to be distracted from his own swirling thoughts. "I'll make it ten if you can make her laugh. She looks so sad."

"And I am an expert at cheering up sad young ladies," O'Donnell said with a wink.

"You're a buffoon."

"Not everyone can seduce a woman with looks alone. Some of us need a winning personality too." With that, O'Donnell walked off in pursuit of Miss Auburn Hair.

Hank watched him go. The poor woman. She had no idea what she was in for.

With O'Donnell gone, his eyes found Rory again. The band started up, and he watched as one man after another took her to the dance floor. Finally convinced that Edward wasn't going to show, Hank waited to take his turn, trying not to appear too eager, even though it killed him. It seemed like every eligible young man from the city's elite was vying for her attention. Her future husband, whoever he ended up being, was likely in attendance tonight. Hank hated all of them.

Unable to look on patiently any longer, he entered the fray. He might not be her future husband, but he was damned well going to dance with her.

"May I have this dance?" Only one man spoke in such low and lovely tones.

"Of course."

Hank had finally asked her to dance. Rory was starting to worry he would keep his distance all night, which would put a significant crimp in her plans. It wasn't as if *she* could approach *him*, but it had been torture wondering if he would avoid her all night because of the risks of getting close with her father in the room.

Hank had to fight his way through several utterly dull society gents to get to her, but he outmaneuvered them with ease and staked his claim.

Charles Willoughby slunk off sulking. Anthony Harding glared. She didn't care.

Hank's hand touched hers, and it was electric. Everything else in the room disappeared.

By luck, the band started a slow, lugubrious foxtrot. His hand kissed her bare back right beneath her shoulder blades, and she shivered in pleasure. As her chest brushed against his in the intimate embrace the dance required, her nipples stiffened, and warmth coiled between her legs. She could hardly wait until she had him all to herself. In his arms, she could lose herself and maybe even forget her father's little speech. How could the man forget to mention her birthday in the middle of her birthday party? Not that he was ever enthusiastic about her birthday. He usually avoided her celebrations entirely.

But coming to her party and then not making one mention of her had to be deliberate. Maybe it was Papa's revenge for her breaking things off with Edward. He'd certainly wasted no time inviting every high-society low-life in search of an heiress to her party. She wished it didn't sting as much as it did.

But she wasn't going to waste another thought on her father, not when she was finally in Hank's arms where she belonged.

As they began to move, their bodies pressed close, his inner thigh brushed against her own through layers of fabric, tantalizing and tempting her, so close to where she wanted him. She bit her lip, needing the pain to bring her back to the present. Her father was in the room, watching all that transpired, plotting how to marry her off to the first fortune hunter he could find with a family name that he found acceptable. She couldn't surrender to the dance, not yet. Later tonight, she would be his, but not now. It was only a dance.

The music built, and Hank pulled her closer. "Happy birthday, princess," he murmured, his lips brushing her ear. She felt the words resonating in her core.

"You can make it happier still," she murmured back. "Ask the front desk for the key to room 512. Tell them your name is Albert Jones. I'll be there at midnight."

He pulled her closer still, the steady rhythm of the music carrying them along as it built toward a climax. "I swore to myself I wouldn't. You're risking too much."

She adjusted her leg's position to brush against his front on the next step. Sure enough, there was a bulge. "No reluctance where it matters," she observed.

"Dammit, Rory," he exclaimed in a whispered hiss. "I'm trying to do the right thing by you."

"Then stop. I'm perfectly capable of deciding what risks I wish to take."

He was silent, his smoldering eyes burning into her as they moved across the dance floor.

"I've taken significant precautions to ensure we won't be discovered. No one will ever know I've been in your room."

Still, he said nothing.

"Will you come?"

He closed his eyes and breathed out. "I shouldn't." But he sounded less certain.

"You'll come. You wouldn't dare disappoint the birthday girl," she said with a confident smile.

The dance was coming to an end. "Goodbye, Rory, and best wishes. I'm leaving after this dance."

"I'll see you tonight, Hank. Don't fail me."

He released her slowly as Aunt Alva strode toward her with a frown, calling out, "Rory dear, I'm afraid I must be going. Come say goodbye."

"I'll be there in a moment," Rory called out, then whispered in his ear. "I'll see you shortly." She didn't wait for an answer before turning away to speak with her aunt.

"Who was that young man?" Aunt Alva asked, narrowing her eyes.

Oh dear. The last thing she wanted right now was for Aunt Alva to draw attention to Hank.

"I have no idea. Just one of the legion of eligible bachelors Papa seems to have invited," Rory answered quickly. "When is the next march? Do you need me to come by to paint signs later this week?"

Aunt Alva pursed her lips and raised an eyebrow. But when she opened her mouth, all she said was, "Come by Sunday afternoon around two. Enjoy the rest of your birthday, my dear."

Rory didn't see Hank leave, but she felt his absence as soon as he was gone.

The rest of the party was a whirlwind. She danced almost without pause for three hours straight before things began to wind down. Her father was among the first to depart.

"Will I see you at home?"

"No, Papa. I took a room here. I knew I'd be too spent to head back uptown."

"Very well. I'll see you tomorrow for breakfast," he said and left. Not so much as a happy birthday, not that she should be surprised after all these years.

Next, Evelyn left on the arm of the self-absorbed shipping magnate her parents kept trying to set her up with. Poor Evelyn! "Goodnight. Have fun," she said with a wink as she headed out. Rory had no doubt Evelyn guessed exactly what she was up to. Thankfully, Rory knew Evelyn would keep her secrets.

"You were marvelous tonight, Evelyn. I couldn't have a better friend. Thank you for everything!"

Evelyn smiled and took her leave. One by one, her dance partners made their excuses and left. One or two persistent ones tried to persuade her to go out with them, but she pleaded exhaustion and headed up to room 511...the one adjoining Hank's.

She'd only done this once before—with Archie. Not that she wanted to think about him with Hank (hopefully!) waiting for her in the next room. But this little adventure was twice as dangerous. A scandal with a man from the same social strata was one thing, but with Hank? The gossip rags would feast on her and her family forever.

Her heart thudded in her chest as she contemplated the risks that they were both taking for this one chance to grasp a bit of heaven. This had to end. They both knew it. After tonight, they would have to go their separate ways. But she needed one perfect night with him to escape the confines of her life for a few hours and get him out of her system once and for all.

Slipping off her shoes, she tiptoed to the door connecting the two rooms and unfastened the lock on her side. She knocked. There was no answer. Did he leave? She was so sure he wouldn't.

She knocked again and pressed her ear to the door, desperately hoping for some sign that she hadn't misjudged. At long last, a bolt clicked. The door opened, and she fell into Hank's waiting arms. Warmth flooded through her body.

He pulled her into his room and kissed her, hard and demanding, with almost bruising force. She answered in kind, her lips and tongue consuming him hungrily. For weeks, she'd been dreaming of this. Ever since that night on the Flatiron, she'd been drowning in desire for this man. No, it started before that. Was it when he took her flying near Washington D.C.?

She needed one last encounter with him to get him out of her system. The intensity of her need was too much to bear. If she could get what she wanted just this once, she could make the memories last a lifetime. They couldn't be together, but they could have this one night to remember always.

Then all thoughts flew from her head as he began kissing down her neck. Her desire became something tangible. It pressed her closer to him, binding them together in a hot, sultry dance. He backed her against the wall so that his entire length pressed against her. The effect of his heat and touch was immediate and overwhelming. She wanted to bite and claw until his clothes lay shredded on the floor. She wanted to lick and suck every inch of exposed flesh. She wanted to feel him everywhere but especially in one particular place that was pulsing with need.

Tugging at the belt around his uniform, she slipped it through the clasp, unbuckling it. Her fingers fumbled at his buttons as his hands drove her mad, travelling up and down her body, caressing her breasts and grasping her buttocks.

He groaned as he slid his hand beneath the fabric of her dress to caress her bare nipple. "No chemise," he murmured as he nipped at her shoulder.

"The cut of the dress wouldn't allow it."

"Good God."

When she tore the last button free, she yanked his jacket down, discarding it on the floor as she started on the buttons of his shirt. He turned her and backed her into the side of a writing desk, shoving a lamp aside to make room for her to sit with her legs spread to accommodate him. The front panel of her skirt hung between her legs, and the side panels slid down, leaving her exposed up to the thighs where her garters peeked through.

Wrapping her legs around his waist, she welcomed his firm, grasping hands, caressing and squeezing her thighs until he reached her garters. He unclipped her silk stockings with ease, tracing the seams at the back with his fingers as he slid them down.

As he knelt at her feet, he reached up and found the part in her sleek, silk undergarments, pressing her open with his hands. Cool air touched her wet folds, and then white heat blinded her as he sucked her into his mouth, torturing her most sensitive place with his devilish tongue.

"Fuck yes," he moaned after taking his first taste.

She arched back at the sensation, leaning on her hands. Fortunately, it was a sturdy desk. The shoulder of her dress slid down to her elbow, exposing one of her breasts.

As he continued his tender torture, he reached up to the other side, sliding the remaining strap off her shoulder so that her dress fell to her waist, exposing her entire chest. As he held her hips, she pinched and teased her own breasts, intensifying the wave of sensation that was overtaking her. She writhed against him as he put a finger inside her, making her shudder.

Closing her eyes, she was in Hank's airplane again, soaring through the air, no engine, only the caress of the wind against her skin. As the ground grew closer and treetops went whipping past, the intensity of the sensation increased. Her senses sharpened as Hank's skilled hand guided them in for a landing. Everything went white as she touched the ground, shuddering to a stop.

Panting, she watched Hank stand up, dressed only in his union suit and pants, an impressive erection tenting the fabric.

She traced her fingers up the bulge, and he took a sharp, hissing breath.

"Fuck," he muttered through gritted teeth, shuddering from head to toe.

"That's my plan," she said, sliding off the bureau, letting her dress drop to the floor, and unhooking her garter belt so that she was completely naked. Then she pulled him by the waist of his pants toward the bed.

"I didn't mean… I don't think we should…"

For God's sake, why was he fighting her on this? He obviously wanted it too. Her hands on his hips, she maneuvered him until his calves hit the bed and began unbuttoning his union suit from the top. "Fuck?"

He gasped hearing her say that word and clutched her convulsively against his arousal. It seemed he liked it when she talked dirty.

"It's my birthday, Hank. I want you inside me."

"God, I want that too, but—"

"I choose my own risks. No one else chooses for me. Besides, I'm wearing protection." At his raised eyebrows, she added, "I have a diaphragm." It hadn't been easy to get, but she was glad of the freedom it offered.

"There's still a risk that—"

It was sweet of him to be so considerate, but really, enough was enough.

"Hush," she said, whispering in his ear and biting his earlobe, making him gasp. She reached the waistband of his pants and slid the arms of his union suit over his shoulder, leaving his delectable, sculpted chest bare for her perusal. Her fingers continued downward, and his pants fell around his ankles. She unbuttoned the last buttons of his union suit and pushed it down so that he was fully revealed.

Taking a step back to enjoy the sight, she said, "My God, you're a beautiful man, and I am one very lucky woman."

His dark hair and dramatic brow reminded her of the movie star, Douglas Fairbanks. His brown eyes were hot coals, flecked with golden flame. But it was his body that was truly breathtaking. He put the Greek statues at the Metropolitan Museum of Art to shame with the chiseled chest and sculpted arms. His legs had muscles she never knew existed. And then there was his cock, standing tall and proud against a spray of coarse black hair. She wanted him inside her now.

"Lay down," she ordered, and he complied.

The sight of him stretched out before her at her command made her feel so powerful. Yes, this was exactly where she wanted this gorgeous specimen of a man. She climbed up and straddled him so that his cock was sliding against her, right where she wanted it. The intimate friction made her gasp as her wetness slicked his cock. She could come just rocking against him like this.

"Oh Christ," he said through gritted teeth.

"That's it. Surrender, Hank. We both know how this is going to end." Judging from the desperate glint in his eye, he was moments away from caving. She needed to hear him say it, needed to know that he needed this every bit as much as she did. Taking him in hand, she rubbed his tip against her opening, and his eyes rolled back in his head. She slid him in ever so slightly then pulled back. "Do you surrender?"

He was silent for a long moment, jaw clenched, and brow furrowed, a pleading look in his eyes. He exhaled slowly. "I surrender."

Yes!

"Thank God," she whispered and slid down onto him, rocking

and taking him deeper with each movement, savoring the triumph of his capitulation. His mouth hung open, and his breathing was shallow as she progressed. The sensation of fullness and deep pleasure was almost too much for her when she had taken him to the hilt. Something about the size and shape of him pressed in a way that made her shudder in ecstasy. As she began to move, he rubbed against a magical spot that she'd never known existed, sending shockwaves out to her fingers and toes.

"You feel. So. Good," she gasped, barely able to form words. "Never felt. Like this. Before."

It was hard to form words or even thoughts when each stroke seemed to shatter her body and soul. It obliterated everything, this bright, crackling connection between them. She moved her hips in a slow and steady rhythm, needing to take her time with the new intensity.

"Me neither," he said, his voice strained and ragged.

She wanted to prolong the moment, but her body had its own ideas. She began quickening her rhythm almost imperceptibly.

"More," she heard herself say, though how she could possibly take more was hard to imagine.

Hank answered by flipping her on her back, to reach new depths within her. Each thrust was a blinding explosion, building toward something bigger still. "Rory," he said with such sweet reverence everything inside her clenched, making him cry out.

"Kiss me," she said, and he did. It was a soft and tender kiss, entirely unlike their furious kisses earlier. It was as if he was trying to convey some unnamed emotion as he took her. Her heart responded to his silent call, falling a little bit in love despite her best intentions. He was offering more than his body, and she wanted it all. Consequences be damned.

"So beautiful," he whispered. "So brave. I've never met anyone like you, so passionate, so daring, so alive. I could have you every night for my whole life, and it wouldn't be enough."

Her heart softened further as a wave of sensation built.

"Please don't let this be the last time." As he said it, she knew she felt the same. This was supposed to be a fling. She was supposed to bed him once and get him out of her system. But somehow it had gotten out of hand and turned into something more. He wanted *her*, not her father's money, not a pretty girl to brag about, not even a quick fuck. Somehow, miraculously, he saw what no one else could see, touched her with a hungry reverence that she'd never experienced before. She had to keep seeing him. She knew already that tonight couldn't possibly be enough.

"It won't be," she said before she could stop herself.

It wasn't supposed to be like this. She was supposed to stay in control. She couldn't afford to have feelings. He was a pilot. Not only would her family never approve, but she was setting herself up for heartbreak. She spent the last month learning exactly how much pain could come from loving a pilot. But dear God, this couldn't stop. She needed so much more.

He kissed her again, drawing her in, savoring lips and tongue, as the wave within her continued to build. Her whole body trembled with the crescendo of sensation. And then it was upon her. Obliterating ecstasy shot through her, sending her to the sweet oblivion of bliss.

As if from a great distance, she felt his thrusts gain strength, and then he groaned and pulled out. Something wet splashed across her belly, and he collapsed beside her.

She floated back down from ecstasy to find him watching her intently. He leaned in for a long, slow kiss. "Happy birthday, Rory Belmont."

She gave him a sly smile. "Why thank you, Hank."

16

Oh, good Lord, he just made love to Rory Belmont. She was still lying there like a goddess with his seed dripping across her belly.

Fighting exhaustion, he made himself get up and go to the bathroom for a warm, damp cloth to clean her up. As he wiped away the pearly liquid, he looked at her. She was absolute perfection. Tossing aside the cloth, he climbed back into bed and pulled her against him so that her head was resting on his chest. Her legs tangled with his, and he knew it wouldn't be long before he wanted her again, no matter how tired he was.

With her in his arms, he couldn't bring himself to think too hard about the foolish thing he'd said. *Please don't let this be the last time.* It had to be the last time. Last time should have been the last time. He came into the evening with such good intentions. He even managed to leave the event without committing to see her. But when he tried to walk out of the hotel, his feet made a different choice. And once he was at the front desk, he had to take the room. And once he was in the room, well...

When he decided to stay, he promised himself this was the

end. But none of that mattered with her naked and snuggled against him. "How long can you stay?"

"All night," she said. "But I need to be home by 8:00 a.m. for breakfast."

He nodded. It was both a luxurious eternity and far too short. She yawned and snuggled closer. "You must be exhausted, princess. Let's get some rest. We have all night."

He turned off the bedside lamp, and they dozed. His dreams were filled with her, and it was no surprise when he woke up several hours later, hard as a rock, and desperate to have her again. Moonlight poured through the window, coating everything in a silver gleam, including her gorgeous curves. He didn't want to wake her, though, so he turned away from her and tried to focus on counting sheep. She must have felt him shift because she nestled against him, spooning him, and began kissing his neck. Her hand wandered down and found his tremendous erection. She said, "Mmm," as she grasped it and began to stroke.

"You're awake?" he murmured.

She laughed. "Yes, and so are you."

He turned around so that he was facing her. "Are you saying you want…?"

"Obviously," she said, hooking an elegant, tapered leg over his hip and drawing him into a long, languorous kiss. "Were you dreaming of me? I was dreaming of you."

"Good dreams I hope," he said kissing her again. He could happily spend a week just kissing her. Her lips were so soft and supple, and she used them so sinfully well.

"See for yourself." She pulled his hand between her legs where he felt her wetness slicking his fingers. Oh God, so wet. His male pride swelled at the thought that he was haunting her dreams, causing other things to swell in response. He immediately began to pet and caress her.

"Oh, I see. Very good dreams. And…uh…what did I do in

these dreams?" She began to squirm against him as he teased and tormented her.

"You started with what you're doing now," she said, "and then you took me, making me come again and again until I dissolved into a thousand stars."

Christ, it made him hard to hear her say things like that.

"I'll make you see stars, princess."

Changing the movement of his hand, he thrust two fingers inside her and curved them to touch the spot he'd discovered earlier, and she convulsed against him. Excellent. Exactly what he wanted. He loved the way she writhed at his touch. In very short order, she was wailing as she came, and he had to kiss her to contain the noise.

"Now give me what I want," she demanded.

"This?" he asked, taking a nipple in his mouth and teasing it with tongue and teeth.

"You are terrible," she said, raking her nails up his back in revenge for his delay.

"No? What about this?" he said, delaying yet again with her other breast. He could play this game all night.

No, he couldn't. Who was he kidding? He could barely contain himself now, but it was so entertaining to thwart her.

She made a throaty noise of frustration.

"Oh, this isn't what you want?"

"You know what I want."

"Yes, but I want to hear you say it."

She took his jaw in her grip and looked straight into his eyes. "I told you, I want you inside me, fucking me until I see stars. Is that what you want to hear?"

"Yes, Your Majesty," he said with a mock salute.

And with that, he positioned himself and sank home. *Oh fuck.* The clenching heat threatened to send him over the edge before they even got started. For a long moment, neither of them moved. All they could do was breathe. She looked back at him, wide-eyed in the silver moonlight, mouth frozen in a small "o."

In that instant, he was hers. His intentions didn't matter. *Please don't let this be the last time. It won't be.* It couldn't be. There was no walking away from this for either of them. Somehow, they would have to do the impossible and traverse the chasm that separated them because they had no other choice. This wasn't going to end simply because they willed it.

The need to move crept up on him, growing and building until he couldn't resist any longer. Her mouth widened as he thrust into her, her lip quivering and her brow furrowed as she took in a shaky breath. He moved slowly, carefully, stoking the fire within her stroke by stroke. She remained speechless, her whole body trembling as they rocked gently together.

As she moved beneath him, she met each thrust with a counterthrust, pulling him deeper and deeper. With delicate fingers, she reached up to his face, cupping his jaw, then running her thumb over his bottom lip. Her gentle touch wove a magic spell that threatened to make his heart explode.

He bent down to kiss her, needing to find a new way to release his overflowing emotions. Being inside her wasn't enough. He needed to be connected in every possible way. Her lips met his with fierce desperation, her tongue driving into his mouth greedily as if he was the air she needed to breathe.

Like the first time he took off in an airplane on his own, he felt an otherworldly sense of rightness, of belonging. This was what he was meant for, why he was born into this world. His purpose in life was to fly airplanes and love Rory Belmont.

Love? Yes, love. What other word could describe the feelings flowing through him? What other force in the universe was this powerful and all-consuming? Certainly not lust. He'd felt lust. It was like a sickness, a fever that took him in its thrall and then broke. With Rory, it wasn't a temporary fever. It was a transmutation. The heat was so much greater. He was being blown and spun like molten glass into someone else entirely, someone permanently linked to her.

A tremor rippled through her, and then another, stronger one. She clenched and pulsed around him, as he struggled to hold back his release. He thrust hard, and she cried out, tipping over the edge into oblivion. He thrust again and again, extending her flight through bliss until he could no longer hold on. At the last moment, he pulled out and spent in the sheets.

As he lay back and caught his breath, he wondered what on earth he was going to do. How could he broach the subject with her without sounding like a lovesick puppy?

"Hank?"

There was something tentative in the way she said his name. Did she somehow sense his thoughts?

"Yes?" He waited.

A long silence.

"What is it, Rory?"

"Have we gone too far?" She settled her head on his chest. It felt like she belonged there.

"What do you mean 'too far'?" He stroked her wild curls, savoring their softness.

"I…" She went silent for a long moment. "I want to keep seeing you."

"I want to keep seeing you too. We'll figure it out somehow, don't worry."

She sighed. "I know we will. It's just that…"

"What?"

Taking a deep breath, she said, "This was supposed to be a fling—one night to get you out of my system. It wasn't supposed to turn into something more."

His heart sank, hearing her speak aloud his own thoughts. But he had been lying to himself all along. Was she? "If you want me to leave you be, I'll do it." It would kill him, but he would.

"That's just it. I don't want you to. I want…something more."

And with those words, everything changed. She didn't want to send him away, never to return. The feeling was mutual, and he didn't have to hide or hold back.

He kissed her fervently, and she responded with equal ardor. "What does 'something more' mean to you?"

"I… I don't know. All I know is I need to see you again. This can't be the end."

He couldn't agree more. "I'll do anything you want. Just tell me what you need from me."

"I don't know yet."

The dangers were great, but this was a risk worth taking.

"Is there anything I could do to make your father less likely to want to murder me?" It was unlikely, but maybe she would have an idea.

She shook her head. "Not unless you can get filthy rich." Unlikely. "And change what family you were born into." Impossible.

"So, no." Damnit.

"I'm sorry. My father's a terrible snob about me. He's not so bad in other areas of his life, but when it comes to family alliances…"

"If I had a daughter, I wouldn't want her anywhere near a guy like me either."

She wrapped her arm around him and traced his shoulder blade. "Why?"

"I know the risks pilots take, even outside the war with no one shooting at us. Airplanes aren't safe, and I wouldn't want my daughter heartbroken like those war widows at the party tonight."

"Oh, Hank." She kissed him sweetly. "Heartbreak seems like a small price to pay for the company of someone as brave and daring—"

"And handsome."

"And handsome," she added with a smile, "as you."

Did that mean she cared enough for her heart to be broken? Discomfort twisted in his belly.

"Rory."

"Hmm?" Her eyes were drooping. He really should let her get some more sleep.

"Don't fall for me. I don't want to cause you pain."

She propped up her chin on his chest so that she could look him in the eye. "Don't tell me what to do, Hank Hawley. I take the risks I choose. It isn't up to you."

He stared. It was all he could do not to laugh. Good God, what a woman. "Does this mean you are falling for me?"

She settled her head back down on his chest, twining her arms and legs around him. "Presumptuous," she said with a yawn. "Are you falling for me?"

"Yes," he answered before he could stop himself. He clenched his jaw, wishing he could take it back. "But it doesn't matter. There's nothing I can do about it. You're as unreachable as ever, princess."

"Well, you can certainly reach me right now," she said with a wicked grin, putting his hand on her breast.

"Don't you need sleep?"

She shrugged. "I have my whole life to sleep. I only have…" She peered at the wind-up alarm clock beside the bed. "…three and a half more hours with you."

He smiled. "How should we use our time?"

"I have some ideas."

And she showed him.

17

*R*ory came into the breakfast room humming the tune from the foxtrot she'd shared with Hank. After a night like that, nothing could bring her down. She'd successfully removed all vestiges of last night's activities and looked as fresh and innocent as a lily. And if she was a bit tired, it was only to be expected after such a long night with so much excitement.

"Good morning, Papa," she said, avoiding looking at him.

"Good morning, Aurora. I thought the party was a great success."

"It was simply smashing. I wish I could do it all over again tonight," she said, sitting and pouring herself a cup of coffee. Thank God he had no idea just how delightful it was.

"Ah, for the energy and vigor of youth!" He gave his newspaper a shake. There was a tray of five different ones sitting beside his chair. August Belmont liked to start his day well informed.

"Says the man that joined the army at the age of sixty-four. Papa, you're going to outlive us all." She served herself a heaping plate of eggs, sausage, and toast.

James, the butler, came in and said, "Excuse me, sir, but there's a Senator Windham here to see you. They say it's urgent."

A warning bell went off in Rory's head at the mention of her former fiancé. How very like Edward to spoil a wonderful morning.

"Edward? Here?" her father asked. "He was supposed to stay away this week and let things cool off. We had an agreement." He folded his newspaper and shoved it to the side.

Oh no. Papa was still trying to mend things with Edward? She thought all the men he'd invited to her birthday meant he'd given up on the 'gentleman' from Connecticut.

"He is most insistent, sir."

"Very well. Show him to my study. I'll be with him shortly." James bowed and departed. "Aurora, you had best make yourself scarce. You've done enough damage with the senator. I don't want you making things worse. We can wait to fix this mess of an engagement until next week when you've both calmed down."

"I think I've lost my appetite," she said, biting back a sharp retort about what a worthless scumbag Edward was. "I'll just finish my coffee and head to my room."

Her father nodded and strode off.

Edward. Why would he choose today of all days to come to see her father? Whatever he was here for, it couldn't be good.

As she was about to leave the breakfast table, James returned. "Miss Belmont, your father has asked to see you in his study immediately, if you would be so kind."

She had a thousand questions but none that could be answered by the poor man sent to deliver the message. "I'll go right away."

Knocking, she was immediately beckoned into her father's inner sanctum. She was rarely granted entry to this hallowed place of business. The entire room was done in dark wood paneling, with built-in bookshelves lining three of the walls. An imposing desk dominated one side of the room, another modern creation by Ruhlmann—more evidence of Eleanor's influence. The more classic Louis XV chairs surrounding the desk were vestiges of her mother's décor.

Her father looked like a storm cloud about to burst. His face was redder than usual, and his brow was deeply furrowed as he looked at her. He clenched his jaw and his fist, as Rory wondered what on earth could have made him so furious.

Edward sat in one of the chairs opposite her father's desk, a smug glint in his eye.

"Aurora June Belmont," her father bellowed.

"What is it, Papa?" She grasped the back of the chair next to Edward, not daring to sit until she knew what was going on.

"I've never been so ashamed in my life." He picked up a marble paper weight and slammed it down again.

"Papa, what happened?" She'd never seen him so furious, not even when the Vanderbilts refused to attend his wedding to Eleanor.

"Edward says you spent last night in the company of a man named Albert Jones. You were heard having…" He paused and stared at the ceiling. "Relations. And it was confirmed that the bed in your hotel room was empty. Do you deny it?"

"Papa, there must be some mistake. I—"

"Yes or no, Aurora. Do you deny having relations with Mr. Jones?"

Was there any way to stall, any possible way to escape? They knew her bedroom was empty and that someone was in the room next to hers, but did they know for certain it was her?

"What makes you think I was the woman in Mr. Jones's bedroom?"

"The Pinkerton I hired heard him use your name," said Edward, looking triumphant.

How dare that snake hire a Pinkerton to trail her? This was beyond outrageous, not that she had a viable excuse. She gave Edward a dirty look then turned to her father.

"Papa, I can explain." Her mind spun, grasping desperately at straws, but there was nothing.

"Can you? I would very much like to hear this explanation."

She didn't have one. She was caught as neatly as a rabbit in a trap. Her shoulders slumped, and she closed her eyes.

"I don't deny it. It was me." At least they didn't know she was with Hank. The damage would be limited to her. This was what she got for fleeing her cage and tasting freedom, even if only for a few hours.

"I'm disgusted, Aurora. Thoroughly, utterly disgusted. That my daughter would do something like this is unthinkable. You're lucky Edward is still willing to marry you."

"I'm sorry, what?" Edward still wanted to marry her despite this? If ever she'd needed proof he was marrying her for money, this was it.

"But I'm not waiting a month," Edward said. "She marries me before a judge today. We'll still have the grand affair in a month, but I want assurance that she is legally mine if I'm going to move forward."

The floor dropped out from beneath her and swallowed her. The rest of her life stretched out before her like the gullet of some dark beast trying to consume her whole. "What makes you think I'll change my mind and marry you now?"

"I caught you red-handed."

"*You* caught me? What were you doing spying on me in the first place?"

"*I* wasn't spying on you. The Pinkerton was. And it's a good thing I hired him to keep tabs on you."

It was all so twisted and wrong. She had no idea Edward was capable of going to such lengths.

"I can't say I approve of spying, Edward," her father said, "though I now understand why you were distrustful. But in the end, none of this matters. Aurora, you're marrying Edward today, and that's final."

She felt something welling up inside her, something big and powerful that she could not deny. "No," she said, stepping around the chair so that it was between her and Edward.

"Did you just say no?" Her father's voice was quiet, deadly calm.

"I won't marry him, Papa. No punishment you could dole out would be worse than spending my life tied to him." And it was true. She would far rather be cast out and disowned than marry Edward after all that had transpired.

"You know what this means, Aurora. I told you what would happen."

"I understand." She was proud of herself for keeping her voice calm and even. She felt as if she were being pummeled by an enormous, dark wave that was going to pull her under any moment.

"I don't understand," Edward said. "August, you said she would marry me."

"I can't legally force her, Edward," her father hissed, emotion finally breaking through into his voice. "But trust me, she'll be back begging. Give it a week, two at most."

"A week or two of what?" Edward demanded. "I want this deal sealed right now."

Her father quelled him with a look, then turned his fury on her.

"Aurora, as of now, you are cut off. You won't receive a penny from me, and you are no longer welcome in this house. If you don't come to your senses in a month's time, I will remove you from my will and permanently disown you. You will no longer be a member of this family. It will be as if you were never born."

Tears dripped down her cheeks. Dammit. She intended to stay calm. "I understand. I'll go pack my things."

"You may take your clothes and personal effects, but you may not take anything of value. All jewelry, art, and antiques stay here. I'll send two servants to oversee your departure and see that you leave the house as soon as is practicable."

With as much dignity as she could muster, she turned and walked out the door.

As she packed, she thought through where to go to stave off panic. Aunt Alva or one of her brothers might take her in, but she didn't want to subject any of them to her father's wrath. Her brothers all worked in the family business, and Alva's husband was a close friend of her father's. She could try Evelyn, but she wouldn't be able to provide any open assistance without putting her own reputation in jeopardy. Did she dare go to Hank?

She needed to see him anyway. If Edward would stoop this low, it was only a matter of time before he worked out that Hank and Albert Jones were one and the same. What he would do, she wasn't sure, but she had to warn Hank.

As she headed out the door with four suitcases, her maid, Kelly, surreptitiously handed her ten dollars. "You've always been generous to me, Miss. I don't want you going out the door with nothing."

Rory stared down at the money in disbelief. The reality of what she was doing suddenly came crashing down on her. She had nothing. Not a cent. No roof over her head, no promise of the next meal, and no family she could turn to. She was a charity case as much as any of the women she'd spoken to for the PBA. Not that she deserved charity. This was all the result of choices she'd made, risks she'd taken with eyes wide open. All her life she'd been cocooned in luxury and privilege. For years, she'd yearned to break free. Well, now she had her wish, and it was devastating.

"Kelly, I don't want to take this, but I can't pretend I don't need it. I'll repay you and more as soon as I'm able." She had to pay for a cab somehow, and it was a long ride out to Mineola. She'd never been more humbled. Throwing her arms around Kelly, she sobbed. Kelly's generosity wrecked her in a way her father's words had not. For the first time in her life, she was ashamed of who she was. What had she ever done to deserve her coddled existence? Kelly was the better woman by far.

It took her several minutes to compose herself so that she could walk out the door with her head held high. Kelly helped her with her bags and flagged down a cab for her. No one else was there to see her off. Rory wondered what all of this might mean for Kelly. Would she lose her job with Rory gone?

Rory's stomach lurched at the thought. "Kelly, I'll make this up to you. I'll make everything up to you, I swear."

"Don't worry about me, Miss. I'll be fine," Kelly said as if she could read Rory's thoughts.

"Not 'Miss.' Just Rory."

Kelly shook her head vigorously.

"Please."

Looking at her long and hard, Kelly finally nodded. "Take care, Rory. Be safe."

Rory got into the cab and drove away for what was likely the last time. *Good riddance*, she thought through the pain. The opulence of the mansions along Park Avenue disgusted her for the first time. How could they all take so much for granted? How could they possibly think they deserved to live like this? How had she thought she deserved it?

As they drove by the warehouses and slums of Queens, instead of shying away, she looked at the faces of the people she saw. Even now, with nothing, she had so much more than these people, toiling in the smoke and summer heat. She had an education. She knew powerful and wealthy people. There was an invisible safety net for her that didn't exist for any of them. She was certain she would find some way to land on her feet.

Wishing she could fix it all, she closed her eyes and realized she was in no position to fix anything until she fixed herself.

As the city turned to the countryside out the cab window, she deliberately turned her thoughts to what lay ahead, to what she was going to say to Hank. It was too much to ask to stay with him. They barely knew each other. Maybe he had a married friend that might be willing to take her in, or he could give her money for a boarding house. She'd pay him back as soon as she got a job.

Speaking of jobs, she was going to need one. A job in a shop was probably the quickest to get, though it likely didn't pay as well as teaching. But it would take time to find a teaching position, and she needed income now. She would have to look for both, she decided.

As they passed Belmont Park, she wiped away a tear. Angry as she was at her father, she was going to miss her family and friends. What would they think when they heard? She didn't want to think about it.

"You all right, Miss?" the cabby asked. He'd been mercifully silent so far.

"I'm just having a bad day."

"Sorry to hear that. I hope it gets better for you."

"Me too." She sighed. It could hardly get worse.

She pulled out the letter from Hank inviting her to the Flatiron to remind herself of the correct address. That night felt like it was ages ago, even though only a month had passed. Back then, the world felt wide open and taking risks felt wonderful. Now, she'd taken the biggest risk of all and lost. But she was finding a strange freedom in that.

She was nobody now, which meant she could be anyone and anything she wanted. She would have to work for it, but she was no stranger to hard work, despite her pampered upbringing. If she could create the Pilots' Benevolent Association from whole cloth in a month, surely, she had the strength, fortitude, and creativity to make a new life for herself.

The cab pulled up in front of a darling mint-green cottage with a large vegetable garden on the side. She wasn't sure what to expect when she decided to come to see Hank, but she didn't expect this. It was adorable with floral curtains fluttering in the windows and two pink rose bushes flanking the door. The cabby helped her bring her suitcases up to the doorstep, and she paid him, then rang the bell.

Hank opened the door, and his jaw dropped open. "Rory, what are you doing here?"

"My father found out. He wanted to force me to marry Edward today. I refused, and he cut me off. I need your help. Can I come in?"

18

Without a second thought, Hank took two of her suitcases and showed her into the house, then came back for the other two. She would probably think his place was a hovel after growing up in a Park Avenue castle, but there was no time to worry about the house. Thank God he'd cleaned the day before!

He led her into his modest parlor, and she sat down on the loveseat. "Can I get you anything? A glass of water? Some tea?"

"You don't have to play host. I just need to talk to you."

Sitting down beside her, he said, "Tell me what happened."

"Edward had someone spying on me."

"He *what*?" That bastard!

"I know. They think I was with Albert Jones last night. They don't know it was you. Yet. But I can't help worrying that they are going to find out, and I'm terrified to think what they might try to do to you."

"Never mind about me. What happened to you?" He leaned forward and put a reassuring hand on her knee. He wasn't scared of Edward Windham.

"I've been cut off. If I come to my senses in time to marry

Edward, Papa says he'll take me back. Otherwise, it's permanent. But I'm not marrying Edward, so it might as well be permanent now."

Poor Rory. If she was anyone else, he would do the right thing right now and propose. He'd ruined her. It was his duty. But with her, he wasn't sure that would be the right thing. Marrying her would permanently destroy any possibility of reconciliation with her family.

"What can I do to help?" he asked.

"I need a place to stay. By any chance, do you have a married friend with a spare room who might be willing to take me in until I have a job and can afford a boarding house? Or would you be willing to lend me money for a boarding house until I get a job? I'll pay you back."

The thought of Rory in a boarding house made him shiver. He couldn't let her do that. "For now, stay here. I'll be gone for the next three days. I'm scheduled to fly down to D.C. We can figure out what to do when I come back."

"Hank, I can't stay here, even with you away. What would people think?"

He blinked. "You've been cut off and disowned because we were caught in bed together, and you're worried what people will think about you staying in my house while I'm gone? Who exactly are you worried about?"

She shook her head. "You're right. I'm being ridiculous. I've already fallen as low as I can go." She tried and failed to blink back tears.

He took her in his arms. "Shh. It's all right. We'll get through this. We'll figure it out. I'll take care of you, princess. You don't have to worry."

"Thank you," she sniffed.

"Have you had lunch? Are you hungry? You must be exhausted. I managed to get some sleep this morning, but it sounds like you didn't sleep at all." Good grief. He wanted to feed her a sandwich and tuck her into bed. Was he turning into his mother?

"I'm not hungry. My stomach is tied in knots right now. A nap sounds heavenly, though. What time do you have to leave?" She wiped away her tears and sniffed. Even with her face red from crying, she was gorgeous.

"Half an hour or so. I have to take the car with me, but you can walk to Main Street if you need something. I'll draw you a little map, and I'll leave you money so you can buy groceries or anything else you need." And then a sudden thought occurred to him. "Do you even know how to cook?"

She gave him a scathing look. "Of course, I know how to cook. I learned in college when I lived off campus with friends. I'm not very good, but I know enough to survive."

He smiled. As he thought, he'd be the one to do all the cooking when they were together. "Let me show you around the house. It isn't very big, but I should give you the grand tour," he said, getting up and offering her a hand.

"This is the parlor. There's nothing useful in here except the telephone. Over here," he said, leading her, "we have the kitchen. The little breakfast nook here is the extent of my dining room. You should be able to find anything you need in the cupboards. Here's the silverware drawer, the spice drawer, the utensil drawer," he said pointing. "And here's the pantry. And there's a door here out to the vegetable garden. Feel free to pick and eat anything that looks ripe while I'm away."

"You garden?" She raised an eyebrow.

"I was raised on a farm. Growing is in my blood." He continued into a narrow hallway. "Here is the bathroom. There's a linen closet in there with supplies and towels. Feel free to help yourself. And here's what I call my study. Really, it's a guest bedroom, but I never have guests."

He opened the door, and she gasped. "This is more like a library than a study. So many books!"

He beamed with pride. "This wall is all engineering. I studied it for a time before the war. These two walls are almost all history. I like to read about the past. Keeps the mind sharp."

"I majored in European history at Smith."

"Did you now? Feel free to peruse at your leisure." *Don't grin too much, Hank. The lady's had a rough day.* "And over here is the bedroom. I assume that requires no explanation."

"It's a lovely house. Thank you for letting me stay." She stifled a yawn.

"You're tired. I should let you rest. I'll leave you alone for a minute to undress and lie down. Then I just need to get my things for the trip."

She smiled gratefully and closed the door. Trying to ignore the tantalizing rustling of fabric, he paced outside the door. A minute later, she called, "You can come in."

He opened the door, and there she was in his bed beneath the patchwork quilt his mother made. She looked so right there, so at home. Somehow his princess fit perfectly in his tiny home and his simple life. He didn't ever want her to leave.

"Seeing you there makes me want to call out sick and climb into bed with you." He'd get an earful about it if he did. The Postal Service wasn't any more understanding about health than they were about weather conditions when it came to excuses not to fly.

"I wish you could, but won't there be trouble if you do? And what if it somehow gets back to Papa and he realizes I'm here? No, you had better go, much as I wish I could curl up with you."

Sadly, she was right. Bending down, he kissed her cheek. "Sweet dreams, princess. I'll see you on Wednesday."

Gathering his clothes quickly, he took one last look at her and left the room. He packed his bag hurriedly and drove to the airfield in a rush. He was just in time to make his one o'clock take-off.

Soaring through the skies, his thoughts were filled with Rory.

What else was he going to think about? Everything in him said he should offer marriage, but he wanted to do what was best for her. Maybe she would find a way to make her father come around without her marrying the senator, but he would never accept Hank. Nonetheless, the thought of marrying her grew on him.

He didn't only feel morally obliged to offer, he realized. He wanted to marry her. Never had anyone felt so right. The thought of her in his house, sleeping in his bed, filled him with warmth and joy. He wanted her in his life to cook for and fuss over. And canoodle with. The thought of her leaving filled him with sadness, even though she'd only just arrived.

Rory wasn't a practical wife. With no experience cooking or keeping house, she was likely to increase his work rather than reduce it. And her tastes were expensive, given that she'd never in her life lived on a budget. He would never be able to offer her Belmont-style wealth, but he could give her a comfortable middle-class life where she'd want for nothing that mattered.

He should think about his career prospects. Glenn Curtiss once offered him double what he made as a pilot to work for his airship company. He'd turned it down because he wasn't ready to give up flying. But if he was going to marry Rory, he needed a job that wasn't trying to kill him. He could still rent a plane from time to time to scratch the itch. Maybe they could eventually buy one of their own if they saved. When he got back, he would reach out to Mr. Curtiss to see if he was still interested.

In the meantime, he needed to pay attention to the plane he was piloting. As his mind wandered, he had veered slightly off course. He needed to adjust quickly and avoid any further mistakes if he was going to make it to Philadelphia before he ran out of fuel. Focusing his attention, he made a beeline for his destination. His engine sputtered as he was landing, but he made it.

The flight to D.C. the next morning was full of turbulence and left him little time for reflection. It was a relief when the journey was over. When he landed in D.C., though, O'Donnell was waiting for him.

"Hawley, just the man I wanted to see. I'd like my ten dollars please."

Hank took off his flying cap and ran his hand through his hair. "What ten dollars?"

"I'll have you know I danced with Ann Prince twice and made her laugh five times. I think I have more than earned my money, thank you very much." He held out his hand expectantly.

Reluctantly, Hank pulled out his billfold and handed over the crisp bill.

"She's moving to Merrick in two weeks," O'Donnell said. "I offered to help her move. I said you and Pritchard would help too. You don't mind, do you? It wouldn't be right to make her pay for movers, a war widow like that."

Hank let out his breath slowly. He was always ready to lend a helping hand to a friend in need, but with everything happening with Rory, he was irritated by the assumption. "Thanks for volunteering me like that. It was really considerate of you."

"My pleasure." O'Donnell grinned. "You seem like you need to do some good deeds to make up for coveting another man's fiancé."

"They aren't engaged anymore." *And I've done more than covet, but no need to go into details.*

"Oh? Do tell." O'Donnell's eyes were wide and round, and his grin grew almost too wide for his face.

"She broke it off once and for all, and now her family is furious with her." *And she's staying in my house. What on earth am I doing here when she's there?*

"I take it this has something to do with you, you heart-breaking sonofabitch?"

Hank sighed and stared at the ground.

"Oh, Hank," O'Donnell said in a falsetto. "You're so dreamy. I've run away from my filthy rich family because I can't live without you. Marry me, Hank. Say you'll be mine forever and ever and ever…"

"Shut up, O'Donnell. Just because she left the last guy doesn't mean she wants to marry me."

O'Donnell gasped in delight. "No, but you want to marry her. I can see it in your eyes. Oh, this is too good to be true. Hawley caught in the parson's trap! Who'd've thunk it?"

Blood rushed to Hank's cheeks. He was blushing like a schoolgirl.

Lowering his voice to a mocking baritone, O'Donnell said, "Marry me, princess. Forget your family and your gobs and gobs of money. Come live in my tiny cottage with me and let me poke you 'til you're bowlegged."

In a flash, irritation turned to fury. "Enough, O'Donnell. Don't you dare talk about her like that!"

"All right, all right," O'Donnell said, backing up with his hands up. "I mean no disrespect to Princess Belmont. Only to you, Hawley."

With a slow exhale, Hank let it go.

"I take it this means you won't be going out with Pritchard and me this evening?" O'Donnell asked.

"No, I will not. If you'll excuse me, I have to make a call to my sister."

O'Donnell walked off whistling like the self-satisfied prick he was. He loved O'Donnell, but sometimes the man went too far.

And now he had a proposal to plan and a family to tell about it.

19

$\mathcal{R}$ory had three days to figure out a job and a place to live before Hank came back and did something foolish like proposing.

The last thing she wanted was for Hank to ask for her hand out of a sense of obligation, but he seemed to be hinting that he might. He seemed the noble sort who would feel he had to take care of her, having contributed toward her ruined reputation. But she chose to do the things that ruined her reputation, and the last thing she wanted was to jump from the infantilizing confines of her father's mansion to the arms of a man who thought he could fix things for her. She was Rory Belmont, and she was perfectly capable of taking care of herself.

She woke up from her nap in the late afternoon with her mind spinning with plans. Her first call was to Evelyn.

"Rory? Is that you? The operator said you're calling from Mineola. Why are you in Mineola?"

Rory heaved a sigh of relief. "Thank God, I reached you. Papa is likely trying to keep it all hush-hush, but I got caught with my pilot. He's cut me off without a cent, insisting that I come back and marry Edward if I don't want to be cut off for good."

"Good gracious! What can I do to help?"

Thank God for Evelyn!

"I need to figure out how to get a job. I was thinking of a secretarial or teaching position, nothing fancy, but enough to eat and get a room somewhere."

There was a moment of silence, then, "I have just the thing. You should take over as Executive Director of the Pilots' Benevolent Association. You did all the work anyway. I was always a figure-head so that your father wouldn't suspect. You could pay yourself a reasonable stipend. Lord knows there's enough money for it."

"How much did we make?" She was almost afraid to ask.

"One hundred and twenty-six thousand dollars."

"One hundred and twenty-six thousand… How are we ever going to spend that much money?" The total requests from the women she'd been in touch with amounted to eight thousand.

"Sounds like the organization needs a paid Executive Director to figure that out. Will you do it? I need someone to take over managing the staff."

"The staff?" When she last spoke to Evelyn, there was no staff.

"You now have an accountant and a secretary. I hired them this morning when I found out the final numbers. I couldn't manage this on my own."

Grinning from ear to ear, she said, "I'll do it. Can you send me a letter, or better yet a telegram, formally offering me the new position? Put down a salary of $1000 annually."

"You'd better make it $3000. We pay the accountant $2000, and you need to make more than him. And I should send you some money too. Will $100 do?"

"I promise I'll pay you back." It seemed exorbitant, but what did she know? This was certainly more than she would make as a teacher. She felt guilty about taking anything from the PBA and silently promised she would give back whatever she didn't need to cover her living expenses. Maybe with a bit of time, she could come up with a better plan, but at the moment, she had to agree this was her best option.

"Don't worry about it, dear. How else can I help?"

"That is more than enough. You are a life saver, my dear." Evelyn had her eternal gratitude for this.

"Where is your pilot, by the way?" Evelyn asked. "What does he have to say about all this? Surely, he has an opinion."

Rory sighed. "He had to fly to Washington D.C., but I think he's going to ask me to marry him when he gets back."

"As he should. What are you going to say?"

What was she going to say? She'd only just gained her independence. She wasn't sure she was ready to give it up so soon.

"I'm not sure."

"He's not marriage material?"

"No, it's not that. Papa wouldn't approve, but who cares what he thinks?" She paused for a long moment. "The thing is I'm free now. No one can tell me what to do. I think I might like some time on my own before I think about tying myself to someone for life."

"Understandable," Evelyn said. "It's wise to take your time now that you have the option to do so. I almost envy you. Not that I'm willing to give everything up like you have, but it must be nice to be captain of your own destiny."

It was terrifying and humbling, but Evelyn wasn't wrong.

"It is. And who needs all that money anyway?"

"Darling, you know I need my diamonds and champagne."

Rory laughed. "Of course."

"Well, I hope you're happy, whatever you decide. Where should I send that telegram?"

Providing the information, Rory said, "You are the best friend a girl could have, you know that?"

"Promise me you'll stay in touch, no matter what happens. Let's meet up once you settle in. I want to hear everything!"

"I promise I'll reach out as soon as I have my feet under me again."

They said their goodbyes and hung up.

Rory wiggled her hips and did a little dance. She was free and had a means of making a living. Now all she had to do was find a home. Mineola would make a fine home. Most of the women she wanted to help lived near airfields, not in the city. Yes, it would keep her near Hank, but that was beside the point. It was practical for her work. That was what mattered most.

And her work mattered. She was determined to use the PBA to help lift those in need. For the first time in her life, she had a sense of purpose, a mission to fulfill. She couldn't fix all of society's ills, but she could make a difference. Maybe she could start to chip away at the heavy debt she felt for a lifetime of oblivious privilege.

Her stomach growled, and she stifled a yawn. It was time to explore Hank's kitchen. He'd doubted her cooking abilities. She wasn't a master chef, but she knew enough to make a decent meal. Opening the icebox, she found milk, eggs, bacon, and some leftover roasted chicken. She took out the chicken and went to see what else she could find. In the pantry, she found potatoes. Out in the garden, she pulled up a couple of carrots. In a cupboard, she found a bottle of whiskey, and she poured herself a dram. She deserved it after what she'd been through today.

Sitting down to her dinner of chicken, mashed potatoes, and carrots a short while later, she was quite pleased with herself. And Hank thought his poor little rich girl couldn't cook. It wasn't the spectacular French cuisine her father's chef cooked, but it was good, hearty fare that filled her belly. It was all she needed to feel full and at peace.

As she sat back at Hank's table, drinking his whiskey and eating his food, she couldn't help but think about the delicious night they'd shared. The consequences were disastrous, but she couldn't bring herself to regret the night itself. Nothing had prepared her for the intensity, the electric heat of their encounter. She wasn't sure she wanted to marry Hank, but she couldn't let him go as a lover. She felt too much when she was with him, and she couldn't imagine anyone else ever making her feel the same.

Perhaps she'd refuse to marry altogether and be his "companion with no strings attached," leaving them both free to live their lives as they saw fit. Hank could fly without worrying about his responsibility to a wife at home. She could have her independence without being burdened by children or a household to care for. It was perfect.

She cleaned up her dinner, washed her face, and went to bed, breathing in his scent from the sheets. Such an intoxicating man. She closed her eyes and imagined him here in bed beside her, his body wrapped around hers. Relaxing in his warm embrace, she felt at home. This little cottage felt cozy and comfortable in a way the mansion where she was raised never had. Everything here was functional. Nothing was for show. But it was beautiful nonetheless, just like the man who lived here.

She drifted off surrounded by him, breathing him in, despite his absence. Never had she slept so soundly.

THE NEXT MORNING, she woke up refreshed and ready for the challenges ahead. A small part of her was still shaky from the shock of yesterday's loss, but her new surroundings and sense of purpose did much to mitigate her lingering distress. If anything, her losses filled her with added determination to succeed in building a life for herself without her father, a life where she did some good in the world. She had a job. She had the telegram in hand confirming it. Papa wanted to teach her a lesson and expected her to come crawling back. Well, she'd show him! Deep down, she knew he wouldn't let her go so easily, but that was a problem for another day. Today, she would set out to find a home, and tomorrow, she would get to work.

After making a simple breakfast of coffee, eggs, and toast, she sat down with pen and paper to draw up a budget. She'd taken a seminar called "Domestic Finances" in college to prepare herself for someday managing a household. Doing some simple math to break down her salary, she decided she could afford to spend up to eighty dollars a month on housing. Knowing very little about local housing costs, she hoped it would be enough, but she knew her salary was generous, so she thought it likely to be adequate.

After cleaning up her dishes, she set out into town to make inquiries. The greengrocer told her to speak to the druggist who told her to speak to the florist.

"Excuse me," she said, passing a profusion of carnations in every color to enter the shop. Inside, there were bundles of every possible flower that was currently in bloom.

A gray-haired man with a mustache like her father's stood behind the counter. He wore a deep plum vest over his pristine shirt. His jacket lay discarded over a chair. His smile was friendly as he said, "Good morning, Miss. Come to buy flowers? We have some beautiful peonies over here. They make a gorgeous center-piece for a dinner table." He spoke with a soft Irish lilt.

"Not today, thank you. I'm new in town, and I'm looking to rent a room. I was told you might know who I might speak to." She smiled her sweetest, most innocent smile.

"Well, Miss, you've come to the right place. It just so happens I have a room to let. There's also a ladies' boarding house two streets over, but I think Mrs. Allen overcharges for what she provides. My family and I live above the shop here, and there's a furnished apartment on the third floor that's vacant. If you don't mind a few stairs, it's bright, clean, cozy, and the hot water works consistently—something I hear can't be said for Mrs. Allen's. We can also offer board if you like."

This sounded perfect. A boarding house would come with all kinds of rules that would constrain her freedom. An apartment of her own where she could come and go as she pleased would be just the thing.

"That sounds perfect, Mr.—"

"Mr. O'Donnell."

"Thank you, Mr. O'Donnell. Might I ask what you are charging for rent? I want to make sure it falls within my budget."

Mr. O'Donnell smiled at her kindly. "We want the right tenant, someone quiet and decent but willing to put up with us. We're talkative folk. If you decide to take meals with us, you'll find that out soon enough. We'd like someone friendly who won't mind our boisterous ways. For the right tenant, we'd charge twenty-five a month. If you want to eat with us, make it thirty-five. Does that sound all right to you, Miss?"

"My name is Rory Belmont, and yes, that all sounds fine to me, ideal even. Might I see the space?"

The man bellowed, "Shannon, can you come tend to the store for a minute? I've some business to attend to."

Moments later, a round older woman with her silver hair in a bun came bustling in, wiping her hand with a dishcloth.

"Good heavens, Finn. You'll wake the dead bellowing like that. What's so important you have to interrupt my cleaning?"

"The young lady here wants to see our apartment to let."

Mrs. O'Donnell looked Rory up and down with a sharp eye. "Shannon O'Donnell, nice to meet you, Miss," she said, holding out a red, calloused hand. "She looks like quality, Finn. Perhaps you'd best let me handle this. You stay with the store, and I'll take her up."

"But Shannon—"

"But nothing. I'm taking her up, and that's final." She turned to Rory. "Come with me, lass, and I'll show you the place."

Stuffing the dish towel in her apron, she turned and walked through a door at the back of the shop. They passed a door and heard someone playing scales on the piano and flubbing it every few notes. "That's my granddaughter practicing piano in the parlor. We're so proud of her musical talent!"

At least the piano was two floors away from where she'd be staying.

They climbed a narrow, dimly lit staircase to a third-floor landing. Pushing open the door, Mrs. O'Donnell ushered her into the apartment and squinted in the bright sunlight. "These back windows face south, so it's very bright up here." They were in a long room that served as a sitting room, dining room, and kitchen.

There were two modest-sized bedrooms and a small bathroom. "Our children used to live up here. They're all grown up now, though, so we let it out. Our last tenant was a family with a two-year-old and a four-year-old, and it was like having puppies upstairs—constant noise of running feet. It drove us crazy, even if they were cute little things. We're hoping our next tenant will be quieter."

"I promise to be quiet as a mouse, Mrs. O'Donnell. This looks like an ideal place for me to stay. I'll sign up for room and board if you don't mind. It's so dull to cook for one." She looked around, feeling very pleased with her new home to be. "When could I move in?"

Mrs. O'Donnell gasped and clapped her hands together. "Oh, I'm so pleased! We'll just need a deposit of fifty dollars and a letter from your employer or your bank to prove you can pay, and you can move in as soon as you like."

"Excellent. I have proof of income and the money right here. I just got a new job, you see." She handed over the telegram and cash, and Mrs. O'Donnell nodded appreciatively.

"Well in that case, you can move in as soon as tomorrow, if you would like."

Rory smiled. "Excellent. I'm staying with a friend at the moment, and I don't want to impose longer than is necessary."

Walking back to Hank's house, she couldn't help but be pleased with how well everything was working out. By tomorrow, she would have fully embarked upon her new life as an independent woman with nothing to tie her down.

20

Hank could hardly wait to get home so that he could propose. He had it all planned out—a romantic dinner, a drive to the airfield, a proposal in front of the Jenny where he met her. Last year, his mother had given him his grandmother's engagement ring in case he ever met the right woman. He never thought he would use it, but now he was glad to have it.

He landed at Belmont Park and handed off the mail. As he was about to get in his Model T and go home to Rory, Major Fleet stopped him.

"Hawley, I need to speak with you a moment."

"Yes, sir. What is it, sir?" he said, saluting.

"I have Glenn Curtiss here, and we were just talking through design modifications to make a new aircraft custom-made for the mail. I was hoping you would share your thoughts. You always have more engineering insights than the rest of the team combined."

Glenn Curtiss. Exactly who he needed to talk to. He followed the major eagerly into the mess hall.

"Mr. Curtiss," the major said, "I believe you've met Hawley here."

"Indeed, I have," he said, standing up and shaking Hank's hand. "I tried to steal him out from under you, but he wouldn't hear of it. He wanted to keep flying."

"I think he's just the man to tell you all about what we need from this new plane," said Major Fleet. "I'll leave you two alone with these design specs." He bowed out and headed for the door.

Part of Hank wished he could follow. Rory was waiting for him at home. But he needed to speak with Curtiss, and he hadn't promised Rory he'd be home at a specific time.

They spent half an hour pouring over the technical details of the design when Curtiss said, "Are you sure you won't work for me? I could use a guy like you. It's not as exciting as flying, but it's a hell of a lot safer. Pays better too."

"Now that you mention it, I have been thinking about getting into a safer line of work." How could he walk past such an obvious opening?

"You don't say. Looking to settle down finally, Hawley?" he asked with a smirk.

"Yes, sir, Mr. Curtiss. I met someone. I don't want her to spend her whole life worrying about whether I'm going to survive my next assignment." For Rory, this was a sacrifice worth making.

Curtiss gave him an all-too-understanding smile. "Well, I'm sure you'll make the little lady happy. She has my thanks if it means I finally get you on my team. Come by my office tomorrow, and we'll work out the details."

"Yes, sir. I will do that. Now if you don't mind, I should be getting home. Someone's expecting me." And if he didn't see her soon, he was going to climb out of his skin.

"Don't let me keep you. I'll see you tomorrow."

Hank had to restrain himself from running to his car, and he drove a trifle faster than he ought on the way home. He rushed in the door and found...an empty house. Where could she have gone?

He looked all around the house and finally saw the note on the table in the breakfast nook.

"Hank,

Thank you so much for letting me stay at your house when I had nowhere else to turn. I am deeply grateful. While you were away, I managed to procure employment and a place to live. I rented the third-floor apartment above the flower shop on Main Street. I would love it if you would call on me when you return.

Yours truly,
Rory"

"Good God," he said aloud. "Rory moved in with the O'Donnells?" He could just see Bill O'Donnell's smug face now. He didn't live with his parents, but Hank was sure he'd be over at their house every night once he found out about Rory. "Christ."

Taking a deep breath, he regrouped. His plan didn't need to change very much. He could still go over, invite her out for an evening walk, and then propose. Retrieving his grandmother's ring from deep in his sock drawer, he shoved it in his pocket and set out for Main Street.

Arriving at the florist, he just caught Mr. O'Donnell as he was closing up. "Mr. O'Donnell, I—"

"I'm so sorry, Hank, but I have to close up. The missus says dinner is almost ready." He was rapidly putting away the day's flowers in an icebox.

"I'm not here for flowers, Mr. O'Donnell. I'm here to see Miss Belmont. I understand she just took the third-floor apartment?" Come to think of it, flowers weren't a bad idea. "Though I would love to buy those roses right there," he said pointing to a bunch that hadn't gone into the icebox yet.

"Lovely girl, Miss Belmont. Very decent sort. Well educated. Offered to teach our Adelaide French if you can believe it. She had her first lesson today and she can already say yes, no, and hello." He grabbed the bunch of roses Hank wanted to buy.

"Wait, Mr. O'Donnell, I'll give you five dollars for those roses."

Mr. O'Donnell paused, narrowing his eyes. "But they're only worth eighty cents."

"Yes, but I need them." Hank tried and failed to keep the desperation out of his voice.

"Oh, aye? A romantic emergency, is it?" Mr. O'Donnell asked with a wide smile.

"Something like that," Hank said, shoving his hands in his pockets and pulling out his billfold.

"Well, since you're such a good friend of our Bill, I'll give them to you this once. One dollar, please."

"You said eighty cents."

"And you said five. I think this is a fair compromise." Mr. O'Donnell wrapped the flowers in paper and tied a bow around them. "Here you are."

"Thank you."

"I take it these are for Miss Belmont?" Mr. O'Donnell asked, going back to closing up the store.

"They are."

Mr. O'Donnell nodded slowly. "I should warn you the missus has other designs. She's determined to make a match for our Bill. Myself, I don't think it's right to meddle in these things, but Shannon does as she pleases, God love her."

Getting impatient, Hank asked, "May I go up to see her now?"

Mr. O'Donnell smiled at his impatience. "If you like. She's with the missus on the second floor helping get dinner ready."

Oh no. Hank had hoped to get her alone, but it looked like he was going to have to pry her away from Mrs. O'Donnell, not an easy feat.

He climbed the stairs with some trepidation, wondering how he was going to get his plans back on track.

The door was open when he arrived on the second-floor

landing, but he gave a little knock anyway. Mrs. O'Donnell came bustling over, wiping her hands on her apron.

"Lieutenant Hawley, what a surprise! And what lovely flowers! Did Finn send those up for me? He's such a romantic, even after all these years."

Rory appeared behind her, watching the scene unfold with great amusement. His heart lurched in his chest. Good Lord, she was beautiful, and to his immense surprise, she looked perfectly content and at home in the O'Donnell's humble kitchen.

"Well, I—"

"I'll just take those and put them in water. Such a sweet and thoughtful man, my Finn." And before he could get a word in edgewise, she whisked them away and deposited them in a vase with some water in the middle of the dinner table.

"Did Bill invite you to join us for dinner, Hank? He might have given me some warning. But never mind that. You're welcome at our table, as always. We can squeeze in an extra seat down by Adelaide. Oh, and I should introduce you to our new tenant. Hank, this is Miss Aurora Belmont. Miss Belmont, this is my son's friend, Lieutenant Hank Hawley," she said, turning from one to the other. "Miss Belmont only moved in yesterday, and she's started teaching little Adelaide to speak French."

At that moment, Adelaide came zooming in, playing airplanes with her brother.

"Adelaide, show our guest how good you are at French," Mrs. O'Donnell called over the ruckus.

"Oooeeeeee," squealed Adelaide as she ran by.

"That means yes in French," Mrs. O'Donnell explained confidentially. "She's very good at French. Learned three words on her first day of studying. Ah, here's our Bill," she said rushing in to smother her son in a hug.

Bill saw Hank and raised an eyebrow. Then he saw Rory, and his eyes went wide, both eyebrows nearly reaching his hairline.

"Bill, meet our new tenant, Miss Aurora Belmont," Mrs.

O'Donnell said, turning to tend to a pot on the stove. Bill's jaw dropped as he looked at each of them in turn, eyes wide as saucers. "You should show her your medals from the war," Mrs. O'Donnell said over her shoulder to Bill. "Take her downstairs and show her," she ordered Bill. "Our Bill is very brave and did our country a great service," she told Rory. She shooed the two of them out the door and grabbed Hank's elbow.

Hank managed to give Bill a dirty look as he was on his way out. Bill shrugged helplessly.

"Hank, would you be a dear and help me put everything on the table?" She began handing Hank pots and trivets, which Hank dutifully laid out.

Mr. O'Donnell appeared in the doorway. "Oh, there you are, dear," Mrs. O'Donnell said. "Thank you so much for sending those roses up with Hank. They're just lovely."

Taking in the table centerpiece, the pot of mashed potatoes Hank was holding, and the absence of Bill and Rory, Mr. O'Donnell gave Hank a sympathetic look. "I take it you'll be joining us for dinner, Hank?" he asked, taking a pot of green beans from his wife and depositing it on the table.

"Yes, it seems I will. Your wife has kindly invited me to join." Mrs. O'Donnell shoved a plate and silverware in his hand after he set down the potatoes.

"If you wouldn't mind, set your own place," Mrs. O'Donnell said. "I know you don't stand on formality, Hank. Right down there next to Adelaide."

Helpless to refuse, he set his place at the foot of the table, next to the cup painted with flowers that marked Adelaide's spot.

"Dinner," bellowed Mrs. O'Donnell. Her voice was truly deafening at full volume.

Up the stairs came Bill and Rory, followed by Bill's sister, Mary, with little Connor and Adelaide in tow. Mrs. O'Donnell steered everyone to their assigned place. Mr. O'Donnell sat at the head of the table. To his left were Rory, Bill, Mary, and Connor.

To his right were Mrs. O'Donnell, Adelaide, and Hank, who was about as far as he could be from Rory.

When they were all seated and served and done saying grace, Mrs. O'Donnell said, "Miss Belmont, you must tell us all about yourself. We'd love to get to know you better."

Rory met Hank's eye for a moment, and they exchanged a panicked look. Then she cleared her throat and said, "I grew up in the city. My father works in banking. My mother died in childbirth when I was born, so I never met her. My father remarried when I was twelve and my stepmother raised me as best she could. I was a bit of a wild child and spent far too much time getting into trouble with my brothers, but my stepmother tamed me."

If Rory was tame, Hank was a monkey's uncle.

"I went to college and studied history," she continued, "and now I work in charity. I run the Pilots' Benevolent Association and manage its endowment."

"What's an endowment?" asked Adelaide.

"It's the money a charity uses to do its work," Rory explained with a smile. It was a good explanation for a child. No need to go into the details about reserved funds and interest and all that nonsense.

"Hear that, Bill?" Mrs. O'Donnell said. "She does work to help the families of pilots. A very impressive young lady, isn't she?"

Bill nodded, his mouth full of roasted chicken.

"When he's not flying, our Bill has an excellent head for business, don't you, dear?" Mrs. O'Donnell said.

Bill glanced at Hank and then at Rory, his eyes still wide as could be. "I helped my father rearrange his shop to bring in more business, and my mother thinks I'm a genius now," he said to Rory, flushing red. Rory smiled at him.

That smile was supposed to be for Hank. This dinner was supposed to be alone with Hank. Everything about this was going wrong.

Clearing his throat, Hank interrupted all those friendly gazes, saying, "Bill, can you pass the green beans?"

Mrs. O'Donnell deftly grabbed the green beans and passed them down without a glance in Hank's direction. Her full attention was on the couple sitting in front of her. Hank could practically see the hearts and cupids circling above their heads in her mind's eye.

How long was this dinner going to last, and how was he going to get Rory alone so that he could propose?

21

It was all too transparent what Mrs. O'Donnell was trying to do, and Rory felt she didn't have much choice but to play along. Bill seemed like a nice enough fellow, but she couldn't help but feel for poor Hank.

"Miss Belmont—" Hank began.

"And where were you staying before you came to us?" Mrs. O'Donnell asked at the same time, drowning Hank out.

"I…er…I was staying at a friend's house. She was very gracious and let me stay while she was away."

"Oh?" said Mrs. O'Donnell. "What's her name? Maybe we know her. We do know practically everyone in this town."

"Well…uh…she moved here recently, so you might not know her yet. Her name is…uh…Darla Hartley. She and I went to college together."

She chanced a glance at Hank, and his mouth twitched as he tried to suppress a smile.

Bill was looking back and forth between the two of them as if trying to discern what exactly they were up to. It seemed like Bill knew or suspected that there was something between her and

Hank…had she seen him somewhere before? He was too percep-tive by half.

"Lieutenant O'Donnell," Rory said to Bill, "how do you and Lieutenant Hawley know each other?"

Bill glanced at Hank before answering, "We met in the army. We were stationed in France together under Major Fleet, and now we both work for the postal service on their new Airmail operation. It's all very experimental. It only started in June."

She thought his face looked familiar. If he was with the airmail, then he was at the fundraiser, and that meant he knew exactly who she was. No wonder he looked so wide-eyed and amused.

"By any chance, did I meet you at the PBA fundraiser earlier this week?" she asked, keeping her voice light and nonchalant.

"Why yes," Bill said. "I don't believe we were introduced, but I was in attendance. A very impressive affair. You must be very pleased with how it all went."

Clearing her throat, she said, "Um, yes. Very pleased."

She wished she could find a quiet moment with him to beg him not to tell who she really was, but there was no opportunity to say anything without the whole table hearing. She would just have to pray he kept his mouth shut.

"And are you any relation of August Belmont's?" he asked, making her choke on a green bean. "I noticed he was in attendance."

She gave Hank a panicked glance. Bill, to her irritation, seemed to know exactly how much he'd ruffled her and seemed to be enjoying himself immensely.

"He's a…um…distant relative. Very supportive of his extended family."

"Did you hear that, Finn?" Mrs. O'Donnell said in a none-too-quiet whisper. "A woman related to August Belmont beneath our roof. Can you imagine?" She looked like a kettle about to whistle from all the excitement.

Rory swallowed hard, trying to think what to say next to distract attention. "Mr. O'Donnell," she said, turning to Bill. "You must be very brave flying the mail back and forth through all kinds of weather. Tell me everything about how it works. I find it fascinating."

Having very little choice, Bill launched into an extended description of the intricacies of airmail service, all the while watching her with a hint of a smile. He was torturing her on purpose. She was sure of it.

When he finished, she followed up with, "Now tell me about the airplanes. I understand the Jennies aren't made for this sort of thing. Is there any thought of replacing them?"

"I don't know the details, but I know the major has been speaking with Glenn Curtiss about a new design. Hank might know more than I do. He's the engineer among us."

Hank looked grateful for the opening to say something, anything in this farce of a dinner. "I spoke with Glenn Curtiss about the new design at length earlier today. The new planes will have purpose-built cargo holds so that we don't have to sit the mail in a cockpit, and they'll have stronger engines and greater fuel capacity. They'll make the daily runs significantly safer and more reliable once they're in service."

Mrs. O'Donnell gave Hank a disapproving look. "I'm sure we don't want to bore Miss Belmont with technical details." Never mind that she'd been nodding in rapt attention moments ago when her son was speaking about the mail service.

"Oh, no, Mrs. O'Donnell. He's not boring me. I love airplanes. That's part of how I ended up running the PBA, you know. I met a pilot who suggested that something should be done for war widows, so I started raising funds, and here we are." And he was sitting right over there.

Hank raised an eyebrow. For all her desire for independence, she was starting to wish she'd opted to stay at Hank's. They could be having an intimate dinner right now, or an intimate something else. Instead, she was stuck in this tightrope walk of a dinner conversation, barely able to speak to him.

Mrs. O'Donnell interrupted her moment of reverie with, "It looks like everyone is done. Would anyone like dessert? I have a lovely apple cherry pie." She began gathering dinner plates, and Rory followed her lead, gathering the plates from her side of the table. In the kitchen, Mrs. O'Donnell murmured confidentially, "I'm so pleased to see you getting on so well with Bill and taking such an interest in his work. He's a very good boy, and he'll make someone a very fine husband."

Rory had to work hard to suppress a laugh. She managed to nod and smile indulgently. Mrs. O'Donnell handed her a pile of small plates, which she took over to the table and began distributing. When she got to Hank, their fingers brushed for a moment, and she flushed with heat. Her eyes flitted to his, which were burning like coals. She jerked back as if burned, determined not to give herself away, having made it this far.

Mrs. O'Donnell doled out the pie. The children, who had kept up a steady stream of chatter throughout the meal with their mother, were suddenly silent. Mary piped up, "Thank you so much for giving Adelaide French lessons, Miss Belmont. Now you'll be a proper young lady, won't you, Adelaide?"

"Oooooeee," exclaimed Adelaide.

"Can you say thank you to Miss Belmont?"

Adelaide gave her mother a resentful look and put down her fork. "Thank you, Miss Belmont, for teaching me French." Then she dove back into her pie. Connor appeared to be wearing more of his pie than he'd eaten. Hank whispered something to him that made him giggle. It warmed her heart to see him be so sweet with the boy.

"What do you think of the pie, Miss Belmont?" Mr. O'Donnell asked. "Shannon won the trophy at the county fair last fall for this pie. We were all very proud of her."

Mrs. O'Donnell grinned and blushed at the compliment.

"It's delicious, Mrs. O'Donnell," Rory said. "You'll have to show me how to make it." She didn't miss Hank giving her another eyebrow from the other end of the table.

As they wrapped up dessert, Bill said, "I really should get going. I have a flight first thing tomorrow."

"Wait," his mother said, halting him in his tracks. "Miss Belmont hasn't seen how pretty the town hall looks in the moonlight. You should take her for a walk."

Bill and Rory stared at each other helplessly.

"You'd like a little walk in the moonlight, wouldn't you dear?" she said to Rory.

"I—," Rory began and stopped. Mrs. O'Donnell watched her expectantly. "I suppose a walk would be quite nice." At least it would be a chance to get out of the house, and perhaps she could manage a few words with Hank.

Bill glanced at Hank with a furrowed brow. Hank was looking daggers at him. With the face of someone on his way to the gallows, Bill offered his arm and led Rory out the door and down the stairs.

They stepped into the street and Bill turned to her. "I'm sorry about my mother. She's a bit much."

Hank burst through the door and charged toward them a moment later. "I'll be taking over from here, O'Donnell."

"Yes, but you'd better let me take her back in when you're done, or my mother will make all kinds of assumptions. You wouldn't want her thinking you're stealing my future bride," O'Donnell said, smirking.

"Give me twenty minutes," Hank said with an exasperated sigh. "I'll meet you back here at the fountain."

He took Rory by the hand and led her away into the dark. They stopped in the alley beside the closed greengrocer, and he pressed her up against the wall and kissed her so furiously her whole body went up in flame. He kissed down her neck and worshipped her chest before returning to her lips and plundering them thoroughly.

"Oh God, Rory. I want you so much. I spent the last three days thinking about nothing but you."

"I want you too, Hank." She couldn't pretend she was any less affected. "But we can't. Not here. Not now."

"I know." He took a step back. "I thought you would be there when I got home. It never occurred to me you would move out before I got back."

"I know, but I had to get my life sorted. I couldn't stay with you. You know that."

"You could if you were my wife. Rory, I didn't intend to propose in an alley. I had a whole plan that fell apart completely. I'll do it properly, I promise, but I need to know."

Oh no. He's kneeling. He's pulling something from his pocket.

"Rory Belmont, will you marry me?" A diamond sparkled in the moonlight.

Every terrible thing the gossip rags had written about her began running through her head, along with Edward's insults, and her father's put-downs. She didn't deserve him, and she couldn't bring herself to accept. But how could she explain in a way that he would understand?

She took a deep, shuddering breath, grasping for a way to answer that wouldn't break his heart.

"Hank, it's so sweet of you to ask. I know you're only doing it out of a sense of obligation. I'm sorry you went to the trouble of buying a ring. But I'm not ready to get married. I only gained my independence a few days ago. I need some time to settle into my new life before I consider anything as drastic as marriage."

He stood slowly, leaning his hand against the wall and pinching the bridge of his nose. Every muscle in his body was rigid. "I'm not offering out of obligation, Rory. I'm in love with you. I want to spend my life with you. I'm lost without you."

He slowly brought his eyes up to meet hers. "I love you, Rory. Please, I'm begging you, say yes."

She cupped his cheek and stroked it with her thumb. "I have feelings for you too, Hank. Maybe it's even love, but I don't know yet. Everything in my life just turned upside down. I feel like I barely know myself. I'm not ready, not yet."

He took a deep, shuddering breath. "But you might be at some point?"

"I don't know. Maybe. Right now, everything is so new. I need time. I care for you, Hank. Honestly, I do."

"Is this because of your family? I know they'll never accept me." His eyes were closed as if bracing himself for a blow.

"It has nothing to do with my family. It's me. I need time to be me without all the pressures and expectations of being who I was. I'm not ready to give up my freedom yet. I only just got it."

"I'm not asking you to give up your freedom. I just want you to let me love you. Please."

A tear dripped down her cheek as she looked at him. She didn't want to hurt him.

"I'll let you know when I'm ready. I promise. If I ever marry anyone, it will be you."

He kissed her again with a little moan. It was the kiss of something ending and something else beginning. She clung to him, wishing she could soothe away his pain.

"I should go," he said, pulling away. "Goodnight, Rory. I love you."

"Goodnight, Hank."

He turned and walked away.

22

Hank woke up with a blistering headache, fully clothed, the ring in his hand. Yes, he had some whiskey last night, but this feeling had nothing to do with what he'd drunk. Rory turned him down. Even after everything that happened to her, she preferred life alone to a life with him.

He'd flubbed the proposal. That much was clear. How could he propose next to a grocery store and expect her to say yes? And after that ridiculous dinner? It was no wonder she refused. He had to do better. He'd gotten impatient, and look where it had gotten him. But if he'd done everything right, if he'd executed his plan perfectly, would her answer have been any different?

He needed to convince her that marriage to him wouldn't mean the end of her freedom, but how could he do that?

There was a knock on the door. Running his hand through his hair and dusting off his wrinkled clothes, he got up and trudged to the door. Opening it and wincing at the sunlight, he saw O'Donnell. Hank forgot he promised him a ride to the airfield today.

"Look what the cat dragged in," O'Donnell said, taking in Hank's appearance. "You look about as happy as she did last night when I walked her home. She explained that her father cut her off, but she wouldn't say why. And she refused to explain what upset her so much when she was talking with you. What happened?"

Hank waved his friend in, started the stove, and put the percolator on for coffee. "It's my fault. We got caught together, and her father cut her off. Then last night, I proposed, and she turned me down. Said she just got her freedom and wasn't ready to give it up yet."

"You *proposed?* Where?"

Hank winced. "In the alley next to the greengrocer."

"Well, there's your problem right there."

Taking a deep breath, Hank said, "Thank you so much for reminding me how badly I fucked it up."

"Yes, you did, but you can fix it. Do it properly. Woo her. I've seen the way you two look at each other. She feels the same way you do. I'm sure of it," O'Donnell said, sitting down in Hank's breakfast nook. "It's only a matter of time before she says yes, you musclebound oaf."

The percolator finally boiled, and Hank poured himself a cup of scalding coffee. "You're a good friend, you know that?" he said, burning his tongue.

"I'm sorry. What was that? I'm not sure I heard correctly." He put his hand to his ear and waited.

Shaking his head, Hank laughed. "I said you're a good friend. Don't make me say it again." He took another sip of coffee, blowing on it this time. "Let me take you to the airfield, or you'll be late."

"Thank you for the ride. My car is in the shop for another week, they say. How is it you and I can build a Jenny from parts in six hours, and it takes Baker's Garage one whole week to fix a measly radiator?"

"I do not know."

They climbed into his Model T and headed for the airfield.

WHEN HANK GOT BACK from dropping off O'Donnell, he ate a proper breakfast, bathed, put on his best suit, and headed out to the offices of Glenn Curtiss.

The Curtiss offices were a hive of activity. The army needed airplanes faster than the manufacturers could make them. Automobile plants were being taken offline and repurposed to produce planes for the war effort. No one was more in demand in the industry than Glenn Curtiss, the mastermind behind the Curtiss Jenny, the most widely used plane in the war effort. It wasn't the most powerful plane, but it was quick and easy to build and maintain, giving it an advantage over more sophisticated models.

When Hank told Mr. Curtiss' secretary he was there to see him, he expected a long wait. But no sooner did he sit down than Mr. Curtiss came out of the office with Major Belmont in tow.

"Hank, boy am I happy to see you! This is Major Belmont." Hank stood and saluted, petrified of what might come next. "Major Belmont, this is Hank Hawley, a talented pilot, and a brilliant engineer of aeronautics. He's advising on the new planes for the Post Office, and I think I may have convinced him to join my team."

"Pleased to meet you, Hank," said Major Belmont without a hint of recognition, even though they had met before.

"Pleased to meet you too, sir," Hank said, shaking his hand, his body flooding with relief. The major didn't know.

"Join us, Hank," said Mr. Curtiss.

"We need more Jennies," said Major Belmont.

"How many?" asked Mr. Curtiss.

"Four hundred."

"Four hundred?" asked Mr. Curtiss, scratching his head. "That'll take six months minimum."

"We can't wait that long."

"Then make the Jennies you have better," Hank interjected, and both men turned to stare at him. "It's much cheaper to upgrade the Jennies you have so that they last longer than to buy more. Put better engines and bigger fuel tanks in the ones you have, and I guarantee you'll reduce the number of new ones you need so that production can catch up with demand. It's simple math."

Mr. Curtiss turned to the major. "See, August? That's the kind of thinking we need around here to keep up with the war effort." He clapped Hank on the back, and Hank grinned. He was going to like this job, even if he wasn't flying.

"Hank, assuming Major Fleet signs off, I want you to lead this project overseeing the upgrades and managing the production of the new planes. You can own it from start to finish. That's how much I trust you." Mr. Curtiss gestured expansively, painting a picture.

That was a lot to take on, but as Hank started to mull it over, he immediately had thoughts on how it could be done. He needed to start with the supply chain for parts, and then...

"See, August? Hasn't even started yet, and he's on the job already."

"Have you resigned your commission yet, young man?" the major asked.

"Not yet. I came today to get the details of the job offer. Once we have that ironed out, I'll be giving notice."

"See that you do posthaste, Hank. The war effort needs you here far more than flying mail." Major Belmont wanted him to quit? That was unexpected. He thought he would get resistance, arguments that the army needed every pilot it could get. He also expected a drawn-out process, but perhaps he could get it expedited. This was going to be easier than anticipated.

"I will, sir," Hank said, hardly able to believe his luck.

"If you'll excuse us a moment, Hank," Mr. Curtiss said, "I need to speak with the major privately. I'll be right back to speak with you."

Hank sat on the sleek sofa outside Glenn Curtiss' office. It looked as modern as the airplanes the company produced. They were ushering in a new era of widespread flying, and he, Hank Hawley, was going to be sitting in the cockpit.

Five minutes later, Major Belmont walked out the office door. Hank leapt to attention, and the major offered a perfunctory nod and left without a word.

Mr. Curtiss beckoned him into his office. "Now, Hank. I want you, and you heard the major. Your country needs you. What will it take for me to get you on board?"

He'd recently gotten a raise to three thousand a year. "Four thousand?"

Mr. Curtiss shook his head. "You have to do better than that, Hank. I don't want the competition stealing you because I'm underpaying you. How does six thousand sound to you?"

Hank nearly fell out of his seat. For six thousand dollars, he could buy a house a year. With six thousand dollars, he could buy his own Jenny in a year or two and take Rory flying all around the country.

"Six thousand sounds grand. But you know I haven't finished my engineering degree yet."

"Doesn't matter. You have deep, practical experience with these machines. Couple that with your engineering mindset, and you are one in a million. Plus, you're a smart business thinker. What you said to the major back there was spot on. I was about to suggest the same myself. If you want to finish your degree, I'll pay for it."

"Thank you, sir. You're too generous." This was truly above and beyond what he ever could have expected.

"No, I'm practical. Plenty of my competitors would love to get their hands on someone like you. It's in my interest to keep you happy. Now, when can you start?"

That depended. "I'll put in the paperwork to resign my commission today. It usually takes ninety days to process, and it could take more. But perhaps you could reach out to your army connections to expedite this?"

"Say no more. Consider it done. This work is essential to the war effort. I'm certain I can convince the brass to move quickly on this." Mr. Curtiss got up and called to his secretary.

"Mabel, I need you to type up an offer letter. Address it to Hank Hawley. H-A-W-L-E-Y, is that right?" Hank nodded. "Offer him six thousand and tuition reimbursement for his Bachelor of Engineering. Give him the job title 'Senior Director.' Have you got that?"

Mabel repeated it all back. "Did I miss anything?"

"No, you've got it. Now go type up two copies, one for Hank here and one for our files."

"Yes, sir." She began typing away.

Hank walked out of the office ten minutes later with that letter burning a hole in his pocket. This was his big break, his ticket to success. He might not be a Belmont, but he would be more than comfortable. Rory would lack for nothing as his wife. He would see to that.

At home, he wrote out his letter of resignation, and he drove out to the airfield to deliver it to Major Fleet. He found the major in his makeshift office just off the hangar.

"Major, might I have a moment?"

"What is it, Hawley? Come in. Sit down."

He came in and seated himself in one of the rickety folding chairs in front of the folding table that served as the major's desk.

"I'm here to tender my resignation."

The major smiled. "You've decided to go work for Curtiss. Major Belmont was here earlier and warned me this would be coming. I can't say I'm happy to lose you, but I wouldn't want to hold back someone as talented as yourself. And I know you can do more for the war there than here. I expect you'll be out of here in record time."

"Thank you, sir. It's been a pleasure working for you."

The major reached across his desk and shook his hand. "It's been a pleasure having you on the team."

Leaning back, he said, "While you're here, I have some news of my own. I'm being reassigned. A man named Charles Willoughby will be taking my place. You and he may not overlap, but I wanted to let you know. There's also talk of transitioning this operation from Army to civilian Postal Service oversight. It will be interesting to see where that goes. Changes are afoot, Hawley, and you've chosen a good time to move on. I'm sure Major Willoughby will do a fine job, but I expect the coming months to be bumpy ones, given the broader politics."

"I'm sorry to see you go, sir. No one but you could have launched airmail service so quickly and kept it going these last few months through all the accidents and emergency landings. It's a big loss, and the men are going to miss you."

Hank had heard about Willoughby and didn't have high hopes. He was supposed to be arrogant and pretentious.

"I'll let you go back to your business, sir. I only stopped by to drop off my letter." Hank stood, and the major shook his hand one more time. Then he left.

On the drive home, he couldn't help thinking about how Rory had turned his life upside down but in the best possible way. Without her, he never would have considered the opportunity with Curtiss, an opportunity that was going to make his career. He couldn't wait to see her again and tell her the good news.

23

At last, Rory was going to have some time alone with Hank. Bill had cleared things up with Mrs. O'Donnell, explaining that Rory was Hank's girl. Mrs. O'Donnell didn't like it, but she brightened considerably when Bill said he'd met someone and promised to bring her around as soon as he was able. It made life at the O'Donnell's significantly easier, but she still missed Hank, who she'd barely seen since she turned down his proposal.

She didn't know what to expect today. Hank said it was a surprise but asked her to wear pants or divided skirts. She hoped this meant they were going up in an airplane. She wore a one-piece, long-sleeved, navy jumpsuit with a single-breasted jacket collar and buttons down the front. The loose legs gathered just above the ankle, and she wore matching low pointed heels. Her hair was tucked beneath a straw cloche hat with a band of navy ribbon.

Hank arrived right on time at noon in his Model T, and he kissed her hand as he helped her in. Warmth suffused her body. For all her complicated emotions about his proposal, she still desired him as much as ever. He seemed to have forgiven her for turning him down. At any rate, he was as attentive as always. His face showed no hint of sadness or disappointment, just a mischievous smile and a dark smolder in his eyes.

He looked quite dashing in his form-fitting shirt with his pants tucked into knee-high boots. He wore a tie, but his jacket lay discarded in the back seat over a picnic basket.

She held onto her hat as he sped as fast as he could go, the windshield barely breaking the wind as they pushed forty miles per hour. Soon they were at the local Mineola airfield, as she had hoped, and he helped her out of the car. She was relieved they weren't headed to the Belmont Park airstrip. There was too much chance of running into her father. Not that Mineola was entirely safe. Papa sometimes came out to Mineola too on Army business.

Hank took the picnic basket out of the back.

"We're going to go for a little flight, if that's all right with you, princess."

She smiled widely as she followed him to the hangar. "Always," she said, taking his arm.

"I rented a Jenny for the afternoon. I checked her over this morning, and we shouldn't have any unfortunate incidents like the last time I took you flying."

She kissed his cheek. "I had a delightful time last time, despite the engine troubles."

"Well today, I'm hoping to give you some thrills without putting you in mortal danger."

"Smashing," she said.

Hank handed her a cap and goggles, and she took off her hat to put them on. Then he helped her into the front cockpit before climbing into the rear. Soon he had the engine roaring and the propeller turning, and they were taking off. The sound made her shiver in anticipation of what was to come. Her whole body vibrated with the plane, making it impossible to ignore the deep longing she felt every time she looked at Hank.

As they climbed into the air, the familiar thrill of risk trickled through her veins. It felt different this time, though. It wasn't an escape anymore. It was a vindication. She no longer wanted to flee her life. She wanted to revel in it. They soared up above Mineola, her new home, and she looked down fondly on the town. She could see the O'Donnell's and Hank's house. It was becoming a familiar geography, and she loved it.

Throwing her arms out, she basked in the sun, loving the way its heat caressed her skin as a cooling breeze blew by. The engine growled beneath her, thrusting them forward through the open skies, and she could sense Hank's gaze on the back of her head.

He brought them down skillfully in a grass field next to a stretch of beach, and the plane shuddered to a halt. There was no one in sight in any direction: no roads, no houses, just them.

The landing was smooth, and as soon as they stopped, she turned around. Giving in to impulse, she slipped off her shoes, climbed on her seat backward, facing Hank, and leaned out over the fuselage, kissing distance from Hank's face. He took full advantage, standing and kissing her slowly, savoring her lips and tongue as if she were a ripe fruit. Hooking his hands under her arms, he pulled her to him until she was perched on the fuselage, her legs on either side of him.

"Do you know how many times I've imagined you sitting like this in front of me as I flew?" he asked. "You're a very distracting co-pilot, even when you aren't there."

She loved how much he wanted her and was delighted that he fantasized about her when he flew. Whether she was ready for matrimony or not, it was clear she would never meet another man that made her feel so much.

His hands traced her curves, coming to rest on her buttocks, and she wrapped her legs around him, needing his hard muscle between her thighs. Other things too. His arousal pressed right where she wanted him, and he groaned as she moved against him. The friction was such a delicious tease.

"You said you wanted to canoodle in a Jenny," he said, kissing her again, deeper and longer.

"Yes, I did," she said, pulling off his tie and unbuttoning his shirt and union suit so that she could touch his delicious chest. Oh, how she loved the feel of him, the taste and smell of him, everything about him. Her fingers trailed over the newly bare skin, exploring. "Mercy, you are a handsome man."

Still too much clothing separated them. He unbuttoned her jumpsuit and pulled it partway down, leaving her in her chemise and corset. Then he pulled it the rest of the way off, and she slid down with him into the cockpit where she straddled him in his seat. His lips traveled to her chest as he gloried in the taste of her skin, loosening her corset and freeing her breasts. "God, I've missed you," he said, taking one nipple in his mouth and tickling it with his tongue.

She moaned as he teased and tormented her breast, abrading her nipple lightly with his teeth. The intensity made her moan. Here she was in the cockpit of a Jenny just like she'd dreamed, and he was devouring her, consuming her, making her tremble. "Oh, Hank."

"Yes, that's it, princess. Say my name. Let me hear it on your lips."

The curling warmth of his voice reached her deepest depths, resonating, vibrating, making her want to do sinful things. "Yes, Hank, please. I need more."

His fingers found the part in her bloomers and began to tantalize her as he continued to make her fantasy come true. This man knew her too well. He handled her with all the tender subtlety he used to fly his plane, and she was melting as his fingers worked their magic.

"Say 'Hank, I want you to touch me,'" he murmured.

"Hank, I want you to touch me." She would do anything at all for him at that moment as long as he didn't stop what he was doing. He was driving her mad.

"Say 'Hank, I want your fingers inside me.'"

"Hank, I want your fingers ins—" In they went, and speech gave way to an extended wail. She came hard against his hand, the control stick of the Jenny grazing her back as she trembled in his lap.

"Now, tell me what you want. I want to hear you say the words," he murmured in her ear.

"Please, I need you inside me. Please, Hank." The hunger inside her could not be contained.

"Yes," he growled as she unbuttoned his trousers and union suit, and he sprang free. "Yes, Rory."

She slid down onto him.

"Fuck," he growled.

The sensation made her eyes roll back in her head. She rode him hard, swiveling her hips and meeting his upward thrusts. God, she wanted this. She wanted him. More, screamed everything inside her. Take all of him. Take everything. Fly through the air with him and never come down.

Her fingernails dug into his back as tremor after tremor took her. "Yes, come for me, princess, right here in the cockpit in the open air where anyone might see if they only knew to look. Show the world you're mine."

"Oh, Hank. Oh, Hank…" A spasm took her, squeezing, pulsing as he continued to thrust into her. The edges of her vision grew dark, and bliss overtook her. He was losing control, and she welcomed it. He thrust hard, and she felt the hot pulsation as he spent inside of her. Fortunately, she was wearing protection because what was happening right now between them was everything.

They collapsed against each other, panting. "I'm sorry I lost control," Hank whispered in her ear. "I shouldn't have come inside you."

"I wanted you to lose control. I know there are risks, but I took precautions. It was worth it. You're worth it."

He looked at her with searching eyes. "Does that mean you've changed your mind?"

Oh dear. He means... For a moment, panic gripped her. Marriage was a trap, even with him, and she wasn't ready to surrender her newfound freedom.

"Let's go have our picnic," she said brightly, hoping to distract him. Standing up, she started to reassemble her clothing as she watched Hank button up. Such a shame to put away all that decadent muscle, but she needed his attention diverted.

As soon as she was dressed, she slid down the side of the plane to the ground. He handed her the picnic basket and jumped down himself, then took it back from her.

Spreading out a blanket on the sand, he unpacked champagne, strawberries, Italian sandwiches cut into bite-sized pieces, and two delicious-looking chocolate cupcakes. All of it looked tasty and tempting.

He poured the champagne into two sturdy, metal and enamel cups. "I hope you don't mind. I thought glasses would be impractical out here."

"Not at all," she said, raising her glass and catching his eye.

He clinked his cup against hers, holding her gaze, and took a sip. She did the same, her eyes dipping to his lips as she drank.

Hank served her a plate of sandwiches and strawberries and handed it to her. "I'm sorry about last week," he began. "I should never have proposed when and where I did. You deserve better."

She listened but said nothing. If he thought her only objection was the circumstances of the proposal, he didn't understand her at all.

"I know this has been a difficult time for you, and your life has turned upside down. I understand why you want time."

That's a relief.

"For my part, I meant what I said. I can't take it back because it's true. But I'm happy to wait for you, Rory. I'll wait as long as it takes. And I won't stop trying until I get a yes."

Her stomach clenched. He was still going to press. Why didn't he understand? He'd had arrangements with women in the past. Why did this need to be different?

"You once told me you preferred no strings attached. Why can't we enjoy each other's company without making commitments?"

"That was before I met you. In case I haven't made it clear, I want you in my life. I want to commit to you. You are the woman I want to wake up with every day for the rest of my life. I know this would mean sacrifice on your part. I'll never be able to give you Belmont wealth, but I can give you a comfortable life, even a few luxuries."

"Hank, that's not—"

"Wait," he said. "Hear me out. I'm quitting the postal service. I resigned my commission earlier this week. Glenn Curtiss offered me a job overseeing a portion of his manufacturing operation. I'm going to make Jennies, Rory. And new aircraft too. I'm going to be at the forefront of aeronautical design. He's offered me six thousand a year, which is enough to live like a king in Mineola. I can give you a good life. I swear I can."

Oh, her poor pilot. So determined to solve all the wrong problems. "I never doubted that we would have a good life together. I hope you aren't giving up flying for my sake. I could never forgive myself if I took you away from what you love."

Hank shook his head. "It's time. I need a job that isn't trying to kill me. And I'm excited about getting to work on these machines I know so well, thinking about how to make them better, faster, more powerful."

"I'm glad," she said, "because nothing *you* do is going to change my mind. My hesitation has nothing to do with you. I care for you, but I need time to learn who I am aside from August Belmont's wayward daughter. I need the freedom to live my life in the way I choose. I can't tie myself down right now. I need to prove to myself I can stand on my own two feet."

"What if there are consequences from today? Even with precautions, there's a chance," he asked quietly.

"If there are, we'll discuss what to do, but for now, I need my freedom."

He nodded slowly, not meeting her eyes. "I'll wait. When you're ready, I'll be here."

She caressed his cheek and kissed him, but he pulled back, resting his forehead against hers. "It hurts, you know. It hurts to be with you and know you aren't mine."

She kissed his forehead. "I'm not anyone else's either. For the first time, I don't belong to someone, and I love it. But Hank, there isn't someone else that's going to take me away from you. We can continue as we have been. Nothing needs to change. Don't you understand?"

"No, I don't, but I'll accept it. For now." He took a bit of sandwich and washed it down with champagne. She did the same. It was an exceptionally good sandwich with prosciutto ham, fresh mozzarella, and perfectly ripe tomatoes.

They ate in companionable silence and watched the waves. She could only hope he understood enough to let her be free.

24

Hank didn't understand why she couldn't say yes, but he was determined to find a way to convince her. Making love to her in the Jenny didn't help matters. It only made him yearn for her more. He needed her in his home, in his bed, in his arms every night forever.

But he didn't want to press too hard and ruin their afternoon. "Much as I hate to say it, we need to get back. I have to return the airplane."

She was breathtaking with the sea breeze in her hair and a mischievous smile on her lips. He wanted to stay here forever, but time would not allow it.

"It's been a truly wonderful afternoon, Hank. I know you must have gone to a great deal of trouble and expense, and I'm deeply flattered."

He had, but he wasn't about to admit it. "It was nothing, princess."

She kissed him with those soft, red, kiss-stung lips. Why did she have to go and do that? It only served to remind him of what he couldn't have.

213

He helped her into her cockpit, reminded her how to open the throttle, and gave the propeller a swing. Climbing into the rear cockpit, vivid memories assailed him of their earlier activities. He pushed them aside to focus on taking off safely.

On the brief trip back, he racked his brain for what to try next in his campaign to win her hand. There had to be some way to convince her. How could he assure her he had no intention of impeding her independence? He didn't want to own her or control her. He only wanted to be free to love her with his whole heart.

Too soon, the airfield at Mineola came into view, and he landed the plane, taxiing back to the hangar.

Instead of driving her home, Hank took her to a park where they could sit together on a bench. He wanted to understand her refusal, even if he couldn't change her mind. "I know I need to be patient, and I'll do my very best. But can you tell me why? Is it because you're afraid of what your father would do? If I was your husband, I could protect you. He'd have no legal right to interfere in your life. I would be your next of kin. As it is, he has too much power over you."

She shook her head and stayed silent for a long moment.

"Rory?"

She lifted her head slowly to meet his gaze. "I'm barely considered a person under the law. It's why I fight for women's suffrage. I don't even have the right to open a bank account in my own name. But if I married you, my legal rights would dwindle even further. A husband and wife are considered one person, legally, with the husband exercising all rights on the wife's behalf. You may say you offer me freedom, but I know the reality of what marriage means."

"And yet you were willing to marry Edward Windham." As soon as he said it, he regretted it and wished he could take it back. The pain in her gaze made him want to crumple up into a ball and be swallowed by a hole in the ground.

Her voice shook as she said, "I thought I had no choice. I know better now, but I genuinely couldn't see an alternative at the time." She put a gentle hand on his cheek. "Hank, I don't want to marry anyone, not even you. Eventually you'd get tired of me and my foolishness, and then where would I be? It's better if we enjoy the connection we have while we can and then go our separate ways before things turn sour."

Hank straightened, hardly able to believe what he was hearing. "You think I'm going to get tired of you? That's why you won't marry me?"

Rory's hand dropped to her lap, and she stared down at it. "My father says I'm the most tiresome female he's ever met," she mumbled.

"Your father is a pompous ass."

A ghost of a smile turned her lips upward. "True. But he isn't wrong. I've been nothing but trouble my whole life. I'm restless and careless. I take too many risks. I'm tiresome, and I know it. You might find my antics endearing now, but eventually they would begin to grate on you as they did on him. And I don't think I could bear to look in your eyes and see resentment."

"You think I would resent you?" Arguments tumbled over each other in his mind, and all he could do was sputter.

"I know you would. Papa does. He's resented my existence from my earliest days. He had no idea how to raise a little girl after losing my mother, so he left me in the care of a series of nannies who I drove away in quick succession with my wild behavior. I've had a lifetime of practice being difficult and unruly. I'd make a terrible wife, and I couldn't bear it if I hurt you."

Taking both her hands in his, he knelt on the ground in front of her. "Rory Belmont, I love you with my whole heart, and nothing is ever going to change that. Your father is a bitter old man who doesn't know what a treasure he has in his daughter. You are so strong and so brave. I love your fierce independence. I love your creativity and drive. I love your mischief. I loved it from the day we first met. Do you think I want a nice, dutiful wife? Do you think I could ever be happy with a conventional marriage after being with you?"

"Hank, I—"

"Yes?"

"Are you sure? I'm a terrible trial. Everyone says so."

"I don't know how I could ever deserve you, but I absolutely cannot live without you. No one else will do, Rory. It has to be you."

"Oh, Hank," she said, tears forming in her eyes. "I can't tell you how much that means to me."

"So you'll marry me?" He held his breath, desperate for her answer.

"I'll consider it. Give me a few days to think it through. I don't want to rush into this."

Progress at last! His heart soared.

"Of course," he said. "I have another run to D.C. tomorrow, and I'll be away for the next three days. But take all the time you need. I love you too much to rush you into anything."

"Oh, Hank, you are the sweetest, most considerate man a woman could ever hope for." She kissed him on the cheek, not daring more in public in broad daylight. Even that chaste peck could be considered scandalous if the wrong person saw it.

"Let me walk you home."

They were silent as they strolled back to the O'Donnell's, her hand on his arm. He'd never been so hopeful and content in his life. She was nearly his. He'd found the magic key to her affection at last.

As they walked down the street, his eye caught on Portman and Sons Law Offices, and an idea struck him. Rory wasn't just worried about him getting tired of her. She was worried about her freedom. What if he allayed that worry too?

"Rory, would you mind if we made one more stop before home?"

Her tentative smile encouraged him. "What do you have in mind?"

"I have an idea about how I can prove that you can marry me and still be your own woman."

Her eyes narrowed, and her smile tightened. "Hank—"

"Please. Just hear me out. With Mr. Portman's help, I think I can put your mind at ease."

She tensed as she cast a dubious glance at the law firm's storefront. "A lawyer? I can't imagine what you have in mind."

Pausing, he took both of her hands and met her gaze. "Men have been making decisions without you your whole life. I don't want to be like them. I want you by my side while we talk about our potential future and lay out the ground rules. I want you to know beyond a shadow of a doubt that all I want from you is your love and companionship. I don't want a cent of your money or an ounce of your freedom, now or ever. I'll commit to it in writing, and you can take all the time you need to decide."

Her lips parted, but no words came out. Was this the right thing to do? He sure as hell hoped so. It was a gamble, but he was willing to try anything at this point.

"Do you trust me?"

With a deep breath, she met his gaze. "Yes."

"Then let's go inside."

Together, they ducked into the cozy, wood-paneled office, and, to Hank's deep relief, they found the elder Mr. Portman free.

"Lieutenant Hawley, isn't it? I've seen you around for years."

"That's right, Mr. Portman," Hank said, shaking his hand.

"And who is this lovely lady you have with you today?"

"This is Miss Aurora Belmont."

Mr. Portman's eyebrows shot up, but he held out his hand to her. "Any relation to August Belmont, the financier?"

Rory sighed and took the old man's hand. "He's my father."

Mr. Portman's eyes were wide as saucers as he shook her hand.

"Well, I'll be a monkey's uncle," the lawyer muttered under his breath. Then he cleared his throat. "Have a seat and make yourselves at home. What can I do for you two today?"

"We need your help with drafting a marriage contract. It needs to contain very particular terms guaranteeing the finances and property rights of Miss Belmont, here, who I'm hoping will agree to be my wife."

Mr. Portman let out a low whistle. "Is there a reason Mr. Belmont isn't involved? Because if you're doing this behind his back, I've got to warn you that his lawyers are better than I am. I'm not sure this will stand up in court without his involvement."

Rory stiffened, and Hank's hackles rose. For God's sake, this was exactly why she didn't trust the men in her life. Even when she was in the room, they tried to circumvent her.

Barely reining in his irritation, Hank answered, "Miss Belmont is more than capable of negotiating on her own behalf."

Rory glanced at him and gave him a private little smile. "Thank you, Hank. Mr. Portman, my father won't be involved in this. If you have any questions regarding my interests, you can ask me directly."

Hank took her hand and squeezed.

"Hmm." Mr. Portman looked back and forth between them with narrowed eyes. "Well, if you're determined to go through with this, I'll draw it up, but don't say I didn't warn you."

It was all Hank could do to check his rising temper. He needed Mr. Portman's help with this document, or he would have marched right out of the office. "It's none of Mr. Belmont's business who Rory chooses to marry. But since I intend the terms to be entirely favorable to her, I don't anticipate a legal challenge."

Mr. Portman let out a long breath and pulled a notepad and pen from his desk drawer. "Very well. What terms are you proposing?"

Hank turned to Rory and looked directly into her gorgeous blue eyes. This was the part where he either won her over or made a complete fool of himself. But he had to try. "Rory, I want you to retain full rights to any money you earn or inherit. You can spend it as you please, and I won't touch it. Furthermore, I want you to have equal rights to all my property, except the farm in Michigan. That belongs to my family, and I can't in good conscience give it to anyone but them. But aside from that, what's mine is yours."

She furrowed her brows. "Hank, you don't have to do this."

Damn it all, this wasn't working.

"Yes, I do." For his own peace of mind as much as for hers, he needed her to know he wanted her for her own sake and not because he was after her father's fortune. "I want you to trust me never to put you in a cage like your father and Edward did. I don't want to trap you, Rory. I want to fly with you."

Her eyes glistened, and a tear ran down her cheek. "Oh, Hank. That's the loveliest thing anyone's ever said to me. I want that too. I hope you know that."

He thumbed away her tear. It was almost a yes. If Mr. Portman wasn't watching, he would have kissed her into oblivion, but unfortunately, they had an audience.

Mr. Portman cleared his throat, and they broke apart. "Any penalties for a broken engagement?"

Well, that ruined the romance of the moment, but it was a question they needed to face. "No, we both need to walk into this freely."

Rory nodded. "Agreed."

"And in case of divorce?"

Hank wiped his hand down over his face. "I pray to God we never need this provision, but I would pay alimony and ensure she had a house of her own to live in."

"Hank, don't be ridiculous. I would never expect you to support me that way." The horrified expression on Rory's face told him he'd gone and put his foot in it.

"I know, princess, but who knows if your father will ever

relent about your inheritance? I need to know you're safe and sound, whether I'm in your life or not."

"I'm perfectly capable of taking care of myself, you know." Her cheeks reddened as she sat ramrod straight.

He was losing ground, but this was something he wouldn't give on. "Yessiree, I do, and I love you for it. But please let me do this for you. If you were anyone else, I would offer this, and I wouldn't feel right cutting you off if things went south between us."

She gave him a long hard look then sighed. "Very well. This is all hypothetical anyway. I'm still considering."

It was a dagger to the heart, but he nodded. He knew she needed space to think, and he intended to give it to her as soon as he finished making his case.

Mr. Portman turned a page in his notebook. "And in case of the untimely death of either party?"

Hank looked at the ceiling, trying to force himself to contemplate what would happen. "She gets everything of mine except the farm in Michigan. That goes to my family. If she passes first, her property and assets should go to whoever she's given them to in her will. I make no claims."

"Don't be absurd. Your money should all go to your family." Of course, she was arguing. She wouldn't be the woman he loved if she didn't.

"Princess, most of this agreement is about giving you what you need to feel safe and respected as my wife. But this piece is what *I* need to feel right about making a lifelong commitment to you."

They stared each other down for a long moment. "Fine. If you must."

Hank sagged back in his chair with relief.

Mr. Portman turned another page. "You would need an updated will in addition to this marriage agreement."

"Of course." Hank looked at his hands, folded in his lap. Wills. How had his marriage proposal ended up in a discussion of wills? But he supposed this was how it had to be. She needed assurance of her freedom, and this was the only way he could think of to do it. "How quickly can you put it together?"

"Two, maybe three days."

He looked up at Mr. Portman. "Do it. Send me a copy and send one to her as soon as it's done. Here are the addresses," he said, writing them down on a notepad.

"Very good, and you are all set. It's been a pleasure doing business with you, Lieutenant Hawley and Miss Bemont. And I wish you luck. If you're crossing August Belmont, you're going to need it."

Yes, they would, but that wasn't going to stop Hank. They said goodbye to Mr. Portman and headed out.

As soon as they were out on the street, he paused. "Did I convince you?"

She reached up and caressed his cheek. "I'm very moved by your gesture. I still need some time to think it through, but you certainly are making it harder and harder to say no."

"Take all the time you need, princess. I'll be right here as soon as you're ready."

She looped her arm through his, and they strolled along Main Street like they'd been doing it all their lives.

When they arrived at the florist shop, Mrs. O'Donnell was outside, fussing with the flower arrangements on display.

"You two look happy," she said with a sharp look but a kind smile. "Do you have good news to share?"

Rory flushed pink at the question, and Hank cleared his throat and stared at his toes.

Mrs. O'Donnell nodded knowingly. "Won't be long before there are wedding bells for you two. Mark my words."

Under the watchful gaze of Mrs. O'Donnell, Hank squeezed

Rory's hand and let her go. "I'll see you soon," he said, not daring any more with an audience.

"I'll see you soon, Hank."

He watched her disappear up the stairs. Just a little bit longer to wait, then—if all went well—she would finally say yes.

25

*R*ory followed the Carnegies' butler down the long hall to the conservatory, seeing the parquet wood floors and the decorative plasterwork on the ceiling as if for the first time. How many workers toiled away for how long to build it all? The opulence she used to take for granted now seemed so excessive and extravagant compared to her simple life in Mineola. Plaster acorns and oak leaves were certainly pretty, but how could one justify the expense when so many city residents struggled for their daily bread?

The scent of the conservatory reached Rory before she entered it—floral notes mixed with rich soil. And there was a freshness to the air that only came from a profusion of growing greenery. As they entered, sunlight filtered through arching glass and then tall branches, leaving dappled patches of shade on the green-tiled floor. The butler led her to an ornate ironwork table shaded by several tall palms and an orange tree laden with ripening fruit, all in terracotta pots large enough to bathe in.

"If you'll pardon me, I'll go fetch Miss Evelyn," the butler said with a bow and left.

Thankfully, the windows were open, and electric ceiling fans created a gentle breeze. Otherwise, the summer heat would have been unbearable. Rory sat back and fanned herself as she waited for her friend. After a long, hot journey on the Long Island Railroad, followed by a taxi ride all the way up to 91st Street, she felt positively wilted.

Evelyn arrived squealing a moment later, and Rory forgot all about her exhaustion.

"My God, darling, I've missed you so!" Evelyn hugged Rory with all her might, and Rory hugged her right back. After all her travails, it was a balm to her soul to see her best friend.

"I've missed you too! It's only been a few weeks, but it feels like an eternity!" In fact, she felt like a completely different person after everything that had transpired. It was a wonder the Carnegies' butler even let her in. "Do your parents know about me? I half thought I would be turned away when I rang the doorbell."

"My parents are in Newport for the season. Papa has a new yacht he's showing off. It's made my life ever so much easier in the meantime. But even if they were here, I wouldn't let them turn you away! You are my dearest friend, and I'm standing by you no matter what."

Her friend's staunch support moved her more than she could say. "Thank you. I know it can't be easy being my friend. I can only imagine what everyone must be saying about me now. I haven't so much as looked at a gossip column since I left. How bad is it?" She bit her lip and braced herself.

"Not as bad as you'd think. Fortunately for you, no one seems to know yet. There's no hiding that you and Edward are on the rocks, but your father seems to have convinced the papers that you're in Europe, visiting friends."

So Papa was still trying to salvage this. It was amazing what money could smooth over.

"Edward and I are finished. After the way he's treated me, I want nothing to do with the man ever again. If Papa thinks he can make me reconsider, he is dead wrong. He's already done his worst, and I'm doing just fine." For a moment, she almost forgot she was talking to Evelyn as the argument she could no longer have with her father played out in her head like a phonograph recording. Her nails dug into her palms beneath the table as her head throbbed with words she'd never get to speak.

Evelyn tilted her head and furrowed her brow. "Are you, dear? Are you sure? I worry about you."

A sudden well of sadness threatened to overwhelm Rory as she considered how to answer. In Mineola where everything was new and different, it was easy to pretend that things were going swimmingly. There was nothing to remind her of what she'd lost. But here with Evelyn, the loss of her former life was a gaping wound she couldn't ignore. Much as she tried to convince herself she didn't want this life anymore, it had hurt her deeply to be torn away from her family and her world so abruptly. She blinked back tears, determined not to let them fall.

"Oh, I'll be all right." She was very proud that she didn't let her chin quiver. "I like my new life. I have work for the PBA to keep me busy. Did you know I've distributed funds to the twenty-three widows we connected with last month and received five new applications?"

This was safer ground. Rory wasn't sure she could hold herself together under sustained scrutiny from her friend.

Evelyn gave her a far-too-knowing look. "That's wonderful, dear. I had no doubt that you would make the PBA a smashing success. But I'm still not certain you're all right."

"I've been writing letters to elected officials about women's suffrage too. That's been keeping me busy."

"Now, Rory, I know that—" Evelyn broke off abruptly as a servant came into view, carrying a tray of lemonade and cookies. She and Rory both smiled politely. It wouldn't do to have the servants suspecting anything was amiss. "Thank you! Just leave it on the table here."

The maid nodded her head and hurried away.

Taking advantage of Evelyn's momentary distraction, Rory poured herself a glass of lemonade. "Excellent timing. I'm parched."

She took a long sip, and the cold, sweet liquid went far to steady her nerves.

"As I was saying…" Evelyn leaned forward and looked Rory in the eyes. "I know that you've given up a great deal. You don't have to pretend with me that it doesn't hurt. I know you don't like to talk about…feelings. You much prefer to lose yourself in a flurry of activity and pretend everything is fine. But if you *did* wish to talk about it, I want you to know that I am here for you."

A tear dripped down Rory's cheek, and she dashed it away. So much for holding herself together. "You are the best friend I could ever have. Do you know that?"

Evelyn grinned. "Oh, I do. And don't you ever forget it!" She reached out and squeezed Rory's shoulder. "Have a cookie and some more lemonade. There are few problems in this world that Mrs. O'Malley's shortbread cookies can't fix."

Grateful, Rory took one and let buttery perfection transport her away from her troubles for a moment.

"There. You see?" Evelyn picked up a cookie and held it up. "Her cookies are magic. You feel better already, don't you?"

Rory nodded and took another cookie.

"Now, let's talk about something more pleasant. How are things going with your pilot?" Evelyn leaned forward and propped her chin on her hands.

Rory chewed thoughtfully as she pondered how to reply. She adored Hank, but things were becoming so messy between them with his repeated proposals and her refusals. "Evelyn?"

"Yes, Rory?" Her friend raised her eyebrows expectantly.

"Would you marry Clyde if he asked you?"

Evelyn sat up straight and frowned, glancing around as if

worried someone might overhear. "My parents would never allow it."

"What if you were in my situation? What if you no longer gave a fig what your parents thought?" Because she didn't. Her father was never going to have a say in who she spent her time with again.

"I suppose it would depend." Evelyn chewed her lip, considering.

"On what?" Rory leaned forward.

"On whether at the end of the day, after all the change and loss, we still made each other happy."

Hank certainly made Rory happy. She was giddy every time she saw him. She wanted to curl up in his arms and never let go. But should she? "You would give up your independence for happiness?"

Evelyn chuckled. "Is that what this is about? You're afraid you won't be your own woman once you wed?"

"Yes." There was no hiding anything from Evelyn. She always saw straight into the heart of the matter.

"That's a perfectly reasonable thing to be concerned about. But have you asked him about it? If he's truly someone who can make you happy, he should respect your freedom. Have you thought about what you might need from him for you to feel comfortable saying yes?"

"That's the thing. He's already bent over backwards and done everything I could possibly want, including drafting legal documents committing that he'll never take a cent from me. But I'm not sure what would take away the hesitation in my heart. Maybe this is about me and not about him. Maybe I'm not ready yet."

If only she could put her finger on what would fix her inconvenient feelings, this would all be so much easier.

Evelyn took both her hands and looked her in the eyes. "Then wait until you're ready. Only you can know what is right for you."

It wasn't the most helpful of answers, but she couldn't say she was surprised. Evelyn was right. This was her decision to make, and no one could make it for her.

"Have you talked to your aunt about this? I'm sure she'd have a thing or two to say about the institution of marriage, considering how poorly things went with her first husband. Something made her decide to marry again, despite all she went through."

"I haven't dared. I'm afraid of how she'll react if she hears about Hank. She'll say I'm throwing my life away for a man. I'm sure of it." Rory loved Aunt Alva so much, and she was so afraid of seeing disapproval in her eyes. Her aunt had given her a stern talking to about not throwing her pearls to swine after the Archie incident. She didn't think she was ready to face Aunt Alva's censure again. At least not yet.

"Don't be so certain. She might surprise you. At the very least, you should let her know you're all right. She reaches out to me almost every day asking if I've heard from you. Please let her know how you're doing so that I can have a little bit of peace."

Rory squeezed Evelyn's hands. "You're right. I should. I'm sorry she's been pestering you. I'll get in touch so that she leaves you alone."

Evelyn squeezed back. "Thank you. She's like a steam locomotive when she's on a mission. There's only so much I can do to hold her back." Relinquishing Rory's hands, Evelyn picked up another cookie. "You know, I do envy you."

That took Rory by surprise. "You do?"

"Mm-hmm. You've broken free. You've won your independence and can do as you please."

"Hardly. I've burned all my bridges, and I'm cobbling together a life as best I can from the ashes. I can choose my future, but I can't undo the past. I'll always be a fallen woman whose family disowned her. I'll never live that down." Try as she might to rise above it, her ruined reputation still weighed her down in quiet moments when there was nothing to distract her. Much as she wanted to be a modern woman who didn't give a damn about convention, she knew the rest of the world did.

Evelyn shook her head. "You'll be a phoenix, rising from the ashes. Mark my words. Nothing is going to keep Rory Belmont down. Speaking of which, is Hank going to teach you how to fly? Because I want to be your first passenger when you get your pilot's license."

Flying. Rory and Hank had talked about it over lunch on the beach the other day. He offered to teach her, regardless of whether she agreed to be his wife. She would have a hard time paying attention to her lessons with him as a teacher, but how could she resist such a generous offer?

"He did. With any luck, I'll be a licensed pilot by the fall."

"That's simply splendid," Evelyn said, clapping her hands together. "What a marvelous man you've found! He sounds like a keeper to me."

Rory smiled. "Yes, he is. And I have no intention of letting him go. I just need to figure out a way to stay with him without feeling like I'm giving up this new life I've discovered."

"I'm certain you'll figure things out," Evelyn winked. "Now tell me more about how things are going with the PBA. I'm dying to know."

For the next hour, they chatted about the future of the PBA and how they were going to expand it beyond New York City. It would be a challenge, but together, they could accomplish just about anything.

As Rory said her goodbyes, she couldn't help reflecting on how different her life was without all the trappings of wealth. Living on her own required a lot of hard work, but it felt more real. In Mineola, everything she wanted done she had to do herself, but every day she earned her place in the world. That was an entirely new experience. Under Papa's roof, she'd never lifted a finger. Everything was done for her. It was good for her to come down from the clouds. What was more, in her new life, she had friends, purpose, and love. And Evelyn was right. She was better off without all the rest.

Something shifted for her during their conversation. A small part of her had been holding back from her new life and clinging to the familiar world she had left behind. But now, she was ready to let it go and embrace new possibilities. She could even picture how she might find her way to saying yes to Hank.

She left the Carnegie mansion with a new spring in her step, ready to face whatever life might bring, even the terrifying, wonderful possibility of love.

2 6

<hr>

The three days away from Rory seemed to stretch to eternity, but at long last, Hank was ready to fly the final stretch back to New York.

"Headed home to your lady love?" O'Donnell asked, putting down his turkey sandwich.

Hank threw away the butcher paper his own sandwich had been wrapped in and took a last swig of muddy coffee before rinsing his mug in the sink of the Bustleton Airport lunchroom. Three other men sat at whitewashed picnic tables enjoying the sandwiches Mrs. Richardson brought them from Cooper's Deli down the street. Hank had eaten his at record speed, desperate to get to his plane and leave Philadelphia behind.

"I can't wait to see her. I think I may have convinced her to finally say yes."

O'Donnell grinned. "Can't understand what she sees in you, myself. But I wish you the best of luck, you old dog."

Hank laughed. "Thank you. I'll need it."

He waved goodbye to his friend and rushed to the locker room to don his leather flight suit, aviator cap, and goggles. Hustling out to his plane, he performed his usual checks, though perhaps he did a more cursory job than usual. After all, he'd just flown the plane from D.C. to Philadelphia. What could possibly have happened to it over a lunch hour? Or really a lunch fifteen minutes.

"Hawley, is that you?" asked Thompson, climbing out of the biplane he'd just landed. "You and I should—"

"Sorry. Gotta go." Hank waved off his friend and practically leaped into the rear cockpit of his Jenny. "Mind swinging the propeller for me?"

Thompson shrugged and gave the propeller a good shove.

Hank opened the throttle and started down the runway. It was a gorgeous, sunny day with only a smattering of clouds. The heat had broken, and the temperature was a mild seventy degrees. He reveled in the feel of the wind on his face.

The countryside sped by beneath him as he flew faster than any car could drive toward the woman that held all his hopes and dreams in her hands.

She would have received the contract by now. Would it be enough to convince her? She was so close to saying yes before he left. He was nearly certain this would nudge her into certainty. But if, for some reason, it didn't work, he'd have to keep trying. How could he help her trust him, or even herself?

It broke his heart to think of her self-doubt. What had her father done that left her so uncertain of her own worth? Here he was, a nobody farm boy from Michigan, and she was worried that *he* was going to get tired of *her*?

If only she could see herself through his eyes. Her strength, determination, and bravery were unmatched. He'd never met another woman so fiery and full of life. What man in his right mind wouldn't want to spend his whole life with her?

Edward, that was who. The bounder. Hank wanted to wring his neck for the damage he'd done. And to think he expected Rory to marry him after everything! The senator from Connecticut had better hope that Hank never crossed his path.

Hank wouldn't be answerable for what he might do if he saw that miserable sonofabitch.

Hank realized he'd been gripping the stick too hard and climbing in altitude. He purposely relaxed his hand and let the plane settle back into its proper course.

Trenton, New Jersey, passed beneath his left wing, a mass of brown roofs interrupting the dappled green of the countryside, as he followed the rail lines northeast toward his destination. He was almost halfway there. Not much longer to wait.

As soon as he landed, he was going to head straight over to the O'Donnell place to see her. Hopefully, Mr. O'Donnell wouldn't have closed up shop yet, and Hank could buy some flowers. He'd take her to dinner at the East Williston Hotel and order their finest champagne. Then he'd take her for a walk in the fairgrounds, stopping at that gazebo he liked with the perfect view of the sunset behind his favorite oak tree.

Kneeling before her, he would say, "Rory, I'm not a poetic man, but I need you to know what is in my heart. Until I met you, I was adrift, and I didn't know it. When my father and brother both died, it was like the ground fell out from beneath me. All I could do was glide along the surface of life, struggling to stay aloft. But when I'm with you, I soar up to the heavens. You lift me up and give me purpose. You are my compass, my true north. Without you, I am lost."

Glancing at his compass, he realized he was talking airplanes again. A man took inspiration from the things around him, and could he help it if every time he tried to talk about something personal it took a particular direction? Fortunately, Rory loved airplanes. She wouldn't mind. She might even get that dreamy look on her face he loved so much.

There was something vulnerable about her in those moments. She was a woman who knew what she wanted, no doubt about that. But sometimes, she took such innocent, childlike delight in things. That smile made his heart dance a jig every time he saw it.

It was so raw, so honest. He wanted to see her smile like that every day for the rest of his life.

And for the first time in several years, he wanted that life to be long and peaceful. No more risk-taking for him. He loved the airmail, but he loved Rory more. Thank God Glenn Curtiss offered him that job. He was keeping his fingers crossed that Major Belmont didn't sabotage it for him somehow. If everything went as he hoped, soon he would be the husband Rory deserved. No more risking his neck for a sack full of mail. He had something to live for now.

Please, God, let her say yes!

He looked down at the winding river of the train tracks, then glanced at his compass, making minute adjustments to his course. The sooner he got home, the sooner he could tell her everything in his heart. And the sooner she could end his agony and give him her answer.

He tried to eek some extra speed out of the airplane, even though he knew he'd pushed it to the limit. The familiar landmarks passed by one by one beneath him with agonizing slowness. He passed Princeton, then Edison, towns he knew far better from the air than on land. Sure, he'd driven through New Jersey on occasion, but from a car, you couldn't see the distinctive shapes of each town—brown against a field of green.

Staten Island passed beneath him, and the skyscrapers of Manhattan loomed off to his left. He was so close. Not long now until he held Rory in his arms, so soft and vital, her sweet scent of magnolias driving him wild. He could practically taste her sweet lips against his own, each curve of her body pressed up against him. They fit so well together. Surely that had to be a sign.

A vivid memory of Rory, naked against him in the cockpit of a Jenny, momentarily flooded his senses. *Oh God.*

No. He had to keep his head. He was flying an airplane for heaven's sake.

Long Island stretched out before him. The racetrack at Belmont Park was just visible in the distance. He began his descent.

The ocean sparkled in the late-day sunshine off to his right as he flew over the factories and rowhouses of outer Queens, gliding over the city's polluted air. The green oval of the racetrack grew large before him, and he coasted down toward home, toward Rory and a future he was now anxious to embrace.

As he made his final descent, the muggy haze of the city in summer enveloped him, and he loved it—even the factory smoke and automobile exhaust. It meant he was close. So close.

He glided low over the stables, banking slightly as he had a hundred times before.

The familiar three-tiered, green grandstand towered over the cheaper bleachers, and the enormous sun canopy loomed over the track in the evening light. Hank thought about the first time he'd come to a race here. It was the Belmont Stakes, and the world-famous racetrack was full to bursting. Over eighteen thousand spectators were there that day, according to the papers. He was seated so far up, he could hardly see the horses, but he didn't care. The crowd's enthusiasm swept him up, and he had a fine old time. And to think he was courting the owner's daughter! Who would ever have dreamed?

A loud snap pulled him abruptly from his reverie.

Hank inhaled sharply. *What the hell?*

The ailerons weren't responding. He couldn't steer.

There was no way to even out. He was coming in sideways.

No. Not now. Not tonight. Rory!

The hair rose on his forearms. He was headed straight for the stands. There was no way to stop. He couldn't get the plane down fast enough to hit grass and use the skid that served as a brake.

Time slowed to a crawl as the airplane careened toward a collision. He always knew this day would come. It was only a matter of time. That was why he took the job from Curtiss. The only way to escape an early death was to quit this crazy job, but he hadn't quit soon enough. Fate was slamming into him today.

He snarled as he desperately tried to work the controls, knowing already they wouldn't respond. Useless.

What was it like for Benny in his last moments? Was this how he died too? Benny's face floated in his mind's eye.

No. He couldn't go like this. Not today. Maybe he could jump. Landing on the dirt had to be better than crashing into the stands. He scrambled to climb out of the cockpit, but it was too late.

The plane slammed into the stands with a sickening explosion of splintering wood and screeching metal ripped from its base. The propeller demolished several rows of seats before flying apart. Hank was only aware that he was in the air once more. As he fell back down, only one thing was in his mind.

Rory, I love you.

Everything went black.

27

*R*ory sat in her bright sitting room, staring at the draft marriage contract in her hands with a huge smile.

"Yes, Hank. I'll be your wife," she whispered, tasting the words, testing them. Did she dare say them aloud to him?

For two days, she mulled over all her worries and objections, and then the draft contract arrived. Even though she knew what it would contain, seeing it all spelled out bowled her over. He knew exactly what she needed. To be free to stand on her own two feet. That was what he was giving her. She could be with him and still stand on her own.

She stood up and spun around, hugging herself. Her delicious pilot was all hers at last. She couldn't wait to tell him. He was supposed to be home this evening, wasn't he?

With a little whoop, she ran into her room and threw open her wardrobe. She needed exactly the right dress for getting engaged—something flirtatious and flowy but not overly formal.

Stripping off the plain cotton frock she was wearing, she changed into a gown that was a deep plum color with fluttering whispers of silk at the shoulders for sleeves, a square neckline, cinched waist, and a flowing skirt whose hem fell to mid-calf. It was decadent without being too showy or revealing. She paired it with gray suede kitten heels and examined the effect in the mirror. Perfect.

Then she sat at her vanity and arranged her hair up in a twist with curled tendrils framing her face. She used a touch of rouge and lip paint and accentuated her eyes with dark eyeliner. Most of her jewelry, she had to leave behind when she left her father's, but she still had the string of pearls from her mother, so she put them on. Lastly, she put on a touch of magnolia scent. She was ready.

Just as she was getting her handbag to walk over to Hank's, there was a knock at her door. Could it be him? Maybe he came straight to see her after he landed.

She opened it and was surprised to see Bill O'Donnell. His face was uncharacteristically somber.

"You're not Hank," she said.

"No, I—" He stopped, glancing at her dress and then her face. Taking a deep breath, he said, "I'm sorry, Rory. I have bad news. There's been an accident."

For a moment, the words didn't register, and then the world narrowed to a pinhole. She grabbed the doorjamb for support.

"Hank?" she asked, knowing the answer before he spoke.

"I'm afraid so. He's at Nassau Hospital."

That meant he was alive. Thank God. "What happened?"

"Something went wrong when he was landing. He plowed into the stands at Belmont. He was thrown from the cockpit and hit his head. He's unconscious. The doctors say it's touch and go."

She grabbed Bill's arm. "I have to see him."

Bill nodded. "I'll take you."

Everything around her seemed far away as Bill walked the few blocks to the hospital with her. It was dusk, and the world was surrounded by deep, insidious blue. It seeped into her, making her shiver despite the sultry summer evening.

When they arrived at the entrance, it felt like she was wading through mud. Her body didn't want to move. She needed to see but didn't want it to be real. Seeing it would mean accepting that it happened, that he was hurt, that she might lose him.

She clung to Bill's arm as he walked her into the hospital and up to the front desk. Bill asked for the room, and the woman told him, "I'm afraid only family members are allowed in at this time."

"She's his fiancée," he bluffed. Little did he know that it was very nearly true.

"Oh, sweetie! I'm so sorry," the woman said. "You can go right in. It's room twelve."

"I'd better go with her," Bill said. "She's not very steady on her feet at the moment."

The woman gave him a look. "You can go in and help her get seated, but then I want you back out here in the waiting area. Understand?"

"Yes, ma'am," he said and steered Rory down the hall.

The sounds of the hospital echoed around her, but she hardly heard them. All her attention was on putting one foot in front of the other so that she could get to Hank. He steered her into a small room with two beds. One was empty, the other had Hank.

She rushed to his side, and Bill backed quietly out of the room. Hank looked so peaceful, as if he was sleeping, except for the bandage around his head. Then she looked closer and saw his left leg was in a cast beneath the covers. "Hank, it's me, Rory. I came as soon as I heard. Can you hear me? Squeeze my hand if you can hear me."

Nothing.

Tears prickled the corners of her eyes. "I wanted to tell you I'll marry you, Hank. I was hoping to tell you today. You finally convinced me." She took his hand and kissed it, then pressed it to her cheek.

She pulled up a chair and sat beside him, holding onto his hand.

"The contract was perfect. You gave me exactly what I needed to feel free and independent. I love you for it."

The words took her by surprise. Hank had said them often enough, but she had resisted. She hadn't spoken of love before, except to family. But that was what Hank was now in her heart: family. He was the man she planned to spend the rest of her life with. Or the rest of his, she thought sadly, looking at his still form on the bed.

This was what Hank always feared. He didn't want to cause the heartbreak and grief that came with accidents like this. Never getting close, he kept everyone at arm's length.

Rory couldn't help but think of the war widows she worked with through the PBA. They had all been through this, though they weren't able to sit beside their husbands' bedsides. It was a luxury to be here, holding his hand.

If she lost him…

No, she wasn't going to think about that. Somehow, she was going to get him through this. He was going to recover. He had to.

"Hank," she tried again. "Hank, it's me. Please show me some sign you're in there."

Then she felt it—the slightest squeeze. "Oh, thank God." She squeezed him back and kissed his hand again.

At that moment, a doctor came in. "Excuse me, young lady. Are you a member of his family?"

"I'm his fiancée," she said, sitting up but refusing to relinquish his hand.

"I see. Well, you can stay while I examine him, but I'll need you to step back."

She got up and pulled her chair against the wall, then sat well out of the way.

The doctor listened to his heart, checked his pulse, opened his eyes and checked them with a light for response. He shook his head and began making notes on his clipboard.

"Can you tell me anything, doctor? Please, I need to know."

The doctor gave her a sympathetic look. "He's had a severe concussion. We stitched up and bandaged his injuries, but it's the internal damage we have to worry about. It's impossible to know what will happen after an accident like this. He could wake up just fine five minutes from now. He could wake up with brain damage. He could stay in a coma indefinitely, or he could pass on. I don't want to alarm you, but I also don't want to hide the truth. I wish I could tell you something more definite, but in cases like this, only time will tell."

Tears streamed down her cheeks. Her eye makeup must look a fright, she thought idly as she attempted to absorb the doctor's words. "Is there anything I can do, doctor?"

"Talk to him. Read to him. Anything to stimulate his brain. People respond to their loved ones differently than strangers. You may have luck where we've failed."

Rory nodded. "Just now, I asked him to give me a sign that he heard me, and he squeezed my hand ever so slightly. I think he heard me."

The doctor smiled at her. "Any reaction is a good sign. Keep talking to him. Maybe you'll get something more."

"Thank you, doctor," she said wiping her tears.

"Of course, my dear. Take care, and I'll be back to check on him in a few hours."

He left, and she took some tissues and water from Hank's bedside and wiped off her eye makeup as best she could, using a compact to check the results. Her face was red and puffy, but at least she no longer had black dripping down her cheeks.

Pulling her chair back over to Hank, she took his hand again.

"Did you know I almost died of pneumonia in this hospital when I was three?" she said, holding his hand to her cheek. "My family has a vacation home on the North Shore, and we were there over Christmas when I got sick. My father says I was in here a whole week. All I remember is the piles of candy my brothers brought me to cheer me up. And I remember the worried look on Papa's face. It's one of the few times I remember him looking worried at me instead of angry. I think he was worried he was going to lose me like he lost Mama. When I finally came home from the hospital, he had bought me a pony, even though I was too young to ride."

Rory caressed Hank's hand. No response.

"Papa's upset, and he's wrong about so many things when it comes to women in general and me in particular. But I hope someday we can reconcile. I don't care about the money, but he's my family. All I've ever wanted is his love. I don't know if I'll ever get it, but I have to hope."

She kissed Hank's hand. "Now you're going to be my family. You're going to be my husband, and I'm going to be your wife. And you had better wake up if you want to have any hope of getting me in your bed. Although I suppose a bed isn't strictly necessary. A rooftop or a Jenny will do."

She felt another squeeze, this one stronger than the last. "When we were growing up, Evelyn used to tease me about marrying a pilot, you know. Or a jockey. Or a racecar driver. Or perhaps a hot air balloonist. I always had a daredevil streak. When she and I race, I almost always win. I want it more, and I'm willing to take bigger chances."

She poured herself a cup of water from the pitcher on Hank's nightstand and took a drink. "Once, we were all at the circus, and after the show, I ran off and found the tent with the trapeze artists. When my nanny found me, I was asking them all about how to join the circus and learn to do tricks just like them. I lost desserts for a week for running away like that."

She took another drink. Her throat was dry from talking. "I just want you to know who it is you're marrying. I would like to say I've settled down since then, but really, I haven't, as you well know. There are so many new and interesting types of trouble to get into. But I promise to be a good and faithful wife. I'll be boring as bread for you if you'll just wake up."

She felt another squeeze. It ran through her like an electric jolt, prodding her to tell more stories. She talked for hours, stopping only to feed him some broth, slowly spooning it into his mouth and making sure he swallowed.

The doctor stopped by, checking his pulse and examining his head injury, but when she asked if there had been any change, the doctor shook his head and left.

At some point, Bill came back and asked if she was ready to go home. She told him she was staying and sent him on his way. Eventually, she drifted off sitting in the chair with her head resting against the bed, her hand still in his. She slept fitfully for hours, having one terrible dream after another until a squeeze on her hand woke her up in the darkness just in time to hear him murmur, "Rory."

Through the mental fog that would not lift, Hank could hear Rory's voice. He faded in and out of awareness. His body wouldn't move. He couldn't so much as lift an eyelid, but he knew she was there. The words she was saying slurred together, so he focused on the rise and fall of her voice and the feel of her hand in his.

What happened? Where was he? Why couldn't he move? He was flying back from Philadelphia and then what? He had no recollection of landing at Belmont Park. Something must have happened to the airplane. He must be hurt. That would explain why he couldn't move. Maybe he was in the hospital?

The haze descended once again, and when his awareness returned, he had to puzzle it out all over again. Then Rory asked him to squeeze her hand. He was sure that was what she'd said. It sounded crystal clear. All he had to do was figure out how to move his hand. His mind called out, but his hand didn't answer. He tried again. Nothing.

She asked again, and, trying with all his might, he managed a twitch. He had to find his way out of this somehow.

Unable to think, he let himself drift with her voice. He

caught snippets of what she was saying. There was something about a trapeze? He tried another squeeze, and she squeezed back.

He drifted off into sleep after that, dreaming of being trapped in his house. He wanted to go out the front door but every time he tried, there was another door, and he ended up right back inside. Finally, he gave up on the door and went out through the window. This time, he succeeded and was standing in the cool night air.

Slowly, he blinked awake. It was dark wherever he was. He was lying in a bed, but it wasn't his bed. Someone's hand was in his.

"Rory," he said aloud, his voice thick and rough. It sounded odd to him, as if someone else was speaking.

"Hank?" she asked in a sleepy voice. "Hank, are you awake?"

"Rory, what happened? Where am I?" Dear God, his head hurt. There was something funny with his leg too.

"Oh, thank God you're awake. I was so worried. You're in the hospital, Hank. You had an accident when you were landing. Bill said something about the steering failing?"

He tried to remember, but it was all a blank. "I remember flying from Philadelphia. I remember seeing…Belmont Park. And then…nothing."

"Don't strain yourself. It's not important. All that matters is that you're awake and all right." She kissed his hand.

"Can you turn on a light? I want to see you. There isn't anyone else in here is there?"

"No, just you." She clicked on a lamp, and there she was, beautiful as ever despite her rumpled hair, or perhaps because of it.

"You're all dressed up." Her dress looked so soft. He wanted to touch her all over in it. Then he tried to move, and a stab of pain pierced his skull. No, there would be no moving.

She smiled, and it was like the sun coming out. "I was planning to go see you."

"You got all dressed up just to see me?" He was one to talk. He'd done the same thing.

"For you and for the occasion."

What occasion? Was it her birthday? Did he miss it?

"I thought I should look nice for our engagement," she said.

"Wait. Does that mean…? Are you saying…?"

"I'm saying yes, Hank."

His breath caught. "You mean…you'll marry me?"

"Yes," she said, and a moment later her lips were on his. His future wife was kissing him for all she was worth, and he was doing the best he could to respond. With some difficulty, he managed to raise his arm and cup the back of her head.

At that moment, a man cleared his throat loudly. "Excuse me, you two. I'll thank you to remember this is a hospital. Lieutenant Hawley, I'm very glad to see you've…er…recovered."

"She's going to marry me, Doc!" He wanted to get up and twirl her around, but of course he could do no such thing.

"Well, yes. That's why we let her in here in the first place, but I won't have any funny business or she's out. This is a respectable institution, and you are in a public place where anyone could walk in. Like me, for instance," he said, giving them both a disapproving look. "I'll overlook it this once, but not again, am I clear?"

"Yes, doctor," they said in unison.

"Besides, you should avoid excitement, Lieutenant Hawley. You may be recovering, but you aren't out of the woods yet. We'll need to monitor you for another day at least before we release you. In the meantime, let's keep things calm and quiet in here, shall we?"

"Yes, doctor," they said again.

"Doctor," Hank called as he started to leave. "How long will it take me to fully recover?"

The doctor folded his clipboard over his chest. "Now that you're awake, I'd say your head should be better in a couple of weeks, around when the stitches come out. Your leg will take six to eight weeks to heal before we can take off that cast."

"Thanks, Doc." It was a bit disappointing to know he'd be in a cast for so long. He hadn't envisioned hobbling down the aisle with crutches. When he imagined marrying Rory, he'd wanted to be her loyal knight, strong and heroic, making up with chivalry for what he lacked in polish. He wanted to kneel before her beauty. He wanted to carry her over thresholds, but he didn't think either of them could wait until he'd fully healed.

"If that's all, then goodnight." And the doctor left them alone.

Rory burst into quiet giggles as soon as he was out of sight. "I think we scandalized the poor man."

"He'll get over it."

"When should we marry?" she asked, squeezing his hand.

He was tempted to say as soon as they got out of here, but he thought better of it. "When would *you* like to marry?"

"As soon as possible. Could we go to City Hall?"

He smiled. He was about to say yes when he remembered. "I promised my mother and sister that if I ever got married, they would be there. Also, I'd like to get this bandage off my head before our wedding day. The cast I can live with, but the bandage... I don't want to look like I might have had brain damage on my wedding day. What would you say to two weeks from now?"

"I suppose I can wait that long," she said with a sideways smile.

"Can you remind me what day it is today?" He was still a bit addled, and his head was starting to throb again.

"Friday. Or at least it was. It's probably Saturday by now. Why?"

He tried to move his head to look at her better, but it hurt too much. "I wanted to make sure I didn't miss a phone call home. I call every Wednesday. If I missed a call, they'd worry."

"I can't wait to meet them. What are they like?"

The question made him pause. It had been so long since he'd talked about them to anyone. He realized he was excited to tell Rory. "Well, Ma is a force of nature. She wakes up every morning before the crack of dawn to start the chores: milking the cows, gathering eggs, and feeding the livestock. Then she moves on to the garden, weeding, fertilizing, and harvesting anything that's ready. We have a small orchard where we grow apples and cherries. When it's harvest season, she's out there with the farm hands, working twice as hard and putting them to shame. When she's done outside, she comes in and cooks and preserves. In our house, everything that can't get eaten or stored gets pickled or preserved."

"I look forward to meeting her. How old is she?"

"Forty-eight and going strong." Ma was going to live forever if only to harangue Hank about how he ought to visit more often. Which he should.

"What about your sister?"

"Kate takes after Ma. Same work ethic and sharp mind. Got her looks from Ma too, though she got Pops' green eyes. Jeremiah had a lot of competition when he set out to court her. Fortunately, she knew how to separate the wheat from the chaff. It didn't hurt that she'd always been a little sweet on him. He's the silent but steady type. Real thoughtful and a good hard worker."

Rory was silent for a moment, then asked, "And your brother? What was he like?"

Benny. If he was going to talk about Benny to anyone, he supposed it should be her. "He was the perfect oldest son. He loved the farm as much as Pops, and he had Ma's work ethic. Pops always worked hard too, but he had a bit of a dreamy side. Ma was always on hand to bring him down from the clouds. Anyhow, Benny was everything I wasn't: steady, reliable, and responsible. He should have lived to inherit the farm. It never should have been me."

Rory stroked the back of his hand with her thumb. It was so

soothing. He didn't want her to ever stop. "And what were you like growing up?"

He laughed, but it hurt, so he stopped quickly. "I was a rascal. Always trying to get out of farm work, playing dangerous games with my friends. Every other day, it seemed like I was scaring my parents half to death, leaping off rooftops and racing carts down hills. I saw a barnstormer pilot when I was at a county fair when I was a teenager, and from that day on, I was hooked. I went to every show of his I could, offering to help him with mechanical problems as they came up. I was always good with machines. When he opened a flight school, he hired me to be a full-time mechanic, and he taught me to fly on the side. That was how I started my career as a pilot."

"Sounds wonderful," she said, stifling a yawn.

"You're tired, princess. And so am I. Let's get some sleep. We can talk more in the morning."

She stole a quick kiss goodnight and collapsed into the chair beside him, falling asleep immediately. He drifted off to sleep on a cloud of contentment.

THE NEXT MORNING, he woke up to Bill O'Donnell loudly whispering, "Rory, Rory..." and giving her shoulder a shake.

"O'Donnell, what in God's name are you doing?" Good grief his head hurt. It felt a little clearer than last night, but his head, and for that matter the rest of his body, ached so much he could hardly move.

"Hawley, you're awake," he said at full volume, making Hank wince. "I thought Rory might want to go home and freshen up after spending all night here."

Rory stirred and stretched like a kitten, making him wish he had her at home in his bed all the more. Not that he was in any state to do anything.

"Hmm? Me?" she said in a sleepy voice.

"Yes, you," he said. "And I have some news for you that you're not going to like."

"I just woke up, O'Donnell. At least let me have some coffee before you bombard me with news." He wasn't sure he was capable of sitting up to drink, but he was damned well going to try.

At that moment, a nurse came in with a breakfast tray. "Eat up, Lieutenant Hawley," she said as she stuffed pillows behind him to raise him to sit. "There you are. If you start to feel light-headed, lie down again for a bit. All right?"

"I will," he promised.

As soon as she was gone, he took a deep drink of the sad, lukewarm coffee from the tray. At least it had caffeine, which was all that really mattered.

"So what's the news?" he asked O'Donnell.

"One of the mechanics cleaning up the accident noticed that one of the wires controlling your steering was cut. Not snapped, mind you, but cut, nice and clean. They called the police who confirmed it looks like a case of sabotage." O'Donnell looked a little too gleeful delivering this juicy and upsetting news.

"Who would want to hurt Hank?" Rory asked.

"Exactly what the police are asking everyone at the airfield this morning. I just came from there. Several people brought up your father. It seems he learned of Hank's identity earlier this week and made some threats in the presence of witnesses. It looks like the police consider him a person of interest in this case."

Rory gasped. "Oh, no. My father was angry, and I have no doubt he would try to do something like ruin Hank's job prospects, but sabotage and murder? He would never!"

Hank was less certain. Major Belmont was a powerful man, and he might think he could get away with something like that.

After all, he practically owned New York City. Even if he was accused, Hank was certain the charges would never stick.

Major Belmont wasn't his only enemy, though. Senator Windham had also made threats, and he was underhanded enough to have arranged spying on Rory in an attempt to force her hand. He also seemed like the sort that might consider himself above the law, and he had more to lose if Rory married Hank.

"When the police find out you've woken up, I'm sure they'll want to interview you. Both of you," he said, turning to Rory. "After all, your romance is the primary motive for someone to want to harm Hank."

Rory's grip on him grew painfully tight. "If someone tried to hurt Hank on my account, they'd better watch out. I'll… I'll… I don't know what I'll do, but I swear I will see justice served." She turned to O'Donnell. "Take me home, Bill. I need to change clothes, and there's someone I need to see. I'll be back this afternoon, Hank. I promise."

Deeply uneasy, Hank said, "Please don't do anything foolish, Rory. If someone's trying to kill me, then you're in danger too. Promise me you won't take any unnecessary risks."

Rory's lips thinned to a tight line. "I promise I'll be back this afternoon, Hank. Be good."

With that, she dragged O'Donnell out the door.

Hank gritted his teeth. That was not the promise he asked for. But Rory had never been one to play it safe. He loved that about her…except when there was a murderer on the loose. This was going to be one long and anxious day, and there wasn't a thing he could do about it.

29

*R*ory hadn't seen Aunt Alva since her birthday party, but it was time to humble herself and make peace with at least part of her family. When she rang at Aunt Alva's front door, the footman led her to the drawing room, which she took as a good sign. At least she wasn't being denied entry.

Aunt Alva wore her most imperious and stern look as she came in and sat across from Rory.

"I've heard some shocking things about you, young lady, and I expect an explanation of where you've disappeared to. I don't hold with what August did, but I'm deeply disappointed in you."

"I'm sorry for disappearing, Aunt Alva." She had to start with an apology, she knew, or Aunt Alva wouldn't listen to anything else. "I'm engaged to a man Papa doesn't approve of. He caught us together and threw me out."

"You should have come to me. I don't approve of some of the things I've heard, but I believe strongly a young woman ought to be free to choose her spouse and ought not to be forced into marriage. I could have helped you."

Aunt Alva's disapproval was a terrible weight around her shoulders. She loved her aunt with all her heart. Somehow, she had to make her understand. "I know, Aunt Alva. I thought about it, and I nearly came here. But I decided it was time for me to try my wings and see if I could survive on my own. I've learned I can. I have a job and a place to live, and I'm doing just fine."

"You aren't staying with your paramour?" One accusing eyebrow rose as she said the words.

"No, I'm not. And he's my fiancé. We're to be married as soon as he's out of the hospital."

"Hospital?"

Rory told her aunt the story of Hank's accident and the police finding evidence of sabotage, as well as their suspicions of her father. "I need your help, Aunt Alva. I want to go see my father and confront him about this, but I don't feel safe going alone. I was hoping you would come with me. I don't believe he did it, but I need to hear him say it."

"I've known your father longer than you have, and he is a ruthless businessman. But I cannot believe he would stoop so low. I'll come with you if you wish because I would like to see you two reconciled. I couldn't begin to guess who is behind this sabotage, but I'm certain it isn't him."

"Thank you, Aunt Alva. That's all I ask." Relief flooded her. With Aunt Alva by her side, she would be safe. She needn't fear her father trying to force her marriage to Edward again.

***

HALF AN HOUR LATER, she and Aunt Alva were escorted into her father's study. He looked to Rory like he was ready to breathe fire when he saw her, but one look from Aunt Alva quelled him. "I'm a busy man, Aurora. The police have already wasted half of my morning with nonsense. I won't have you wasting the other half. If you've come to beg me to relent, you've wasted your time."

"I've come to tell you I'm doing just fine without your money, and I have no intention of asking anything of you ever again. I also wanted to let you know I'll be marrying Hank as soon as he's out of the hospital. I take it the police told you why he's there?" She gave her father a sharp look over his enormous desk, holding his gaze and not looking away. She needed to see every tiny reaction right now.

Please let him be innocent.

"Yes, yes. Someone sabotaged his airplane. And they think I have something to do with it because I lost my temper when I learned the true identity of Albert Jones. Ridiculous."

She caught his eye again and held it. "Is it, Papa?"

The silence stretched out as they stared each other down.

"Aurora, I loathe the man for the liberties he's taken with you, but I'm not a murderer. I swear to you I had nothing to do with this. And I'm deeply distressed you would think such a thing."

She continued to hold his gaze. "I want to believe you, Papa."

"When a man is my enemy, I confront him. I don't hide in the dark and secretly try to do him harm. Sabotage is cowardly. Have you ever known me to be a coward?"

Taking a deep breath, she shook her head. "You aren't a coward. I know that."

"Then I ask you to take my word that it wasn't me. Ask that young man of yours who his enemies are. It must be someone else he's gravely offended. Hardly a surprise, given his behavior with you. Now are we done here? I have more important things to attend to than the spurious suspicions of my runaway daughter."

"I didn't run away, Papa. You sent me away." She took Aunt Alva's hand for support.

"And you refused to come back. The clock is ticking, young lady. If you don't come to your senses and marry Edward, then you are no longer my daughter."

Blood rushed to her cheeks as she clenched her fists. "I have a right to choose who I spend my life with, and I will never ever agree to spend it with Edward."

Aunt Alva stepped between them. "August, it isn't right to try to force her to do your bidding. She's a grown woman, and she's proven she can live without your help, or mine for that matter. I don't like this pilot of hers any more than you do, but under the circumstances, don't you think it would be best if he made an honest woman of her and wed her? If Edward Windham is still after her despite all that's happened, then he is only after the money. Do you truly want her married to someone like that?"

"I think it shows how honorable Edward is that he's willing to stand by the engagement despite all that has transpired."

Rory shuddered. "I'm not marrying Edward, no matter what you do to me," she said, taking Aunt Alva's hand again.

"August, I think it's time you let it go," Aunt Alva said gently but firmly.

He stormed around his desk and towered above Alva, who was undaunted. "I will not let it go. She's *my* daughter, and I don't appreciate your meddling, Alva. I will do everything in my power that is legal to put an end to this nonsense with the pilot and to marry her to Edward, as has been planned all along. I cannot force her, and I cannot murder him, even though at the moment I'd rather like to do both. But I am not waving the white flag of surrender. Not yet."

Alva turned to Rory. "I think we're done here, don't you?"

Rory nodded, and they swiftly exited the premises, stopping only briefly to find her former maid Kelly, who was working in the kitchen now that Rory was gone. Rory paid her back and thanked her profusely before hurrying out the door.

As they got into Aunt Alva's car, Rory felt tears starting to roll down her cheeks. Wiping them away, she said, "At least I managed to remain stoic while we were inside."

To think until a few weeks ago, that had been her home. It broke her heart to walk those familiar halls again and feel like a stranger. Standing amid all that opulence, she was surprised to find she didn't miss it. She was happier than she'd ever been, living in her modest apartment above a flower shop. And she was going to marry her pilot, no matter what anyone thought.

"Thank you, Aunt Alva. I don't think I could have faced him alone."

Alva patted her hand. "Unreasonable man. I do wish you weren't marrying so far beneath you, dear, but it's the only thing to be done at this point. Too many people know you've been carrying on with him. It's the only solution. If only your father would come to his senses and realize it! But enough about him. What about you? Are you going to leave behind that hovel you're living in and come stay with me, or have you, too, departed from your senses?"

Wiping away the last of her tears, she answered, "It's not a hovel. It's perfectly pleasant, and I'm going back to it this afternoon. I promised Hank I would check on him at the hospital."

Aunt Alva shook her head in disapproval. "How are you getting back to Mineola?"

"The same way I got here. By train."

"Saints alive! No, my dear. At the very least, you must let me send you in my car."

Rory laughed. "You act as if I'm in danger from bandits on the Long Island Railroad."

Fanning herself, Aunt Alva said, "Well, it is the countryside, dear."

"All right, I'll take the car."

"Percival," she said to the driver. "Drop me off at home and take Miss Belmont to Mineola, please."

"Yes, ma'am."

Soon, Rory was driving through the Long Island countryside with the windows down and the wind in her hair. Her heart felt lighter with every mile they drove away from Manhattan. Out here, her father's threats dwindled in her mind, and her confidence in her own course of action returned. In a short while, she would see Hank, and everything would be better. Maybe she could even steal a kiss when no one was looking.

Arriving at the hospital, she thanked the driver and rushed inside. Hank was still in room twelve, and he was sitting up, which was a positive development. Sitting was difficult when she left him this morning. He even managed to turn his head when she came in.

Who cared what the doctor thought? She had to kiss him. Checking quickly that no one was looking, she pressed her lips to his and gave him a proper greeting.

"If this is how you say hello, I'm very much looking forward to getting married," he said as she released him.

She smiled, cheeks aflame.

"Where did you go this morning?" he asked, concern in his eyes. "I was worried you might go see your father."

She looked at her hands, unable to meet his gaze. "I did," she said quietly. "I went to Aunt Alva first, and I brought her with me. She's the only person I know who intimidates Papa. I had to speak with him. I had to know if..." She couldn't finish the sentence.

"Did he try to force you to do anything? Because I'll—"

"You'll what? You're lying in a hospital bed." She laughed incredulously.

"I'd think of something."

She shook her head. "I was safe with Aunt Alva. Hank, I don't think it was him. He said sabotage is cowardly, and he's right. My father is many things, but a coward is not one of them. Did you know he's one of the oldest men ever to receive a commission from the Army? He was sixty-four years old when he signed up to fight. The man relishes confrontation. He always has. I can't believe he would do something so underhanded."

"Even if he's innocent, I don't like that you took the risk of going to see him."

She put a hand on his. "I choose my risks, Hank. He's my father. I had to know."

"I accept that, but I don't have to like it," he said, squeezing her hand. "Has he given up yet on getting you to marry Windham?"

She shook her head. "The man is stubborn. Even Aunt Alva thinks you and I should wed, and she's almost as stuffy about these things as he is. I'd like to invite her to the wedding, by the way. And of course, I'll invite Evelyn and some of my suffragette friends."

He smiled. "Anything that makes you happy, princess. You should invite that widow you helped, Ann Prince, too. O'Donnell is sweet on her. I assume the entire O'Donnell family is invited."

"And you'll be inviting your fellow pilots?"

"And Major Fleet, and a few of the mechanics."

"We need to make a list. I'll go see if I can borrow a pen and paper."

She went out to the front desk and asked. The attendant obliged, and Rory hurried back.

"All right, let's see," she said, settling down by his bedside table to write. "My aunt, Evelyn and my other suffragette friends, the O'Donnells, and who else?"

At that moment, a police inspector knocked on the door. "Excuse me, Lieutenant Hawley? I'd like to ask you a few questions. And, young lady, may I ask your name?"

"Aurora Belmont, his fiancée."

The inspector nodded. "Pleased to meet you, Miss Belmont. I'm afraid we have some questions for you too."

Rory swallowed hard. She wanted to help, but she'd rather have dental surgery than answer questions about how she split with Edward. Nonetheless, there was nothing she wouldn't endure to see justice served to anyone who hurt Hank.

30

Hank didn't like the police interviewing Rory, but at least he could be present while they did it. He didn't like her going to see her father either. He was supposed to be the one by her side, standing up for her, not some aunt he'd met for five seconds and never spoken a word to. He was a man of action, her loyal knight. Being stuck in bed while so much was happening around him was maddening.

"Officer—" he said.

"Inspector Green," the man corrected.

"Inspector Green, what would you like to know?"

"Who can you think of that might have a grudge against you at the moment?" He took out a notepad and pencil.

"I don't have many enemies, inspector. I've always steered clear of trouble. But my engagement to Miss Belmont has caused some bitterness with her father and her former fiancé."

Hank shifted, pushing himself a little higher. His head still ached dully in the background, and he had an itch on his leg inside the cast that was driving him mad.

"For the record, that would be Major August Belmont and Senator Edward Windham of Connecticut?"

"Correct."

He tried to shift his leg within the cast to get at the itch, but pain shot through him when he moved.

"Are you all right, Lieutenant Hawley? I can give you a minute and interview Miss Belmont first."

He must have winced. This was all so frustrating. "I'm fine, just a little sore all over. You know, from being thrown from an airplane. Keep going."

"Have either of those gentlemen made threats against you?"

Hank smiled bitterly. "Both of them. Senator Windham threatened me in Washington D.C. about a month ago, and from what I hear, Major Belmont threatened me a little less than a week ago after learning of my relationship with Rory."

The inspector made a note. "Do you have reason to believe either of them would carry through with their threats?"

Hank squirmed again, trying to get comfortable, but nothing felt right.

"I thought they would try to damage me professionally or have me sent back to the front. I never anticipated something like this."

The inspector tapped his pen. "And for the record, why specifically did they have reason to resent you, to the best of your knowledge?"

"Major Belmont wants his daughter to marry the senator, not a nobody like me."

Clearing his throat, the inspector prompted, "And Senator Windham?"

"The senator stood to gain access to a significant fortune by marrying Miss Belmont. I've ruined his hopes both romantically and financially."

"Thank you, that will do for now, Lieutenant Hawley," the inspector said, turning a page in his notebook.

"Miss Belmont."

"Yes?"

She twisted her hands in her lap. Hank reached out, took her hand, and held it, wanting to give her all the support he could.

"Do you know of anyone aside from your father and the senator that might want to hurt Lieutenant Hawley?"

"No," she answered firmly.

"And why specifically might they be angry with Lieutenant Hawley?"

She looked at Hank and looked at her own hands. He'd purposefully left out any information that might be humiliating to her. Was she worried it might come out?

"What Hank said was true. My father doesn't want me to marry Hank, and Edward stands to lose a substantial fortune if we don't wed."

"And when did you get engaged to Lieutenant Hawley, Miss Belmont?"

Oh dear. The inspector was going to dig. Hank squeezed Rory's hand tighter.

She gave him a worried glance and said, "This morning."

"I see," said the inspector, scribbling frantically. "So well after the threats to Lieutenant Hawley. Do you have any idea why they might have threatened Lieutenant Hawley if you weren't yet engaged?"

Her eyes were wide, and her hands clenched as she looked at him and then back at the inspector. She let out a tiny sigh.

"I would ask you to keep this private, but they had reason to believe I had been intimate with him."

"And were you intimate with Lieutenant Hawley?"

"Yes," she said so quietly she was barely audible. Her face was bright red. "Edward jumped to the wrong conclusion before anything happened, but soon after, things progressed between us."

"And how did your father find out about Lieutenant Hawley?"

"Edward had someone spying on me. A Pinkerton he hired heard us together in a hotel room and told Edward. Edward told my father. He tried to use it as an excuse to move up the wedding and prevent any more incidents."

"Very interesting."

Rory was shaking now. It broke Hank's heart to see her like this, as if she hadn't already been through enough today with the encounter with her father.

The inspector gave her a kindly smile. "Just a few more questions, Miss Belmont. We're almost done. What did your father do when he found out about you and Lieutenant Hawley?"

A tear dripped down her cheek. "He threw me out of the house and cut me off. He said the only way I could come back was if I agreed to marry Edward."

"And instead, you decided to marry Lieutenant Hawley, is that correct?"

She straightened her back and wiped away her tears. "I decided to live independently. I secured a job and a home of my own. I agreed to marry Lieutenant Hawley only after he gave me certain assurances about our marriage."

"I see, Miss Belmont," he said, continuing to jot down notes in his pad. Then he closed his notebook. "Thank you for your cooperation. Please rest assured that I have no intention of mentioning any personal details to anyone unless it is necessary to build our case. If I can preserve your privacy and dignity, I will."

"I appreciate that, Inspector."

As soon as the inspector was gone, Hank pulled Rory into a hug. "I'm so sorry you had to go through that, princess."

"I'm all right, Hank. It was important. Your safety is more important to me than my dignity. Besides, the people I care about most already know."

He knew if he pressed, she would only remind him it was her choice, so he let it go. It didn't stop him from wanting to wring the neck of everyone that ever made her cry. She was stronger and braver than any woman he'd known, but he wished she didn't have to be. He wished she could be allowed to follow her own compass without everyone standing in judgment all the time.

Moments after the inspector left, a new doctor came in to check on him. After a cursory exam, he declared, "If you continue to improve like this, I'll let you go home tomorrow morning. Is there someone who can help you out for the next few weeks as you recover?"

"Yes," Rory answered for him.

"Good. Between his leg and his concussion, he'll need to be off his feet as much as possible."

Hank had several thoughts on things he could do off his feet with Rory. But he shoved them away. "I'm right here, you know. I'm sure I can manage just fine."

The doctor stared at him and turned to Rory. "Watch out for him. The ones who think they're fine are always the worst patients."

"I will, doctor," she said.

He made a few notes on his chart and said, "Well then, I'll see you again this evening, Lieutenant Hawley."

With that, the doctor left.

Rory sat back and failed to stifle a yawn.

"You should go home, princess. You've had a rough day, and you barely slept. Go home. Eat. Sleep. You can come back tomorrow morning to bring me home."

She looked like she was about to object but decided against it. "All right, I'll go if you promise to rest too. I know if I stick around, I'll only get us in trouble again."

Her eyes traveled to his lips, and she swallowed.

"Yes, you had better go," he said, his gaze dipping to her lips and then her breasts and then her hips. He sat still for a moment, unable to drag his eyes away, then shook himself and winced. "I should rest," he said as much to himself as to her.

"I'll see you tomorrow," she said, standing to go.

He caught her hand and kissed it. "I love you." It was too much to hope that she would say it back, but he needed to speak his heart.

"I love you too," she said quietly with a subtle smile just for him.

Rory loved him! His heart soared. He watched, breathless, as she kissed him on the forehead and left. Then he leaned back and closed his eyes.

You lucky bastard, he thought to himself as he lay there. He never imagined he'd find himself with someone like Rory. If he ever got married, he imagined it would be to a nice farm girl or a shop girl, someone staid and reliable who kept him in check. They'd move back to Michigan and the farm to live a quiet family life. A monotonous life, if he were being honest with himself. With Rory, life would be anything but monotonous.

She loved him. She said the words. He'd hoped but never dared to expect that she would. The marriage agreement worked its magic, he supposed. He never thought a legal document could be so romantic. Rory needed someone who understood her, who could offer her thrills and excitement but also the assurance of independence. He finally understood that, and now she was his.

His reverie was interrupted by a knock. "Hawley, are you awake in there?"

O'Donnell. Of course.

"I'm awake now," Hank grumbled as he pushed himself up to sitting.

"Excellent. There's someone I'd like you to meet."

"I hope you don't mind," said a feminine voice he didn't recognize. "If we're disturbing you, we'll go."

O'Donnell appeared around the curtain, towing the war widow with the green eyes and auburn hair, who wore a touching look of concern.

"Hawley, this is Ann Prince. You may remember that I met her at Rory's birthday. When I told her what happened, she asked to come and visit you. I can't imagine what for, you tiny-brained baboon."

"Bill," she admonished. "The man is injured."

Hank laughed. "Don't take him seriously. I never do."

"I hope you don't mind my intrusion," she said. "I…" She paused and looked at O'Donnell who gave her an encouraging nod. "I didn't get to see my husband at the end. He was hospitalized for injuries but caught a fever that killed him. I had things that I wanted to say but never had the chance. I wanted to speak to you because I wanted you to know I think you're very brave."

"He's brave? What about me?" O'Donnell objected.

"You are too. But what I mean to say is I don't blame flying for my husband's death. We both knew the dangers that came with being a pilot. I loved him for facing them valiantly every day in the service of our country. I know he worried that he was risking too much with a new wife at home. He didn't want to leave me heartbroken and alone. But if I had it to do over again, I would still have married him, even knowing how little time I had with him."

She dabbed a tear away with her handkerchief.

"Bill told me about you and Miss Belmont. I wanted to tell you that you don't have to choose between love and flying. You probably think you do, especially after this. But women who love pilots know the risks. We chose brave men who explore the skies and push the boundaries of human achievement. We don't love pilots despite their chosen vocation. We love them because of it. Whatever you choose to do next, don't give up flying for Miss Belmont. Make the right decision for you, and she'll love you for it."

Hank didn't know what to say. His whole adult life, he'd feared commitment because of his choice to be a pilot, and now that he was ready to commit, he was certain he had to give it up. But if a war widow who had been through the worst possible tragedy didn't think he should quit, perhaps it was worth rethinking. He'd already put in the paperwork to resign his commission and told Glenn Curtiss he accepted the job. Maybe he could speak to Curtiss about being a test pilot as part of his duties. If he didn't have to choose between love and flying, then he wanted both.

He looked up at Mrs. Prince. She wiped away her tears with O'Donnell by her side, holding her hand.

"Thank you for sharing, Mrs. Prince. I appreciate your kind words more than you'll ever know. I know it can't have been easy to come here today."

"It wasn't, but as soon as Bill told me, I knew I had to." She clutched O'Donnell's hand, and Hank didn't miss O'Donnell's big puppy-dog eyes as he looked at her.

"I hope it has given you some comfort and relief to speak what was in your heart. I know your husband would have been deeply moved, hearing what you have to say. I know I was."

"That's very kind of you. We should let you rest. Thanks again for hearing me out."

She turned to look at O'Donnell, beaming.

Hank smiled. "I'll be sure to invite you both to the wedding."

"Wedding?" O'Donnell said in a high-pitched voice.

"She finally accepted my proposal. We're planning to marry as soon as I get this bandage off my head."

O'Donnell looked like he was going to combust from excitement. "He's getting married! Did you hear that?" he said to Mrs. Prince, who smiled shyly. "Hank Hawley is getting married. I never thought I'd see the day. Can I tell Pritchard and Thompson?"

"You can tell whoever you want."

O'Donnell took Mrs. Prince by the waist and spun her around. "I can tell whoever I want. Did you hear that?" He kissed her on the cheek, and she turned bright red.

"Bill," she said, grinning and shaking her head, "we should let your friend get some rest."

"I'll see you later, Hawley. Congratulations, buddy! I'm truly happy for you."

They left him alone, murmuring to each other as they walked out the door. He couldn't help wondering how long it would be before those two walked down the aisle together.

31

*R*ory walked to the hospital just after sunrise, anxious to get him home and have him all to herself. The woman at the front desk recognized her and waved her through.

Hank was just waking up. She kissed his forehead and caressed his bristly cheek.

"I need a shave," he said as she pulled away. "And a bath," he said, sniffing. "I'm sorry you're seeing me like this."

She furrowed her brow and shook her head. "Nonsense."

"Rory, how would you feel if I asked Mr. Curtiss about being a test pilot from time to time so that I don't have to give up flying?"

She grinned from ear to ear. "Simply smashing, darling. There's nothing more dashing than a test pilot."

"Oh? Any test pilots I should know about?"

"Absurd." As if she'd look at anyone else when she had Hank.

"And you wouldn't worry about my safety?" There was something behind his eyes that made her think this was a desperately important question.

"Of course, I'd worry. How could I not? But when has a little risk ever bothered me? I think it's a grand idea."

The look in his eyes made her want to throw caution to the wind and kiss him to pieces right then.

A nurse came in with a breakfast tray. Hank practically dove for the coffee.

"Thank you, nurse," he said.

She gave him a kind nod.

"Mmm. Better than yesterday. Nice and hot."

"Don't burn your tongue," warned the nurse. "You have enough injuries as it is."

With a smile, she left them alone.

Moments later, the doctor who caught them kissing came in. He looked from one to the other with a censorious gaze and then turned to Hank. "You have recovered sufficiently that we can allow you to go home. It will take another few weeks for your head to fully recover. During that time, you must get plenty of rest and avoid exerting yourself in any way." The doctor looked back and forth between the two of them with narrowed eyes. "Nor should you let yourself get upset. You can come back two weeks from today to have your stitches out. You should change your bandage daily. I'll give you some cream to put on your head wound as well as the bandages you need."

He flipped a page on the chart and gave Hank another pointed look.

"Your leg will take longer to heal. You'll be in that cast for six to eight weeks. During that time, you must use crutches to walk, and you must make sure not to get your cast wet when you bathe. Do you understand?"

Hank nodded.

"You will come back here for a check-up at six weeks, and we will determine whether the cast is ready to come off."

"Yes, doctor."

"I'll be right back with your—"

He was interrupted by a commotion outside, and a moment

later, her father strode into the room. Her whole body went rigid at the sight of him.

"Aurora, what are you doing here? It's indecent for you to be here at this hour."

"What am I doing here? What are *you* doing here, Papa? Haven't you done enough already?" It was only with difficulty that she resisted the urge to throw things at him.

"You said yesterday you were going to marry as soon as he was out of the hospital. I thought I had better hurry if I was going to catch him before it was too late." Turning to Hank, he said, "I know I said you wouldn't get a cent from me, but this has to stop. Young man, what is it going to cost me to convince you not to marry Aurora?"

She clenched her fists and faced him down. "Papa, I am not a racehorse you can buy and sell. You threw me out, and I am never coming back, no matter what you do."

"No amount of money will convince me not to marry Rory," Hank said, swinging his leg down with difficulty and using his crutches to stand. Even hunched on crutches, he loomed over her father. "For the last time, I don't want your money, Major."

"Nonsense," her father said. "Every man has his price."

"Papa, stop. Enough. Do you remember when you married Eleanor, and the Vanderbilts threatened to end their contract with your company? Did it stop you?"

"Of course not. I fail to see your point," he fumed.

"My point is that I love Hank, and nothing you say or do will change my mind about marrying him, nor will it change his," she said, looking at Hank. "We love each other like you and Eleanor did, and we're willing to face the consequences. The sooner you accept that, the better."

The doctor rushed in and implored, "Ladies and gentlemen, this is a hospital. I'll thank you to keep your voices down, or I'm going to call the police."

"No need to call us. We're right here," said Inspector Green, striding into the room. "Major Belmont, if you don't leave right away, I'm going to place you under arrest. You're still under suspicion for the sabotage of Mr. Hawley's plane, and even you aren't above the law."

"Wait! No! Papa didn't do it," she said.

"Can you prove that, Miss Belmont?"

"Well, no, but—"

"Your father had motive and opportunity, being a Major with significant access to both the pilots and the airplanes. However, his secretary and his wife have vouched for his whereabouts over the last week. Whether they can be trusted to be truthful is an open question. Until concrete evidence of guilt or innocence emerges, he will continue to be a person of interest. Mr. Belmont, I suggest you consider your next actions very carefully."

Her father stepped right up to the inspector and stared him down with a steely gaze. The inspector didn't budge.

"Leave, Major," said Inspector Green. "I have my handcuffs ready if you refuse to cooperate."

Rory watched as her father sized up the inspector and then looked at the two officers flanking the door. He was outmatched, and he knew it. "I will cooperate, as I seem to have no choice, but I promise you will pay for your insolence."

"Threatening me is unwise, Major. It just makes things look worse for you."

Rory watched, speechless, as her father was escorted out of the hospital by the police.

Hank sat down hard on the bed, looking exhausted from even that short moment of standing. She rushed to him. "Are you all right? Did you hurt yourself standing up like that?"

"I'm all right. Just a little unsteady on my feet is all, princess. I'm more worried about you."

She sat next to him and took his hand. "I'll be fine." Or as fine as one could be with a father under suspicion for attempted murder of one's fiancé.

The doctor cleared his throat. "Uh, well, a nurse will bring you some cream and extra bandages, and then you will be free to go. There's a note here saying the Army covered the cost of your stay, since the accident happened while you were in active service. So, there's no need to worry about payment. But you are under the strictest of orders to rest, Lieutenant Hawley. Are we clear?"

"Yes doctor."

"Very well. I'll leave you be. Best wishes for a speedy recovery, Lieutenant Hawley."

A nurse came in a few minutes later to finish his discharge, and they were free to go. They headed back to his house together at last. After all that had transpired, she wanted nothing more than a nice long afternoon alone with the man she loved.

"Lunch smells delicious, princess—worlds better than that swill they served at the hospital."

They sat down together in his breakfast nook, and she couldn't hold back a grin of pride.

"I'm impressed," he said after his first few bites. "Who knew the princess of New York knew how to cook?"

"I'm not completely useless, Hank. You may have noticed I have an independent streak. I like to do things for myself. Just because I didn't have to didn't mean I didn't want to learn. I'll have you know I can also change a flat tire on a car, keep household accounts, and mend clothing."

Hank grinned. "You never cease to surprise me, Rory," he said, taking her hand and kissing it. "I'm a very lucky man."

His velvety voice sent heat straight to her core, and she leaned close, brushing her lips against his. "Yes, you are."

He pulled her closer and kissed her deep and hard, exactly like she wanted him to. This was the kiss she'd been dreaming of ever since she decided to say yes, and she savored every moment of it.

A knock on the door interrupted them, much to her annoyance. Reluctantly, she released him. "I'll get it."

Opening the door, she saw Edward, unshaven and wild-eyed, accompanied by her father. Before she could register what was happening, Edward shoved her out of the way and headed straight for Hank, pulling back his fist.

"No," she screamed and threw herself at Edward, knocking him sideways. He was her worst nightmare made flesh, and she had no intention of letting him anywhere near the man she loved with all her heart.

"Edward, for the love of God, what are you doing? I thought you were coming to apologize to Rory." Her father ran toward them and tried to pull her away from Edward, but she wouldn't let go.

"Get off me, you bitch," Edward growled, trying to free himself from her clutches.

She wrapped her arms around his torso as tightly as she could, trapping his arms. Edward might be bigger and stronger than she was, but no one was going to touch her Hank.

They wrestled in an awkward dance and ran into her father, knocking him backwards to the floor. Hank hoisted himself from his seat.

"I've been wanting to do this for a long time, Senator." Hank's fist flew, and there was a horrifying crack as Edward slumped against her, knocked unconscious. Releasing her hold, she let her former fiancé crumple in a heap on the floor.

"Christ, that felt good," Hank said, leaning on the table for support. "We should tie him up before he wakes up. I've got some rope in the basement." He pointed to the door on the other side of the kitchen.

"Good God. I had no idea he was going to attack Lieutenant

Hawley. You must believe me, Aurora." Her father staggered to his feet.

Giving Papa a dirty look, Rory turned her back on him and hurried downstairs, spotting the rope almost immediately. Rope in hand, she tore back up the stairs. Edward lay motionless and face down on the kitchen tiles. She tied the tightest knot she could manage around his wrists, securing them behind his back. As she finished, Edward began to groan.

"You can't do this to me. I'm a senator." Edward tried to roll over but couldn't quite make it. "I'll have you arrested!"

That was rich!

Hank guffawed. "You're the one trespassing on my private property and assaulting my fiancée. And I'm pretty sure you're responsible for my little accident the other day. In fact, Rory, why don't you go call Inspector Green, and we'll see who gets arrested when he shows up. I'll keep your father and the good senator company while you call."

Rory headed to the other room, pushing past her father, and picked up the phone. She asked the operator for the inspector. Fortunately, Inspector Green answered immediately. As briefly as she could, she explained the situation.

"We've been looking for the senator. I'll be right over," the inspector said and hung up.

Ten minutes later, he arrived. Rory let him in, and he took in the scene with Edward still lying prone on the floor, bleeding from his nose, and her father glowering at Edward from an armchair.

"Thank God you're here, Inspector," Edward said. "Look what they've done to me. I'm a senator, for Christ's sake!"

Inspector Green put his hands on his hips and loomed over Edward. "I don't think you'll be in politics much longer, *Senator*. You're under arrest for trespassing, assault, tampering with government property, and attempted murder."

"What do you mean, 'attempted murder'? Obviously, I've been set up. Can't you see I'm the victim here?"

Inspector Green shook his head and raised an eyebrow. "I just received word from our colleagues in D.C. that a Pinkerton agent you hired decided to sing. He says you bribed a mechanic to sabotage the airplane when the Pinkerton refused to do it himself. We're still tracking the mechanic down, but rest assured he will be brought to justice for his part in this. You're safe now, Lieutenant Hawley."

Rory took a deep breath and let it out slowly. "I knew my father was innocent. He's not the sort of man that would stoop to sabotage. I could imagine him threatening Hank with a shotgun before I could see him hiring others do his dirty work."

"Thank you for your work, Inspector," Hank said. "I'll rest easier knowing that the perpetrator has been found and locked up. I know this can't have been an easy case for you, given the people involved. I'm grateful for your diligence."

"All part of the job, Lieutenant Hawley." The inspector pulled Edward to his feet and shoved him none too gently toward the door. "If you don't mind, I'm going to go lock this fellow up."

As the inspector left with his prisoner, Hank hobbled to the sitting room, propping his injured leg on the ottoman. Rory moved their coffee cups and poured a cup with a splash of milk for her father. Her heart was still pumping furiously from the confrontation, and she took deep and even breaths to slow it down.

Papa took the coffee cup silently, looked around the modest sitting room, and sighed, shaking his head. "You've made a pleasant home here, it seems, despite my best efforts to thwart you."

Rory gritted her teeth and took a seat beside Hank on the floral sofa, wondering what offensive nonsense her father would spout next.

Clearing his throat, Papa said, "This has given me a great deal to think about. I confess I'm quite shocked about Edward. I'm sorry I let him anywhere near you, Aurora. I had no idea what kind of man he was, or I certainly wouldn't have brought him here today."

Rory nodded but remained silent. Her father's apologies were rare as rubies, but this was still too little too late.

Her father took a sip of coffee. "I can't say I approve of the man you've chosen to marry, but I took to heart what you said about me and Eleanor. And, you may not know it, but your mother's parents didn't approve of her marrying me either."

Rory stopped breathing. Papa never mentioned Mama out loud.

"I know I don't speak about your mother much," he continued, staring at his shoes. "You're so much like her it hurts. I loved her with all my heart, you know. I'm sure you don't think I have a heart after everything that's happened, but I do. My heart broke the day she died, and I haven't been the same man since. I… I lost the love of my life the day you were born."

Something clicked in Rory's mind. "My birthday. Ever since I was little, I wondered why you could hardly stand to look at me on my birthday." She was still angry with him, but her heart ached at the thought of her father seeing his loss every time he looked at her.

"It's not your fault, of course, that you remind me of what I lost. I haven't been the father I should have been to you. I know that." He looked up into her eyes, and the pain she saw there made her gasp.

"I'll try to be better," he said earnestly. "Starting today. I know you want to marry this young man."

"Yes, Papa," she said, holding his gaze, hardly able to believe what she was hearing.

"I don't approve of what he's done, but he could hardly have done it without your active cooperation. I appreciate that he's now doing the right thing and offering marriage."

Was he saying he was willing to accept their union at long last?

With a tentative smile, Rory said, "He's done more than that, Papa. You should see our marriage contract."

"I have it right here," said Hank, retrieving it from a side table and handing it to her father.

"He's promising not to touch any money I make or inherit. He's promised to give me my independence so that our marriage is one of equals rather than one where I am entirely dependent on him."

Her father flipped through the agreement swiftly, with avid attention. Then he looked up at Hank. "Perhaps I've underestimated you, young man. I thought you were after my money, but this proves you aren't. I don't like the liberties you've taken with my daughter, but perhaps you're more honorable than I thought. Under the circumstances, I suppose I must give my blessing for this marriage."

Rory squealed and hugged Hank, planting a kiss on his bristly cheek. Then she got up and hugged her father, whose muscles went rigid, but after a moment, he relaxed and patted her back. This was more than she'd ever dared hope. "Oh, Papa, thank you! I love him ever so much, and I love you too. It's been awful being estranged from you like this. I know you're going to love Hank once you get to know him. He's so smart and brave."

"Perhaps I will," he said with a strained smile. "In the meantime, I hope you'll agree to come home at least until the wedding."

"I can't, Papa. I have to stay out here to help Hank as he recovers."

"At least tell me you're going to keep the wedding arrangements we already made for your marriage to Edward. The date is only two and a half weeks away. There's no reason for you to waste all the effort and expense we've already gone to. We've already reserved Trinity Church for the wedding and rented out Delmonico's for the reception."

Rory gave Hank an inquiring look. He shrugged and smiled. "All right, Papa. We'll go through with the big wedding if you insist. That's when we were planning to wed anyway."

"Wonderful," her father said. "I hope you can forgive me for being so pigheaded."

"Of course, Papa. And I hope you can forgive me for being so impulsive. It is more my fault than Hank's. I gave him very little choice."

"I can imagine." He gave Hank a commiserating look. "I apologize for…well, I apologize, Lieutenant. I tried to get Glenn Curtiss to rescind his job offer, but he was adamant that he had to have you on his staff. He even went so far as to suggest that it was unpatriotic to try to stand in the way. Major Fleet wouldn't hear a word against you either."

"Papa!" How dare he try to interfere in Hank's life like that!

"I'm very sorry. I was being an ass and doing the same thing to you that the Vanderbilts did to me when I married Eleanor. Young man, I hope you will forgive me."

"Of course, sir." Hank held out his hand, and Papa shook it.

"I'm glad that's all water under the bridge now. I should be going. I have business to attend to, now that this nonsense has all been resolved. I wish you two the best, and I hope to see you soon. Don't be a stranger before the wedding, or after, for that matter." He turned to go and mumbled so low she hardly heard him, "I love you, Rory."

What did he just say? She never thought she'd hear those three beautiful words from her father, not in a million years. "I love you too, Papa!"

Before she could throw her arms around his neck and hug

him, he was gone. Of course, he was. Papa had never been comfortable with sentiment. But he'd said it. Her heart was full.

Hank wrapped his arms around her from behind as the door closed. "I'm glad you two made up."

"So am I." Gladder than she could ever say. Her life was so full of love, and she couldn't wait to see what the future held.

3 2

his was Hank's first time at Delmonico's, and he couldn't wait to leave. The dark wood-paneled walls of the curious, triangular-shaped space oozed sophistication. The steak had been excellent, the baked Alaska intriguing, and the service superbly snooty. But all he wanted was to be alone with his wife.

He smiled. His wife. That gorgeous woman spinning around the room, charming everyone in sight, was all his. He was stuck at the table, his leg preventing both dancing and mingling, but this evening was never about him. This was her night to shine. He couldn't begrudge her, even if he was antsy to leave.

For their wedding night, they reserved the same room at the Waldorf where he'd stayed as "Albert Jones" on her birthday. Their honeymoon in Europe, courtesy of Aunt Alva, was postponed until he recovered from his broken leg. Tomorrow, they were headed back to his place, but tonight would be a night to remember.

Some cousin twirled Rory around as her current dance partner. All Hank could do was admire from a distance.

"You look lonely over here, Hank. I've come to cheer you up."

Ma.

Hank smiled.

"Have a seat. Join me. I'm so glad you and Kate were able to come out for the wedding." Ma was dressed in her finest, complete with a bustle, which was about a decade out of fashion. Nonetheless, she was a good-looking woman for her age and had no lack of interest from the older gentlemen in attendance, not that she paid them any mind.

"Wouldn't miss it for the world. Never thought you'd marry a swell, but I'm happy for you. You two are the cutest little love-birds I've ever seen."

"Where's Kate?"

Ma waved her hand dismissively. "She's over there some-where talking to a young woman named Evelyn about suffrage. I'd like to have the right to vote as much as the next woman, but do they have to talk politics at a wedding?"

Hank laughed. Little did Ma know that Evelyn was a force of nature who did as she pleased, much like Rory herself. "There are only so many comments one can make about how lovely the ceremony was. If it makes them happy, they are welcome to it."

Ma accepted a glass of champagne from a passing waiter. "It was a lovely ceremony. And mercifully short. Was that on purpose?"

"Yes. I may be on the mend, but I can only stand for so long on those crutches." He was rather proud of himself for making it through the whole thing without incident. It helped that his beautiful bride completely distracted him. She was breathtaking in her dress. It was a bit daring, but then so was Rory. It had sheer sleeves, and sheer fabric dripped down to her ankles, while the satin skirt beneath only reached down to mid-calf. It hugged her shape almost as much as the dress she wore for her birthday. He couldn't wait to peel it off her.

"I see you can't keep your eyes off her," his mother observed. "I can't blame you. I'm not sure how I feel about that dress. It's a bit revealing for my taste, but she sure does wear it well." She took a sip of champagne. "Who is that couple over there? Is that your best man?" she asked, pointing at O'Donnell and Ann Prince. "They look almost as in love as the two of you."

"Yes, Bill is my best man, and I agree with you. I'm very happy for them." He'd been watching, and they had danced every dance together so far.

The song finished, and Rory made her way over. "Mrs. Hawley, I'm so glad you're keeping Hank company for me," she said. "I think I've abandoned him long enough, don't you?"

Ma smiled and winked. "Goodnight, Hank. I'll see you tomorrow in Mineola." She got up and walked in Kate's direction.

"I think it's time for us to leave for the Waldorf, don't you?" Rory said with a conspiratorial smile.

"I do," he said, standing up on his crutches. Together, they made a grand exit, nodding and waving at everyone as their guests cheered them on.

Her father's car and driver took them up to the Waldorf, and they hurried up to their room.

Alone at last.

He took off his jacket and vest, removed his cufflinks, and sat down on the bed to remove his one shoe. Then he sat back and watched as Rory pulled pin after pin out of her hair, removing her veil so that she could join him.

Her back was to him, and he had a lovely view of her shapely posterior. She glanced over her shoulder flirtatiously.

"Don't stop, princess. I was enjoying the view."

She pulled out the last pin and flourished the lacey confection. "Shall I do the dance of the seven veils for you?" She fluttered her eyelashes and wound the veil around her.

"Come here, you minx. I had a different kind of dancing in mind."

She sauntered over, letting the veil fall to the floor.

"Then unwrap me," she said, leaning in and nipping at his ear.

He traced the bare expanse of her back down until he found buttons, and he slipped one after another through its hole, slowly, methodically, nuzzling her neck as he worked. He could smell the faint hint of magnolias on her skin as he kissed and licked. The smell of her was more intoxicating than the finest whiskey.

He was hard from the moment she straddled him. The little sounds she made as he finished the last of the buttons only served to enflame him further. When he was done, he pulled the dress over her head in one swift movement, leaving her in her corset, bloomers, and stockings. "No chemise?" he asked, palming her perfect, bare breasts.

"No chemise," she said, arching her back as he lowered his lips to worship her breasts, taking time to fully explore each one. When her breathing grew ragged, he paused and unhooked her stockings from her garters. Then he untied her corset.

"Take it off," he ordered, and she stood up and removed her corset and bloomers so that she was naked except for her stockings. When she started to roll them down, he said, "Stop. Keep them."

Smiling, she returned to the bed, straddling him once again. "My turn. You're wearing too many clothes."

She unbuttoned his shirt, then his pants, then his union suit, following fingers with lips. After kissing her way down his chest, she licked the tip of his cock as it sprang free, and he nearly jumped out of his skin.

"Christ, Rory. You're driving me wild."

With a sly grin, she crawled backward and pulled off his pants and sock and then his union suit, peeling it over the cast.

Straddling him once again, she said, "Hank, I need you." His cock jumped at her words. Reaching between her folds, he found her soaking wet. She rocked against his hand as he made her dance—slowly at first and then quicker. He needed to see her pleasure. It was everything to him at that moment. She was everything—the love of his life, the siren of his dreams. Nothing compared to the sight of her trembling at his touch, utterly at his mercy.

She writhed and moaned, gyrating against him as he teased and tormented her sensitive bud, driving her higher and higher until she was begging for him.

"Give me more." Oh, God. Her face as she said those words. Enflamed lips parted, eyes filled with fire. She whimpered as he slid in one finger and then the other, curling them to touch the spot that he knew drove her mad. She was almost there. Just a little bit more and…

She cried out, shaking and quivering, as he felt the pulsation of her release on his fingers. "I want you inside me."

His cock wanted inside of her too, but he forced himself to pause.

"Before we start, do you want me to pull out or stay when I come?"

"Stay. Please," she said with a sweet smile.

"With pleasure," he said, laying back. "I'm all yours, princess."

She climbed on top of him and took his cock in hand, coating him in her juices before sliding down onto him. As she took him in, his eyes rolled back in his head. She felt so fucking good. His wife. His partner forever. "I love you, Rory," he groaned.

"I love you too, Hank," she said as she began to move. Once again, he felt the electric connection between the two of them. Every movement she made shot through every one of his extremities, and he could feel her body responding to him. In that moment, he lost track of where his body ended and hers began. They were one body, one soul, moving together, taking each other to greater and greater heights. They flew through the heavens, soaring above the clouds and up to the stars. A white heat consumed him as he felt the spasms of her fruition, and he exploded like a shooting star, falling through the sky.

She slid to his side and curled against him. "I love you," she whispered against his chest.

"I love you too," he whispered back.

As he lay beside her, his whole life came into focus, the risks he'd taken, the path he'd chosen. There was no need to run from it anymore. She loved him. He didn't need danger to fill the empty place in his heart. He didn't need to flee love because of the dangers he'd chosen. He could simply love and be loved for who he was. He was home at last.

"Ma, Kate, it's so good to see you," Rory yelled after they parked the Jenny behind the barn. It had been eight months since the wedding, and they were in Michigan at last. A brisk April breeze blew as they took off their caps, goggles, and flying suits. Rory was delighted to get her first view of the Michigan farm at long last.

"I still can't believe your father-in-law gave you an airplane as a wedding gift," Ma said to Hank.

"Neither can I," he answered.

Two boys came running out of the house yelling "Uncle Hank, Uncle Hank!"

"Can you show us the airplane, Uncle Hank?" asked the older boy.

"Pete, I swear you've grown at least a foot since I last saw you," Hank said.

"I growed too," said the younger boy. "Papa says I'm four feet."

"Amazing, Tom! Keep growing like that, and you're going to catch up with your brother," said Hank.

"No, he won't," said Pete. "I'll always be taller."

"Not necessarily," said Kate. "When you're both grown, he might be even taller than you."

Pete gave her an alarmed look. "Well, I'll always be older than Tom. He can't catch up with me there."

"Very true," Kate assured him.

"Who're you?" Tom said, pointing at Rory.

"It's rude to point," said Pete, shoving Tom in the shoulder.

"Boys," warned Kate. "That's your Aunt Rory. She lives in New York with Uncle Hank."

"Aunt Rory, do you fly in airplanes all the time?" Pete asked.

"I fly a lot," said Rory, smiling at the question. "I'm working on getting my pilot's license, but Hank and I don't fly all the time. Sometimes we walk. Sometimes we drive. Sometimes we even stay in one place and don't go anywhere at all."

Much as she liked flying, staying in one place with Hank had undeniable appeal.

"Where's Jeremiah?" Hank asked.

"Had to go to town. He'll be back soon, don't worry," Kate said.

The boys squealed in delight as they clambered up into the two cockpits.

"I think you just made their year," said Ma. "This is better than Christmas."

Kate came up next to Rory. "Hank has always been good with the boys. It's a pleasure to see them together."

"Yes, it is," said Rory. "It's only a matter of time before we have little ones of our own. It's good to see he's ready." They'd done nothing to prevent the arrival of children. There was a chance she was expecting right now. Her monthlies were a few days late. She didn't want to say anything until she was sure, though.

"How are things going on the suffrage front? Please tell your friend Evelyn I said hello. She and I have been corresponding since the wedding."

"I don't want to jinx it, but I think something is shifting.

Women have played such an important role on the home front all through the war."

"I hope and pray you're right, Rory," Kate said, crossing her arms as she watched her boys scramble all over the airplane with their uncle. "Ma and I work just as hard as Jeremiah to keep this place running. If we can work like men, why shouldn't we have the same say as men in how our country is run?"

Rory smiled. "I agree."

"And women should have a right to their money too. I envy the agreement you have with Hank. I love Jeremiah, and he respects me. He doesn't have the best head for figures, though. I take care of most of the business end of running this farm, and yet I'm the one who lives on an allowance because that's how things have always been done. And then there's the fact that Hank owns the farm because Pops thought a woman couldn't handle it. Ma put her blood, sweat, and tears into this place same as Pops. I think it's shameful he only left her the money and not the farm."

Rory began to wish she could bring Kate back to New York to join the cause. "Have you thought about organizing the other women in the area to advocate for suffrage?"

"I have," said Kate. "There's six of us so far, and I think our numbers will grow if we can just convince these farmers' wives to think beyond the next harvest."

Jeremiah drove up just then and saw everyone gathered around the plane. "Hank, Rory, it's so good to have you here!" He walked with a slight limp as he made his way to shake hands with Hank.

Kate followed Rory's gaze. "He had a tractor accident five years ago. It kept him back from the war, so I'm almost grateful. It hasn't slowed him down one bit, though it pains him from time to time."

Rory nodded and watched as the two men wrangled the boys down from the airplane with the promise of treats from Jeremiah if they cooperated. They all went inside, and Jeremiah handed them each a lollipop from the general store.

"You spoil them," Kate said.

"And you should be glad I do, or they'd be sleeping in that airplane tonight."

They all sat down, and Ma served everyone coffee. Hank took a deep sip and smiled. He looked completely at home.

"While we're all here gathered together," he said, "there's something I'd like to tell you."

All eyes turned to him. Rory knew what was coming, but her heart beat faster with anticipation.

"I've decided to give you three the farm," he said to Ma, Kate, and Jeremiah. "I checked with a lawyer, and he says you can share ownership if you set it up as a business. Each of you can own a one-third share. It's not fair for me to own it when you're doing all the work. My life is in Mineola, and it's going to stay that way, especially with my new job with the Curtiss Aeroplane and Motor Company. I should have done this long ago, and I'm sorry it took me so long to realize it."

Ma's eyes went wide. Kate clutched Jeremiah's hand while staring at Hank. Jeremiah furrowed his brow. "It's yours by right, Hank," he said. "Kate and I have been saving up the money to buy you out. Are you sure you want to give it to us without getting anything in return?"

"I'm sure," he said, smiling. "I had my lawyer write up the paperwork before we left. We just have to file it with the county to make it legal."

Ma took a deep breath and fanned herself with her hand. "That's mighty generous of you, Hank. Mighty generous. Thank you, son. It means a lot to me. It hasn't been easy since losing your father. And Benny. I understand why your father set things up as he did, but I think he underestimated the women in this family."

Hank smiled. "Rory taught me some important lessons about what it means to be supportive of the women in my life."

"And I hope you know, son, that you will always be welcome here. I know you've been reluctant to visit. Maybe not being responsible for the farm anymore will make it a bit easier?"

She gave him a sly grin.

"I want to see my grandchildren regularly," she said, her eyes flicking to Rory then back again.

"I think you may be right, Ma. It's a weight off my shoulders to let this place go. It never should have been mine in the first place. I should have realized that a lot sooner."

LATER THAT EVENING, Hank and Rory sat together on a porch swing with a knitted blanket over their laps, looking out at the stars. Rory rested her head on his shoulder, unable to imagine more perfect contentment. "I'm so proud of what you did today. It was the right thing to do."

"Yes, it was, and I never would have seen it if not for you. I would have kept beating myself up about how I was failing to live up to my responsibilities and ignoring the obvious solution."

"It means a lot to me that you not only gave me my independence when I asked but that you volunteered to give your family theirs too. It means you truly understand and weren't just doing it to humor me. I'm a very lucky woman."

He pulled her closer and kissed her head. "And I'm a very lucky man. I love you, princess."

"I love you too, Hank."

She saw a shooting star in the clear night sky, and then another, and she didn't make a wish because she knew she had everything she ever wanted right here.

ACKNOWLEDGMENTS

This book has been years in the making. It all started with a visit to Long Island's Cradle of Aviation Museum in 2021. I was captivated by an exhibit on the origins of the U.S. Airmail operation. These pilots were flying wood and fabric airplanes with open cockpits and no radios, navigating with paper topographical maps in all weather, all year round. It was utter madness. Their bravery and optimism made them legends in their day, and you could see their swagger in the old black and white photos. (Look up Wild Bill Hopson. You'll thank me.) I thought, "Someone should write a romance series about these guys." When I found that no one had, I set out to write the books I wanted to read.

I have a lot of people to thank for helping me get this book out into the world. Here is my best effort at making a list. A big thanks to Sarah, Vicky, Natalie, and Ruth who read the complete manuscript and shared their thoughts. Thanks to my Long Island Romance Writers critique group who read large portions of it. Thanks to Passionate Ink for seeing promise in my opening chapter and giving me a Passionate Plume contest award. Thanks to Claudia, my RAMP mentor, who went through my manuscript with a fine-tooth comb, as well as my RAMP critique partners, Anika and Ashley. Also thank you, Jeannie, for your excellent feedback on Rory's character arc. Thanks to Ed, the docent from the Cradle of Aviation Museum, who helped me make the flight scenes and airplane descriptions as accurate as possible. Many thanks to my agent, Jason, for helping me polish on Air Affair and find a home for it. And, of course, a huge thank you to my editor, Sally, for seeing the promise in my book and making it the best it can be. Last, but certainly not least, hugs and love to Chris for all your love and support every step of the way. You are all wonderful, and I am deeply grateful for the help you've given me on the path to getting this published!

ALSO BY LESLIE VOLLARD

Mile-High Madmen

Air Affair

Landing Love

ABOUT THE AUTHOR

Leslie Vollard writes award-winning historical romance spanning from the medieval period to the early 20th century. Romance reigns supreme in her steamy novels about how love conquers all. A 2023 Passionate Plume winner and 2025 Romance through the Ages finalist, she lives on Long Island with her delightfully nerdy husband and cat. She loves gardening, baking, and reading love poems in dead languages.

A small press bound by the belief that every voice matters.

Sign up for our newsletter to learn about new releases and more.
https://oliver-heberbooks.com/subscribe/

Follow us on social media:

facebook.com/oliverheberbooks
instagram.com/oliverheberbooks
amazon.com/oliverheberbooks
youtube.com/@OliverHeberBooksPublisher